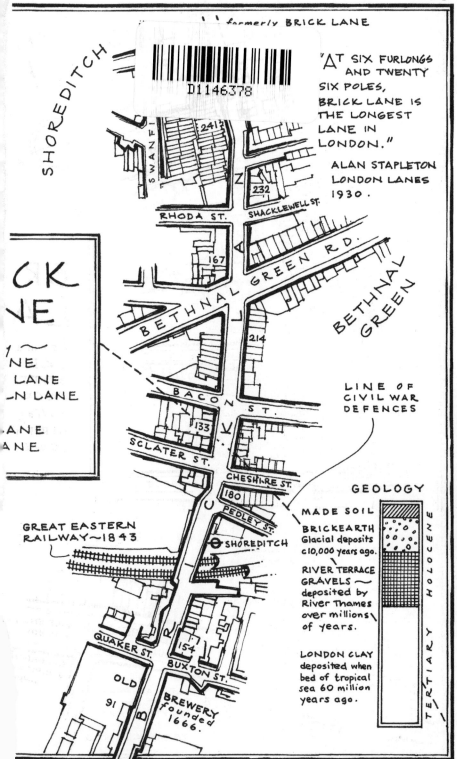

P.T.O

formerly BRICK LANE

D1146378

SHOREDITCH

"AT SIX FURLONGS AND TWENTY SIX POLES, BRICK LANE IS THE LONGEST LANE IN LONDON."

ALAN STAPLETON LONDON LANES 1930.

241

SWANF...

232

Z

RHODA ST.   SHACKLEWELL ST.

167

BETHNAL GREEN RD.

BETHNAL GREEN

214

CK
NE

~
NE
LANE
N LANE

ANE
ANE

BACON ST.

LINE OF CIVIL WAR DEFENCES

133   V

SCLATER ST.

CHESHIRE ST.

180

GEOLOGY

PEDLEY ST.

GREAT EASTERN RAILWAY ~ 1843

SHOREDITCH

MADE SOIL

BRICKEARTH Glacial deposits c 10,000 years ago.

RIVER TERRACE GRAVELS ~ deposited by River Thames over millions of years.

LONDON CLAY deposited when bed of tropical sea 60 million years ago.

HOLOCENE

TERTIARY

QUAKER ST.

154

BUXTON ST.

OLD

91   B

BREWERY founded 1666.

An Acre of
Barren Ground

JEREMY GAVRON

With artwork by Temple Clark

Scribner

CAMDEN LIBRARIES

First published in Great Britain by Scribner, 2005
An imprint of Simon & Schuster UK Ltd
A Viacom Company

1 3 5 7 9 10 8 6 4 2

Simon & Schuster UK Ltd
Africa House
64 –78 Kingsway
London WC2B 6AH

www.simonsays.co.uk

Simon & Schuster Australia
Sydney

A CIP catalogue record for this book is available from the British Library

Hardback ISBN: 0-7432-5971-8
EAN: 9780743259712
Trade paperback ISBN: 0-7432-6854-7
EAN: 9780743268547

Typeset by M Rules
Printed and bound in Great Britain
by The Bath Press, Bath

For my father

Now would I give a thousand furlongs of sea for an acre of barren ground.

WILLIAM SHAKESPEARE, *THE TEMPEST*

It was probably only a creak or a groan of the trees, but wolves and bears and sometimes even men stole through those shadows, and when it came again the boar gulped down whole the acorn it had a moment earlier taken between its teeth and skittered away from the edge of the forest. While it made its way along the track the acorn passed through its stomach into its gut. The other nuts it had eaten that morning it had masticated before swallowing and they were soon being digested, but even the boar's intestinal acids could not penetrate the hard waxy shell of the whole acorn. South of the forest the land grew drier, the vegetation a tangle of broom and furze dotted with spindly birch, though later in the day the earth softened again under the boar's hooves and it came to a spring where it stopped to drink. The water loosened its bowels and shortly afterwards it evacuated the acorn in a pile of steaming dung at the edge of the path, before continuing on its way.

Feldman's Post Office

1 Whitechapel Road

Feldman's, as it was known, stood on the corner of Osborn Street and Whitechapel Road. On the upper floor Dr Leon Feldman had his medical surgery, while below was his brother Isaac's Foreign Bank and Post Office, where the immigrants of Whitechapel came to collect letters, send telegrams, change their last rubles into shillings, or, if they were working, and had left relatives behind them, their shillings into ruble drafts to remit home. The sign of the post office hung over the broad pavement of Whitechapel Road, above notices and advertisements in long lines of Oriental characters, but the doors opened on to the narrower sidewalk of Osborn Street, and it was here, every day except the Sabbath, that one or more members of a family could be found, from seven o'clock in the morning, when the post office opened, until ten o'clock at night, when it closed. Sometimes the father was there alone, or with a boy of about eight years; sometimes it was the mother, a baby in her arms, a girl at her side; though in the early morning and evening, when the post office was at its busiest, they were usually all there together. They stood a little aside from the doors, so as not to be in the way of the customers passing in and out, but close enough to be able to peer into their faces, and from time to time one of them would give a little cry and reach out to tug at a sleeve, invariably of a man approaching middle age, with red hair, and sometimes a red beard.

To the customers quickening their step as they walked past, the father in his drooping hat and threadbare coat (the source, it seemed, to any who lingered too closely, of the pungent odour that hung about them), the mother in her plain brown dress, tufts of shorn hair poking out from beneath her scarf, and the moon-faced children had the unmistakable appearance of new arrivals, which they were. As the father told anyone who would stop to listen, he was Moses Levovitz and this was his wife Rachel. They had travelled by cart and train and foot and boat from the town of Dunsk in northern Lithuania, where Moses had been a slaughterer; though, he quickly added, he had put that trade behind him. Before they left he had sold his practice and his knives. He had meant to sell his coat too, and buy a new one to travel in, but once their passage had been paid for, and all other matters settled, there had been scarcely enough money for the journey, and while Rachel had washed the old coat twice, the olfactory memory of the moist packages of gizzards and chicken claws that Moses had brought home in his pockets still clung obstinately to its fibres.

This little speech Moses had made many times since they had left home, and though he continued to repeat it, his words struggled to carry even the fragile hopefulness with which he had originally imbued them. Sometimes, when he came to the part about the coat, and the packages, instead of the relief he had not so long ago felt he would have to turn his head away, blinking at the memory of coming home with those prizes to their rented room behind the Dunsk bathhouse, for Rachel to cook on the stove in the corner, where the children would later sleep, warm and snug even in winter, while Moses and Rachel stretched out on feather mattresses on the wooden table which Rachel's father, a carpenter, had made for her dowry.

That Moses had not meant to be a slaughterer was true. He had studied for three years at theological college before his father died of smallpox and he had been forced to come home and take up a trade. But slaughtering was pious and learned work and if at first he had been troubled by the sight of blood, he applied himself to his apprenticeship and passed his exams. By then he was married and a father and he drew satisfaction from supporting his family; from his knowledge of the laws and the sureness of his hand. It was rare that he spoiled good meat or could not suggest a way to save flesh sullied by an unexpected lump on the heart or a nail found in the gullet; and if he was seldom paid with the best cuts of meat, only the children of the richest men in the town ate as well as his, and usually he came home with a few coins jangling in his pocket as well.

When the first of the townspeople announced they were leaving for America, Moses had responded with scorn. Their leaving seemed to him a betrayal of their fathers who lay in the little cemetery, shaded by trees, at the edge of the town. A betrayal of His will. Had He commanded them to throw away their old lives and sail across the fathomless seas to this America? Of course, Moses had not seen America for himself. But he saw who was going: the sinners, the ignoramuses, the no-goods, like his wife's brother, Wolf Vitkin, who had borrowed money from everyone, including Moses, and vanished without so much as a thank you. For two years they had heard nothing from him and had begun to despair – Rachel that her brother was dead, Moses that he would never be repaid his money – when a letter arrived. Wolf, or rather Wally, as he signed himself – Wally Vital – was living in Hoboken, New Jersey. He was working in a fruit store and earning more in a week than he had ever earned in a month at home. He could not yet repay his debt, for he was saving up to buy his own store, but if they could make their own way to America he would repay them tenfold by giving Moses a job in his store. Moses read the letter in silence, pausing only to grunt at the signature, before handing it back to Rachel. But that night, after Rachel was asleep, Moses was unable to concentrate on his reading, and setting down his holy book he crept across the room and took the letter from the pocket of Rachel's dress and carried it back to his corner, where he read it again by the yellow light of his candle, especially the part about how in America a man might make himself anew.

In the two years since Wolf's departure, another twenty homes had fallen empty. With every farewell, the piety of those left behind had grown more fierce, but so too had the

poverty. Fewer animals were killed, and when Moses's services were called upon, his customers became angry if he so
much as suggested that they might pay him even in part in
money. Was not slaughtering a religious duty? It was enough
that they should give him a piece of their Sabbath chicken or
their wedding goat. Moses took what was offered and
walked home through the narrow lanes of the town, the
odour of death lingering after him.

In the early days of his apprenticeship, Moses had feared
he was too soft to be a slaughterer. The first time he had
watched an animal killed he had fainted and when he had
made his own first cut he had been forced to turn away so
that his vomit did not fall on the chicken. His master had
assured him he would grow hardened to it and in time he
had. But now his old sensitivities returned. When his knife
sliced through the soft tissues of the neck and struck the
hard sinew of the oesophagus, he found the bile rising again
in his own throat. He began to suffer from bad dreams.
One night he dreamed he was called out to slaughter a
chicken, but instead of cutting its throat he tucked it under
his arm and ran to the forest, where he let it go, watching it
scuttle away through the trees. In his dream he had felt joy
at this act, but when he woke he was gripped by dread at
what it might mean. He grew afraid of sleeping, staying up
long into the night, searching his holy books for answers,
until he would finally fall asleep too exhausted to dream, or
to remember his dreams.

He was still in bed one morning, his family eating their
breakfast around him, when his neighbour came to ask him

to kill his goat. Moses rubbed his eyes and poured water over his fingers as he said his prayers. Slowly he drank a glass of tea. He had killed many goats but this animal he had known since it was a kid. For six years it had been tied to a post outside his door, keeping the lane clean with its rummaging, and, until its udders had dried up, good-naturedly yielding up its warm milk, which Moses had drunk on more than a few occasions. Taking out his box of knives, Moses tested the second longest blade on the flesh and nail of his thumb. He had whetted it the previous day and there were no notches. He left the other knives in the box and walked outside with this one in his hand. Usually he tied an animal's legs together to cast it to the ground, but when he put his hand on the goat it lay down under his touch. Muttering the prayers and benedictions, Moses bent over the creature. The goat, lying patiently beneath him, looked up with its large brown eyes and when he lowered his knife to its throat, it turned its head under his hand and with its rough tongue gently licked the soft skin of his wrist.

Once the news got out that they were leaving, Moses did not need to go to a travel agent to buy tickets. The agents came to them, bringing gifts of sweet cakes, offering the safest, most comfortable, cheapest passage. Their home was rented but they sold everything else: their crockery, Moses's books, their feather mattresses, the table Rachel's father had made. For two days Rachel cooked biscuits as emergency rations for the journey. Finally it was time to leave. A wagon carried them to the railhead. From there they rode first the little kettle, as the small local train was called, and then the great mainline train to the German border, where, as they had no papers, they joined with a group of others in paying a smuggler to take them through the woods into Germany. A last train journey brought them to Hamburg, where they looked on the sea for the first time. For nineteen days they waited in a warehouse on the docks, at a charge of a ruble a day. They were bled almost dry by the time their names were called.

Docked between two much larger vessels, their ship seemed worryingly small and old, paint flaking off its sides, its metalwork shadowed with rust. But another passenger said that small ships cut through the water faster and Moses was reassured. They carried their bags down a set of narrow steps into a low dark hold with rough wooden bunks nailed three-deep along the walls. The first day and a half at sea the ship rolled from side to side, and though Rachel managed to keep the baby fed and make the children suck on slices of orange, Moses could do no more than lie on his bunk, struggling up only to hurry through his prayers or to lurch over to a bucket in the corner. But on the afternoon of the second day the rolling stopped and one by one the passengers climbed the steps from the hold. The deck was piled with freight but Moses found some space in a narrow corridor between stacks of boxes and crates lashed down under canvas. Rachel shared out the last orange and gave each of them one of her biscuits. The sailors brought round a bucket of water. When the sun came out the children climbed on to a crate and sat with their legs dangling down. There were other passengers on either side of them and soon Rachel and Moses were swapping stories of the old lives they had left behind and the new ones awaiting them ahead in the golden land of America. Later the wind picked up and it grew colder with the approaching dusk. The women took the children down into the hold and the men held a service on the deck.

When it was over, Moses did not immediately head below but picked his way between the boxes, stepping over ropes. He did not go quite to the edge of the ship, for all that stood between the deck and the fathomless depths was a flimsy railing, but standing a few feet back and holding on to a piece of canvas, he peered out at the waters through which they were cleaving, wine-dark under the setting sun.

When he climbed down the steps his two older children were already asleep, and Rachel was lying on her side, turned away from him, with the baby. He bent over the children and looked at their faces, David still and peaceful, Tsippe's brows knotted in a frown, her breathing quicker. He took off his coat and boots, and lay behind Rachel, feeling the heat of her body through their clothes. The bunk was hard – a hundred times already Rachel had bemoaned the sale of their feather mattresses – but in a moment Moses was asleep and he slept without dreaming.

At first he did not know what had woken him. But then the sound came again, a long low boom vibrating through the hold. He opened his eyes to see passengers fumbling to dress and in a moment he was doing the same himself. Up on deck, thick cloaks of fog were drifting over the ship and he stood at the rail staring out blindly. A shape loomed out of

10

the mist and vanished again. It must be another ship. It could not be America so soon, even in such a small, fast vessel. But more shapes, solid and square, were appearing out of the swirls of silver and he was straining forward, searching for the great statue of a lady he had been told about, when a sailor walked down the deck behind them, calling out in German that they should prepare to disembark.

Moses hurried into the hold and helped Rachel pack up their bags and dress the children. A few minutes later they were descending the gangplank on to a foggy wharf. He asked a man beside him what was happening, but no one knew. There was no one on the docks who spoke Yiddish or German and none of the passengers could speak any English. Finally one of them must have found a way to make a question understood, for a terrible word now passed among them. London. This was London.

How long they waited on the docks, growing steadily damper in the drizzle, Moses did not know. The day grew neither lighter nor darker, the rain neither ceasing nor turning into a proper downpour. It seemed they might stay here for ever, but then a man appeared out of the fog and spoke Yiddish to them. They crowded round him, all talking at once, so that he had to shout to make himself heard. He was from a shelter, he said, when they had quieted. He had brought a cart to take their luggage. All their questions would be answered there. Bags were piled on to the cart and they trudged behind it through the muffled streets, buildings drifting in and out of the mist, people slipping by like ghosts.

Eventually they arrived at the shelter. Inside it was warm

and dry and brightly lit. In a dining room with a high ceiling and rows of tables they were given a hot meal, their first since they had left Germany. Afterwards, waiting to see the superintendent, Rachel and Moses agreed it would not be so bad to have to stay here for a few days, until they had sorted out their onward passage.

When it was their turn they were ushered into the superintendent's office and Moses immediately began to relate their story. The superintendent let him speak for a few moments and then held up his hand. He did not need to be told. He had heard the same story a thousand times. The shelter paid for advertisements in the newspapers at home but still it kept happening. These agents were all crooks.

You must help us reach America, Rachel said.

The superintendent turned to her with a helpless shrug. What should I do? he said. Buy you new tickets? Do you know what would happen if they heard at home that in London they were giving away free passages to America?

He looked back and forth between Rachel and Moses.

Of course, he said, leaning forward, his eyes narrowing, If you were willing to consider returning home—

Moses turned to his wife, but she only clutched the baby and tightened her mouth.

The shelter, it turned out, was full, but a room had been found for them elsewhere, and later in the afternoon they were back out on the streets, this time carrying their bags, with the help of a guide from the shelter. The fog had lifted a little, though not so much that they were not nearly run down by a horse and cart as they crossed a great thoroughfare as broad as a river. Shortly afterwards they turned down a narrow alley and a few steps on stopped at a door. They followed their guide into the house and up two rickety flights of stairs to a room, where they put down their bags and the guide dropped a few coins into Moses's hand. They could stay here for a week or two, he said, but then they would have to find their own accommodation.

The room was about the size of the one they had left behind at home, with two cots pushed up against the walls, though there was no stove and only a small, badly made table and a single chair. Rachel handed the baby to Tsippe and taking the money from Moses's hand said she was going out to buy some food. When she was gone Moses went over to the window and rubbed at the dirty glass with his sleeve, though even then he could not see the street below, only the faint impressions of other windows in a brick wall a few feet away. While Tsippe comforted the baby and David went out to explore the house, Moses remained at the window, swaying gently back and forth, his lips moving in the soft singsong of prayer.

When Rachel returned, they ate a supper of bread and fried fish, washed down with water from a tap David had discovered in a yard at the back of the house. Afterwards they went to bed. Moses slept little. He lay listening to shouts and clatterings and other noises he could not identify, some from far away, others apparently so close he thought more than once that they were coming from within the room, though when he opened his eyes he saw only the blank walls, pale with the glow of the city.

In the morning, when they had eaten the rest of the bread and fish, Rachel cleared a space on the table and spread out their assets. The last of the money from home added up to twelve rubles and forty-three kopeks. The value of the English money she could not calculate exactly, but she had learned enough from her shopping the previous evening to know it was not much more than the rubles. There was not enough even for one passage to America, let alone four. At least their situation was clear. When Rachel had fed the baby she would go out with the children to send a telegram to her brother. In the meantime Moses must find work.

There was no reason to delay, so Moses put on his coat and slipped three copper coins Rachel gave him into his pocket. He kissed the children and went out of the door and down the stairs. Outside it was as if the fog had never been, the sky above clear and bright, though no sunlight penetrated to the alley floor. On either side were rows of identical houses, joined seamlessly together, people standing in some of the doorways and leaning out of windows. Moses looked at them expectantly as he began walking, ready for the greetings and questions a stranger would have been offered at home, but no one even glanced at him, except for a small boy who looked up for a moment before going back to his game of knocking a stone on the cobbled ground.

At the end of the alley Moses came out on to the great thoroughfare they had crossed the previous evening. In the clear light it was even broader and busier that he had imagined, dense with traffic and noise, and flinching at the mere thought of crossing it he turned instead down the wide pavement, walking between the shops on one side, their doors flung open, and the stalls on the other thick with fruit and hats and birdcages and other goods. Hearing Yiddish spoken as he passed a second-hand boot stall, he stopped and greeted the stallkeeper, who, when he discovered Moses had no interest in making a purchase, chased him away, waving a boot at him.

Shaken by this, and discovering himself by a little café, Moses went inside and ordered himself a hot tea and a roll, which he paid for with one of the coins Rachel had given him.

He was resting against the counter, chewing on the roll, when his eyes met those of another man.

You are newly arrived? the man said in Yiddish, though it was a Yiddish different in accent and expression from Moses's own.

Yes, Moses said, swallowing his mouthful. How did you know?

The man shrugged. A lucky guess.

We arrived yesterday, Moses said. I am Moses Levovitz from the town of . . .

When he had finished his story, he said, Now I must find work.

The man eyed him.

That is not so easy.

No? Moses's spirits sank.

Of course—

When the man hesitated, Moses held up his hands. Please, he said. If you know of anything.

15

I did hear of something, the man said. But I doubt they would hire someone so green.

I have children, Moses said. A baby.

Hastily he wiped the crumbs from his beard and brushed them from his front, regretting once again that he had not been able to buy a new coat.

What money do you have? the man said.

Moses reached into his pocket and held out the two remaining copper coins for the man to see.

Tuppence? Is that all?

Moses was considering whether to tell him about the shillings and rubles Rachel had, when the man sighed and told him to come along and strode out of the café.

Moses took a last gulp of his tea and hurried after him. The man walked quickly, weaving through the crowds on the pavement, so that several times Moses nearly lost him, though each time the man was waiting for him. After a time they turned down an alley somewhat like the one Moses had left barely an hour earlier, though smaller and darker. At a door they stopped.

Give me the money, the man said.

Moses hesistated.

You want this job or not?

Moses took out the coins and gave them to the man.

Wait here, the man said, pushing through the door and closing it behind him.

Moses waited in the alley. A little further up two women were talking on a doorstep. From somewhere close by he heard the whirr and clatter of work. Time passed and

Moses realized he hadn't even asked what the job was. What if it was something unclean? He looked about nervously and knocked on the door. It gave slightly under his knuckles and when he pushed it, it swung open. He walked through into a corridor, which led to another door at its end. This, too, opened when he pressed it and he found himself looking out into a yard strewn with debris. Against the far wall, a box was propped. Moses hurried over and climbing on to it looked over the wall into another empty alley.

Rachel and the children were already there when Moses arrived back at the room. Rachel had sent the telegram and, as the post office was also a bank, had changed their rubles into shillings. Moses reported on his own efforts, though he did not mention the man he had met in the café or his loss of the two coins.

Rachel frowned. We need to find somebody we know, she said. To help us.

But who? Moses said. Everyone went to America.

Not everyone, Rachel said pointedly. Did you not walk the streets? Among all these thousands of people there must be someone we know.

Moses did not reply, but a little later he said, Passover.

What are you talking about Passover?

Passover Nurick, he said. He was born on Passover. I studied with him at college. I used to take Sabbath meals with his family. I think he came to London.

You think?

It must be eight or nine years ago. I met his mother some

time later. I am sure she said he came to London. He had his own business and was doing well.

Then we must find this Passover Nurick, Rachel said firmly. But how?

We will ask at the shelter. They wrote down our names. If this Nurick is in London they will have written down his name too.

The next morning they walked back to the shelter, dashing across the wide thoroughfare, and waited again until the superintendent was free to see them. He explained that the shelter had only been open three years so if this Nurick had arrived before then his name would not be in their records. However, he promised to ask around. If Nurick was in London it was probable he was still in this area and someone would know the name.

It was Friday, the Sabbath eve. On the way home as well as more bread and fish, Rachel bought some tea and sugar – for David had discovered that they shared the use of a gas stove in a small kitchen on the floor below them – and some small cakes and candles for the candlestick, one of the few possessions they had not sold but brought with them. That night they lit the candles and celebrated the Sabbath.

The superintendent had told them to come back in a week. Each day Rachel went to the post office to see if Wolf had replied to her telegram, while Moses continued to look for work. One morning he asked at a pickle stall a moment after the proprietor had received word that his assistant was sick and was given a day's employment selling cucumbers and herring, for which he was paid with a sixpenny piece and a parcel of bruised cucumbers. But that was the best of his luck. Two mornings he got up early to attend the work market, an informal gathering on Whitechapel Road known more familiarly as the pig market, but here there were always ten men seeking work for every employer and the bosses wanted men skilled in practices Moses had not even heard of, let alone possessed: pressing, machining, undermachining. This last made Moses think of the great mechanical contraptions he had seen on the docks in Germany and he imagined himself crawling under these, all the time in danger of being crushed to death.

After his second time at the pig market, Moses was standing on the pavement on Whitechapel Road, wondering what next to do, when he felt a tug on the sleeve of his coat. He looked round to see an old man so doubled over beneath a great bundle on his back that he had to twist his head on its side to look up at Moses.

I'll give you threepence for it, the old man said, rubbing the material between his finger and thumb.

Moses stared at him.

Fourpence then. That's more than it's worth.

You want to buy this coat? Moses eventually said, but the old man had given up on him and let go of his sleeve. Moses watched him shuffle away into the crowds until his bobbing bundle disappeared behind the heads and hats.

On the Wednesday, they received a reply from Wolf. He had sent the minimum five words. Cash tied up, job awaiting.

The next morning, unable to wait another day, they walked down to the shelter again. The superintendent saw them standing outside his office and stopped to speak to them. He apologized gently but while he had made various enquiries no one knew of any Passover Nurick.

They walked home in silence, hardly aware even of crossing once more over Whitechapel Road. When they reached the room Rachel sat down to feed the baby while Moses took out one of the two small volumes of holy writings he had brought with him and began to read with David.

After a time, Rachel said, Perhaps this Nurick has changed his name, like Wolf.

That may be true, Moses said. But what good does that do us if we do not know his new name?

But Rachel was not listening.

Tell me again what his mother said, she asked.

That he was in London. That he had his own business. That he was doing well.

How did she know this?

I don't know, Moses said. He wrote to her I suppose. Yes, that is right. I remember now. Every two months he sent her a letter and always there was some money in it for her.

There you have it, Rachel cried, her eyes so bright that Moses worried she was sickening.

Have what?

Nurick, she said. Every two months he sends a letter with money. Where does he go to send this letter? Where does he change this money that he puts in it?

A white van

half-way up Osborn Street

Look, just stop, all right, Joe.

Stop what?

This – she gestured towards the cavernous interior of the van behind them – thing.

We're nearly there, man.

Yeah, and we've got to sort this out first.

There's nothing to sort.

They were slowing to a halt, but only in the traffic approaching the lights. Shuffling towards them along the pavement of Whitechapel High Street was an old man in a skull cap, a white beard trimmed around the curve of his jaw. She watched him stop and lean on his stick, his long shirt rippling in the breeze.

You're just going to walk in there with two thousand pounds?

Yeah.

And they're not going to ask where it came from?

I'll tell them I earned it.

What? she said. Delivering furniture?

Or borrowed it. I don't know, man. Or won it on the lottery.

She looked at her brother. He was staring ahead through the windscreen, his brow furrowed beneath the black shock of his hair, gelled into dozens of little glossy spikes.

Oh, that'll please them, she said. Their son the gambler? You're supposed to be the good Muslim in the family. It's all Amma ever talks about on the phone. How you go to that mosque—

Don't start that, he said. You don't know nothing about that.

Joe—

And don't call me that. My name is Johar.

The lights had turned green and though the car in front had not moved yet, he started gunning the engine.

All right, she said, softening her voice. Johar. Now please can we stop. We have to talk about this.

It's what he wanted.

Then we'll get the money somewhere else. We can use my loans, I'll get a job or something. My next instalment is in a few weeks.

He'll be in Manor Park in a few weeks, dogs shitting on him, swastikas on his grave.

The traffic was moving now and he nosed the van inside the line of cars continuing down Whitechapel Road and accelerated past them towards the turning into Osborn Street.

Abba can borrow till then, she said, almost shouting the last of the words over the roar of the engine.

He swung the wheel towards her and the van lurched around the corner. She reached out with her hand for something to hold on to and a force seemed to hit them from the front and she was flung into the hard embrace of her seat belt.

Slowly the van ceased its juddering.

She glared at him. What was that about? she said.

You wanted to stop.

Her bag had leaped from her lap, spilling her notes over her feet. She leaned forward and was stopped by a pain in her chest where the seat belt had caught her. It was one of those old ones, without any spring in it. She undid it and bent down gingerly.

Abba's up to his neck, he said quietly. He can't pay off what he's in for as it is.

She pushed her notes back into her bag and leaned back in her seat, reaching up to her chest with the tips of her fingers. She had woken to a different day. When her phone had vibrated she had been sitting in the library, her notes spread out in front of her. At first she had thought the line was breaking up, and even when she understood what her father's trembling voice was saying all she could think was that Dada couldn't have died today, that she had an essay to hand in by the morning, and though she had told her father which bus Johar should meet and gone back to her room and changed out of her jeans she had taken her notes and her laptop with her on to the bus. She had planned to continue the essay on the way, finish it at night, after everyone else was asleep, like she used to study, the flat quiet, no demands to watch the rice, iron her father's shirt, find her brother's school tie, though she had spent the journey with her laptop unopened on her lap, staring out of the window.

We can't sit here, he said. They're waiting.

I thought it was going to be about you, she said, turning towards him. It's why I answered my mobile. That's what I think every time it rings.

Well don't.

Abba would take you back you know, she said. I'll talk to him for you. With you helping him he could make something out of that business.

Yeah, man, he said. You get to be the rich lawyer and I get the fucking shmutter trade.

There's other jobs, then.

What? Flipping burgers in McDonald's? Or serving in a curry house, eh? You want popadom, sir? He put on an accent. Plain or spicy? I don't have your qualifications, or have you forgotten that, Kalpona?

You could go to college, she said. They've got schemes for adult learning. You used to be clever at school.

What? And I'm stupid now?

I didn't say that, she said, shooting him a look, the movement catching in her chest. She let her eyes close, touching herself where she felt the pain.

I'll help you apply for a loan, she said. You could use that money.

That money's for Dada.

She pressed into her bruised flesh, wondering if she hadn't done something more serious, cracked a rib maybe, a bit of bone pushing into her lungs, or her heart

You think he'd have wanted it? she said.

You know he did.

I mean that money. Where it comes from.

All money's dirty, man.

Dada worked for what he earned.

She thought of her grandfather's wound, the jagged white scar on his big brown hand.

Yeah and where did it get him?

These last years she had hardly talked to him, had seen him only as this disapproving old man shuffling from sleep to prayers to the lavatory, but when they were young she had thought him the biggest man in the world. Had loved nothing so much as to be lifted up in his scarred hands and sat on his lap, nestling into his chest, his smell like fur, while he told stories of home, of the lands that went on for ever, covered half the year in water, the other half in rice. It wasn't until she was twelve years old and she saw a photograph of paddy in a geography book at school that she realized that fields of rice meant green plants not a carpet of white grains like snow.

What about Amma and Abba? she said. You think they won't know? They may be naive, Abba may not be very good at business, but they're not stupid. You walk in with that money and it won't be Dada going home on that plane it'll be you.

Yeah, well, that wouldn't be so bad.

Oh, come on, Joe, you hated it when we went home. You didn't take off your earphones the whole month. You cried when Dada tried to make you wear a lungi.

I was only a kid.

It wasn't even three years ago.

At least I didn't have to be taken into town so I could go to a proper toilet.

I was suffering from constipation, she said. I went to see a doctor.

Yeah, man.

The memory of the hole in the ground, clouds of mosquitoes ghosting up as she squatted over it, children giggling at her through the gaps in the bamboo, shuddered through her.

We're not talking about a holiday, she said. You won't have a ticket back. You'll be watched everywhere you go. They'll marry you off to some village girl.

Yeah, well, I've been thinking about it myself, haven't I.

What? she said. Getting married?

Going home.

A horn sounded loudly somewhere close by.

Home? To Bangladesh?

No, he said. The North fucking Pole. His black eyes flickered at her. I hate this place. There's nothing here for me.

That's not true, she said, but her words were drowned out by the horn sounding long and loud.

She opened her mouth to say it again but the pain was spreading across her chest.

Fuck off.

She bent forward, holding herself.

Fuck off, he shouted.

She gasped at the air, wondering if she was dying, if this was what it had felt like for Dada.

Then her chest heaved and a whooping bark burst out of her, followed by another, and another.

What did you say? he shouted, though she had made no sound other than her barks, which were slowing now, so she could finally take a breath of air into her lungs.

Something was dripping off her nose and she put her hand up to her face and felt it was wet.

What did you fucking say?

She looked at him through her blurred eyes. His head and half his body were out of the window, as if he couldn't even bear to be in the same van as her.

Giant's Leg

42 Osborn Street

Let all know that we, by the prompting of charity, give
and grant to the venerable prior and canons of the new
hospital of St Mary without Bishopsgate sole use of the
spring known as Snecockswell by the lane on the eastern
side of Lolesworth field; and do grant licence to the same
parties to enclose said spring and to excavate across the
field that lies in the demesne of the manor of the bishop a
culvert to carry the water to the hospital for the refresh-
ment and profit of the poor and the sick there.

REGISTER OF JOHN DE CHISHULLE, BISHOP OF LONDON,

1278

There were giants in the earth in those days; and also
after that, when the sons of God came in unto the daughters of men, and they bare children to them, the same
became mighty men which were of old, men of renown.

GENESIS, 6.4

Item, I bequeath to the prior of St Mary Spital such
monies as will hire five canons to celebrate divine service
daily for ten years in the chapel, wherein are displayed the

28

great bones of an ancient and the bolt of lightning that killed him, for my soul, the souls of my parents and all the souls for which I am bound.

THE LAST WILL AND TESTAMENT OF JAMES LE BOTILLER,
1308

By virtue of our office we decree that the prior of St Mary Spital shall be permitted to employ and take in twelve lay sisters to relieve the canons a portion of their duties.

REGISTER OF WILLIAM GRAY, BISHOP OF LONDON, 1346

A stalwart swain . . .

galloped through a fair forest . . .

There flourished herbs of every sort,
Like licorice and ginger-root . . .
And nutmegs which you put in ale . . .

And birds were singing, I must say...
The throstlecock piped up his lay...

And when he heard the throstle sing,
The knight was filled with love-longing.

O Saint Mary, Heaven bless me!

Until there came a burly giant,
His name it was Sir Oliphaunt . . .

The giant pelted him thereat
With stones from a terrible sling.

GEOFFREY CHAUCER, *SIR TOPAZ, THE CANTERBURY TALES*,
1392

Moreover that the beds of the hospital should be provided first and foremost for the poor and the ill and not such pilgrims, no matter from how far they travel, nor how generous they be.

VISITATION ROLLS, ST MARY SPITAL, 1461

Act for the Dissolution of the Greater Monasteries.

1539

The vestry assembled was informed that the church is now purified of all graven images, pictures of saints, priestly relics, crosses and popish candles, and that the organ shall be sold by the churchwardens, as they may to the best advantage.

MINUTE BOOK OF ST MARY MATFELON, 1571

I myself, more than 40 years since, in the parish church of St Mary Matfelon in Whitechapel, have seen hanged up in chains of iron upon a pillar of stone the shank-bone of a man (as it is said) of 28 inches and a half in length by rule, that is more than after the proportion of five shank bones of any man now living, and also a stone arrow-head larger than a man's fist that was found with the bone and was said to have been the death of the giant.

JOHN STOW, *SURVEY OF LONDON*, 1598

In antique times . . .
a savage nation dwelt,
Of hideous giants

Until that Brutus anciently derived
From royal stock of old Aeneas's line
. . . here arrived

. . . ere he had established his throne,
And spread his empire to the utmost shore,
He fought great battles with his savage foe,
In which he left them defeated evermore,
And many giants left on groaning floor;
That well can witness yet unto this day.

EDMUND SPENSER, *THE FAERIE QUEENE*, 1590

True Bill, heard before Henry Brampston, esq, J.P., that in a tavern known by the sign of the Giant's Leg in Whitechapel, co. Midd., upon Saturday the six-and-twentieth day of March, about eleven o'clock in the evening, Thomas Loxon, alias Lee, horse-gelder, did wound one William Peverell in the head with a heavy flint stone kept for show in that place so that his life was despaired of.

MIDDLESEX COUNTY RECORDS, 1596

Oppose thy steadfast-gazing eyes to mine,
See if thou canst outface me with thy looks:
Set limb to limb, and thou art far the lesser;
Thy hand is but a finger to my fist,
Thy leg a stick compared with this truncheon.

WILLIAM SHAKESPEARE, *HENRY IV PART 2*, 1597

May we very well think that what are said to be the bones of giants may be the huge limbs of monstrous sea creatures such as we do know swim in the very waters about this isle.

WILLIAM CAMDEN, *BRITANNIA*, 1607

Just as agate when polished sometimes shows representations of natural objects such as flowers, and stalagmites and stalactites take on the form of trees, so within rocks and soil nature makes playful imitations of things which live and die under the sun.

JEAN PUTRODE, *LUSUS NATURAE: LA VRAI EXPLICATION*
DE LE GÉANT DE BRICK LANE, 1698

How the elephant came here is the question. For my own part I take it to have been brought over with many others by the Romans in the reign of Claudius the emperor, and conjecture it was killed in some fight by a Briton. For not far from the place where it was found, a British weapon made of a flint stone fastened into a shaft of a good length, which was a weapon very common amongst the ancient Britons, was also dug up, they having not at that time the use of iron or brass, as the Romans had.

JOHN BAGFORD, PREFACE TO *LELAND'S COLLECTANEA*,
1704

No. 187 in my Catalogue of Quadrupeds and their parts, acquired from a public house near London, is another os femoris of an elephant, of 22 and 7/10 inches, taken up from an unknown depth among brick-earth and gravel in the digging of the foundations of the public house in the last century.

SIR HANS SLOANE, *RELICS OF THE UNIVERSAL DELUGE,*

1728

Upon Sloane's death, his collection, which amounted to more than 71,000 objects, comprising 23,000 coins and medals, 338 volumes of dried plants, and many animal and human skeletons, artefacts from the ancient world and other curiosities, was bought by the crown and became the founding core of the British Museum, which opened in Montagu House in Bloomsbury in 1756 . . . The transfer of the botanical and zoological collections to the Natural History Museum in South Kensington was completed in 1883.

ARTHUR MERRY, *THE INSTITUTIONS OF LONDON,* 1895

The bellies of the pachyderms grumbled with fear, until the greatest of the patriarchs among them charged forward, thrusting his upwardly curving tusks at his assailants in his efforts to protect the females and infants behind him. But our palaeolithic hunter was clever and determined, and by making feints and shouting and waving their rude spears, they were successful in separating a female from the herd; so beginning the chase that would end with her blood spilled across the snow.

GEORGE FEATHERSTONE FRGS, *THE DEATH OF A*

MAMMOTH IN WHITECHAPEL, 1901

P. Norwich & Co.

30 Brick Lane

When Inspector Abberline arrived back in Whitechapel, within hours of the discovery of the body the early editions of the evening newspapers were already dubbing the 'third victim of the maniac', he was confident that it would not be long before he would apprehend the murderer. Following the case from Scotland Yard as he had, he knew that the investigation had produced no firm leads. No reliable witness had come forward claiming to have caught a glimpse of the killer. No murder weapon had been discovered. Examination of the corpses and the crime scenes had yielded no significant clues. Forensic science was not yet the invaluable tool it was to become – Scotland Yard did not have its own science laboratory until 1934 – but a policeman could still benefit from science in various ways. The capability of toxicologists to identify poisons had secured several famous convictions by this time, while handwriting analysis had proved invaluable in more than one high-profile trial. But the Whitechapel victims had been stabbed to death, not poisoned, and no sample of the killer's writing had – at least as yet – been left at the crime scenes. Nor had any cigarette ash, which might have been examined under a microscope, nor any part of the killer's false teeth, nor any of his footprints. That fingerprints may have been left on one or more of the bodies, or their clothes, seems probable, considering all the blood, but none were taken. A study of fingerprinting as a forensic tool had been carried out by this time, by a Scottish doctor, but he lived in Japan, and it would be another four years before Scotland Yard began to use the technique. Nevertheless, in an interview he gave to *Cassell's Saturday Journal* shortly after his retirement, Abberline recalled he had set about pursuing 'his investigations connected with the murders with the greatest certainty'.

In the late summer of 1888 Abberline was forty-five years old. No photograph of him survives but newspaper sketches show him as stout and balding, with bushy sidewhiskers. In his memoirs, Walter Dew, later to become famous for catching the poisoner Crippen, but then a detective-sergeant in H Division, the Whitechapel police district, described Abberline as resembling a bank manager or a solicitor more than a detective. It was a – no doubt usefully – deceptive appearance. Abberline had been a policeman since 1862, with the Metropolitan Police since 1863, and attached to H Division from 1873. By the time of his transfer to Scotland Yard in 1887, he had spent fourteen years in Whitechapel, nine of them as the local head of the newly created Criminal Investigations Department. His reputation can be judged from the farewell dinner held for him at the Unicorn Tavern in Shoreditch, at which he was presented with a purse of gold and a watch engraved 'from the inhabitants of Spitalfields, Whitechapel etc., as a mark of their esteem and regard'. One speech-maker described him as 'the very ideal of a faithful, conscientious and upright officer', while the superintendent of H Division bemoaned his loss to Whitechapel, 'for a better officer there could not be'. When the body of Mary Ann 'Polly' Nichols was discovered in the early hours of the last day of August, her throat cut, her abdomen sliced open, stab wounds to her 'private parts', with the previous two killings no closer to being solved and a horde of journalists descending on Whitechapel, it was inevitable that Scotland Yard should turn to Detective Inspector Frederick George Abberline.

As his cab carried him eastwards from Scotland Yard across London that afternoon, it is fair to assume Abberline's thoughts were concentrated on the second and third murders. Despite the continuing claims of the press, the police had by then discounted any connection between the first and the latter two killings. The first victim, Emma Smith, was – like the others, it was true – a mature women who had fallen on hard times and taken to selling herself: an 'unfortunate' in the parlance of the time. But while the mode of her attack was horrific, it was not unprecedented in the violent alleys and rookeries that made up H Division. Walking the streets at night, she had been robbed and 'a blunt instrument inserted with great force up her vagina'. The wound was to prove fatal, but not until two days later, by which time she had been able to give police a description of her three attackers, including one 'of nineteen years'. For some time after the other newspapers concluded the killer was a 'single fiend', the *Daily Telegraph* continued to support the view that all three murders were the work of one of the gangs of young criminals known to steal with menaces from prostitutes – and in the case of Emma Smith the *Telegraph* was probably right. The deaths of Martha Tabram and Polly Nichols were, however, different in profile. Both were attacked while out soliciting for custom, but neither was left with any breath to tell her story. Each was stabbed repeatedly until she was dead. Yet neither appeared to have been robbed, raped or sexually assaulted. As far as the police could discover there was no conceivable motive for either crime.

The investigation into Martha Tabram's death, nearly four weeks earlier, had initially thrown up the possibility that one or more soldiers had been involved, but this had led nowhere, and further enquiries had produced no more worthwhile leads. The Polly Nichols case was only hours old by the time Abberline arrived in Whitechapel, but already it was proving equally frustrating. The body had been discovered at 3.40 that morning outside stables in Buck's Row, an alley north of Whitechapel Road, close to the London Hospital. By 3.45 the first policeman was on the scene. Shortly after four, Dr Henry Llewellyn, a surgeon on the police books, had arrived to examine the corpse. In the next hour, before the sun rose, Walter Purkis, the manager of the railway wharf, whose rooms overlooked the stable gates, had been woken from his bed and questioned, as had Mrs Green, a widow who lived in the first of the row of cottages across the alley. Statements were taken from the watchmen at two factories further along Buck's Row, and from three nightshift workers, who were interviewed separately, their stories matching up. A step-by-step search of Buck's Row was conducted as soon as it was light and this was subsequently extended into Brady Street at the eastern end of Buck's Row, and Court Street to the west. Later in the morning the railway wharf was searched, as were the yards of the railway, and its tracks, north and east, for several hundred yards in either direction; and through that day statements were taken from every one of the twenty-five cottages along Buck's Row, as well as from the caretaker of the nearby school, who said he had woken in the night with such an eerie feeling that he had had to make himself a cup of tea before he could get back to sleep – a story which appeared on the front page of *The Star* the following morning. But other than that, not a single person had anything to offer the police. The killer had apparently come unseen into the alley, committed his unholy deed undisturbed, and disappeared without trace.

Apart from a far more minute searching of the crime scene and examination of the corpse, and perhaps the use of computers to process information, the procedures carried out in the investigation into the killing of Polly Nichols were not so different from those which would be followed today. House to house calls were made in an increasingly broad circle around Buck's Row. The common lodging houses where Polly Nichols and women like her stayed were visited. Questions were asked in coffee houses, pubs and beer shops.

Word was put out that the usual small rewards were available for good information, and every possible lead, however unlikely, was followed up. The police used, in other words, what all good police investigation relies on: legwork. But legwork of this type is a blunt instrument, dependent on chance. What Abberline's arrival in H Division brought to the case was something more discriminating. As the reporter who interviewed him for *Cassell's Saturday Journal* wrote, 'There is no exaggeration in the statement that, whenever a robbery or offence against the law had been committed in the district, the detective knew where to find his man.' Abberline's knowledge of crime was, he added, 'extensive and peculiar'. Fourteen years of investigating crime in H Division had given him unrivalled 'friendly relations with the shady folk' of this crowded corner of east London. Someone in Whitechapel had to know something and whoever and wherever he was, Abberline's network of contacts would surely lead the detective to him.

In all those years, however, Abberline had never worked a case like this. Arriving in Whitechapel that first afternoon, he had to elbow his way through a crowd to reach the front doors of Commercial Street police station. When he went to see the corpse of Polly Nichols at the workhouse infirmary deadhouse he found another throng at the green gates on Old Montague Street. On Buck's Row, though the body had been taken away, and the blood mopped up by the stable hands, he had to clear away a party of gentlewomen sightseers from the West End before he could look on the scene of the crime. The killings were the talk of the East End and everyone seemed to have an idea of who, or what, had committed them. That day and through the days that followed there was scarcely a moment when a detective at Commercial Street or Leman Street police station was not taking down a statement from a member of the public offering a name or a theory or a clue. Every morning the post brought letters promising the same. 'The desire of the East Enders to assist the police was so keen and the number of statements made so great,' *Cassell's Saturday Journal* would later record, 'that the Inspector almost broke down under the pressure.'

Equally burdensome was the press. Dozens of newspapermen had been sent down to the East End and all of them had column inches to fill whether or not there was anything new to write. They hung about outside the police stations and sat in pubs with their notepads open, buying drinks for anyone willing to concoct wilder and wilder stories, which, whether or not they made the morning edition, were soon adding to the rumours spreading like fog through the lanes and alleys of Whitechapel. The killer was a vampire from Transylvania, an escaped ape, 'half-beast, half-man' as one newspaper put it. Then, on the morning of Abberline's sixth day back, *The Star* published an exclusive front-page story. Under a banner headline – 'Leather Apron' – it reported: 'The strange character who prowls about Whitechapel after midnight – universal fear among women – slippered feet and a sharp leather-knife.' The newspaper claimed to have interviewed dozens of prostitutes, all of whom told the same story. None knew this Leather Apron's real name but by all accounts he is five feet four or five inches in height and wears a dark, close-fitting cap. He is thickset, and has an unusually thick neck. His hair is black, and closely clipped, his age being about 38–40. He has a small, black moustache. The distinguishing feature of his costume is a leather apron, which he always wears, and from which he gets his nickname. His expression is sinister, and seems to be full of terror for the women who describe it. His eyes are small and glittering. His lips are usually parted in a grin which is not only not reassuring, but utterly repellent.

His method was to follow a prostitute down a dark alley and pull out a knife and threaten to 'rip her up'. It was a full and powerful portrait and it was soon being repeated in other newspapers, and in the beer shops and kitchens of Whitechapel. The only flaw was that there was not a scrap of evidence to suggest that Leather Apron even existed, let alone that he had anything to do with the murders.

Nevertheless, policemen had to be assigned to speak to the reporter and chase down the prostitutes quoted. By now extra men had been drafted in from Scotland Yard and the City of London police force and Abberline had scores of constables and dozens of detectives in Whitechapel. He himself was working virtually round the clock. 'His anxiety to bring the murderer to justice led him,' *Cassell's Saturday Journal* would report, 'after occupying his whole day in directing his staff, to pass his time in the streets until early morning, driving home, fagged and weary at 5 a.m.' His days were taken up with paperwork and co-ordinating the investigation and it may only have been in the evening and at night that he was able to pay visits to his most valued 'noses', or informers, and other 'shady folk' he wanted to speak to personally; men like old Arky Claypole and Tommy Wilson, the 'canary trainer'. Abberline was, of course, a policeman and villains like Wilson were long-time adversaries, but in this case their interests coincided, for it was the shady folks' manor too, after all, that was being turned upside down, a uniformed man on every corner, a plain-clothes detective in every beer shop. The villains wanted the killer found and life to get back to normal almost as much as Abberline did. Yet by the end of Abberline's first week back in H Division the police were no closer to finding the killer than they had been seven days earlier. 'Not an atom of evidence,' read a report to Scotland Yard dated Friday, 7 September, 'can be obtained to connect any person with the crimes.' Riding home late that night Abberline must have wondered whether the investigation would ever turn up a lead, only to be woken a few hours later with news of the one piece of evidence he had not desired.

The body of Annie Chapman had been discovered shortly after dawn, by a carman named John Davis, in the backyard of 29 Hanbury Street, where he rented a room. As the day progressed her story was pieced together. Like the previous victims she had once been married with children, but drink and tragedy had broken up her family. One child had died, another was born or became a cripple and the marriage ended. Her husband continued to send her ten shillings a week, which she supplemented by selling flowers and her own crochet work, but when he died she took to selling herself. Earlier on the night of her death she was in possession of fivepence, enough to pay for her bed at Crossingham's Lodging House on Dorset Street, but she spent it on drink, and at 1.30 a.m. the lodging house manager sent her out to earn some more cash.

Once again the police machinery cranked into gear. Annie's body was examined on the scene and taken to the workhouse infirmary deadhouse for a post mortem. The yard where she was found was searched. The residents of 29 Hanbury Street were interviewed, as were those of the adjoining houses. Policemen were sent out again to the lodging houses and pubs to conduct enquiries. This time, though, as the day, and the investigation, proceeded a series of clues emerged. The first was the testimony of Mrs Elizabeth Long. She had been walking along Hanbury Street on her way to Spitalfields market at about 5.30 that morning – she remembered the time from the striking of the Black Eagle brewery clock – when close to the side door of number 29, which led along a passageway to the backyard, she had seen a man and a woman. As she passed she heard the man say, 'Will you,' and the woman reply, 'Yes'. She did not hear any more but she had a clear sight of the woman, whom she identified as the deceased. The man she saw only from the back, but that was enough for her to say that he was 'dark complexioned' and wearing a 'dark coat', that he was over forty, and that he 'looked to me like a foreigner'. Asked if he was a working man she replied he seemed 'shabby genteel'.

The second clue came from the post mortem report which

Dr George Phillips, the police surgeon, delivered that after-noon. His findings indicated that, as with the previous two murders, the victim had been the subject of multiple stab wounds to neck and body. In this case, however, he had found something else: that 'the upper part of the vagina and the posterior two thirds of the bladder had been entirely removed. No trace of these parts could be found.' Moreover, this excision, he reported, had in his opinion been carried out by someone with expertise in or at least a reasonable knowledge of anatomy.

The third clue had been found in a corner of the yard, under a tap, apparently washed clean: it was a leather apron.

As each of these pieces of evidence was brought in front of Abberline he put out strict instructions that they should not be revealed to the press. Since the murder of Polly Nichols, and particularly since *The Star* had run its story about Leather Apron, the police had feared an outbreak of public disorder in Whitechapel. *The Star* had not actually specified that Leather Apron was foreign, or Jewish, but its descrip-tion would have left little doubt in its readers' minds, particularly in the East End, that he was meant to be a for-eign Jew. There had long been a small community of Jews in the East End but in the past few years tens of thousands of Russian Jews had been arriving in London, fleeing persecu-tion at home, and most of them had settled in and around Whitechapel. Even before the killings, tensions had been rising between native East Enders and the new arrivals, who tended to congregate on particular streets or parts of streets, setting up their shops and businesses, speaking their own tongue, eating their own food and dressing in their particular clothes, and despite Abberline's efforts dark rumours began to spread that afternoon through the streets of H Division. 'It was repeatedly asserted,' the *East London Observer* reported, 'that no Englishman could have perpetrated such a horrible crime as that of Hanbury Street, therefore the crowds proceeded to threaten and abuse such of the unfortunate Hebrews as they found on the streets.' By evening the abuse turned into violence enough that the *Daily News* would report that the police surgeon and his assistant 'were out of their beds nearly all Saturday night in attendance on cases of assault, some of them of the most serious character, arising directly or indirectly out of the intense excitement occasioned by discussing the murder'. It was only as the gas jets were turned off and the public houses closed in the hour before midnight that the crowds broke up and the people hurried home, leaving the streets quiet, for no one was eager to be about in the darkness.

For Abberline, a new murder on his hands, Scotland Yard on his back, these troubles were a diversion of police resources just when they were most needed, and a distraction for himself. It must have been a relief when he could finally leave the station and head out for his nightly perambulations through the mostly deserted streets. Abberline left no record of his thoughts that night but it is not hard to put together what must have been passing through his mind. Still nagging at him must have been the failure of his 'extensive and peculiar' contacts in Whitechapel to throw up even the slightest clue. A few months earlier, a young doctor, Arthur Conan Doyle, had published a first story about a private detective in *The Strand* magazine. In 'A Study in Scarlet', the detective, Sherlock Holmes, outlines his philosophy to his associate, Dr Watson: 'How often have I said to you that whenever you have eliminated the possible, what remains, however improbable, must be the truth.' Whether Abberline had read this story we do not know, but more relevant in this case is that Conan Doyle – for all his protagonist's mockery of policemen – must in part have based Holmes's methods upon what he had heard about the practice of detectives such as Abberline. Applying Holmesian logic – which might as well have been Abberlinian logic – to the killings, the fact that a detective with unrivalled knowledge of Whitechapel could find no hint of the murderer in Whitechapel led to the inevitable conclusion that the killer must not be of Whitechapel.

Yet how could an outsider have come three times into Whitechapel, committed three bloody murders and left again without once being seen? True, Mrs Long may have briefly seen him the previous morning, but that was before the murder, before he had sliced open the victim and cut out her womb. By the time he had left the yard behind 29 Hanbury Street, the sun was up. It was a Saturday, market morning, and the streets were busy with people. The killer must have been splattered with blood. He was carrying a knife, not to mention what he had taken from Annie Chapman's body. It was a considerable distance from Hanbury Street out of Whitechapel. Yet no one had seen anything of him.

In his wanderings that night, it seems inexorable that Abberline would have been drawn back to the house at Hanbury Street. From there, it was only a few more steps to Brick Lane, where, turning right, he would have come after another couple of hundred yards, to the Frying Pan pub, where Polly Nichols was seen on the night she died, and a little further down to the corner of Osborn Street and Old Montague Street, where Emma Smith was attacked. If so, he would have walked through the heart of what had become the Jewish quarter of Whitechapel. What Abberline thought of the foreign Jews in general we can only guess. That he was keen to protect them from public disorder we know. Probably his views were similar to those of the East End policemen interviewed by the social researcher, Charles Booth, around this time. 'They are dirty and messy,' one of them told Booth, 'but regular rent payers and respecters of authority.' 'They make a street look bad but their influence has been quieting to the district,' said another. There were, of course, Jewish criminals. A common London slang word for a thief was gonoph, a Yiddish word. But on the whole the Jews were considered, apart from their love of gambling, to be law-abiding and peaceful. Yet that night, walking past houses lit up after the Sabbath, Jewish men standing in the doorways smoking, Abberline must have wondered how little he knew these people; how mysterious to him were the thoughts going on behind the black eyes watching him as he strode by. The Whitechapel Abberline knew was the English Whitechapel, but here was another, newer, Whitechapel, a Whitechapel outside his experience, beyond his imagination – like the murders themselves, unprecedented in all his years as a policeman, unEnglish.

What time Abberline finally went home to bed that night we do not know. What we do know is that the next morning he issued to the press an official description of a suspect: 'A man who entered a passage of the house at which the murder was committed of a prostitute on the 8th September. Age 37; height, 5ft 7in; rather dark beard and moustache. Dress – shirt, dark vest and trousers, dark coat. Spoke with a foreign accent.' Abberline also gave orders for enquiries to be made at every Jewish butcher's, slaughterhouse, leather shop and cobblers in Whitechapel.

It was, the arresting officer's report would record, 3.44 that afternoon when the suspect was apprehended. He had been chanced upon during a routine call at a small Jewish butcher's on Brick Lane. The attention of the policemen, Sub-Inspector Rose and Sergeant Thick, had been drawn to him when they were showing around a photograph of the body of Polly Nichols, none yet being available of Annie Chapman, and the suspect had 'blanched and looked ready to be sick, behaviour we considered suspicious for a man in the butchers' trade'. Marking his close resemblance, in looks, and clothes, to the description put out by Abberline that morning, Sergeant Thick had searched the suspect and found 'secreted in a pocket, wrapped in newspaper soaked through, unidentified organs, still fresh.'

Exit

Brick Lane at Chicksand Street

At the far end of the yard, behind the galleries, near the old back gate that was kept locked to prevent spectators from sneaking in without paying, was a half-hidden door that led into what had once been the stables, but was now used as a store and repository of things broken and no longer useful, and it was here, when she was finished with, that she was brought back, blood oozing from her wounds, hobbling painfully from a large gash on her right calf, though not so slowly that she might earn another painful tug on the chain attached to the collar around her neck. Sometimes he washed her before he put her into the cage, but she sensed he would not do so on this occasion, or more properly smelled, from the odour on his breath; the same odour that had been thick in the air, along with the other reeks of men, where she had been. Nevertheless, she hunkered down hopefully, for even the rough touch of his hand was more than nothing, but he prodded her with his stick, speaking harshly to her, and she shuffled inside, the door clanking behind her, hearing his footsteps to the stable door, which he shut behind him too, shutting out the light.

The roof of the cage was too low for her to sit upright and she swivelled round on her haunches, sniffing for the water, but he had forgotten to put her bucket in the cage. It stood a few feet away. She pressed her shoulder to the bars and pawed at the bucket, but she could not reach it. Eventually she sat back and licked at her wounds, the effort at least bringing some of her own moisture into her dry mouth. Soon she slept.

She smelled him in her sleep, and he became part of her dreams, so that when she woke and the smell was still there she was startled and drew back into the cage, twitching her nose and blinking her eyes open, squinting at the light. Space had been cleared on an old, charred table that stood against the wall, and a box set beside it, on which he was sitting, bent over the table. At first she thought he was asleep, but by the gleam of the lamp beside him she saw him move, and she heard the scratching noise she was to come to associate with him. She lay watching him, wary of his presence, and his noise. After a time he lifted his head and she saw his pale face. He had a feather in his hand and he dipped it into a small pot and then began his scratching again.

Slowly her fear subsided and she became aware of her thirst. She pressed up to the bars and reached out again towards the bucket, patting at the air. When she gave up and sat back on her haunches she saw that he was watching her. He spoke to her, his voice gentle, but still she drew back into the cage. He stood up and walked around the table towards her and she growled at him, to warn him. He stopped beside the bucket and picked it up, speaking to her as he did so and bringing it slowly to the cage, where he set it down. She growled at him again and he backed away and sat down at the table. While he watched her she did not move forward to the water, though her thirst was a heat in her throat. She waited until he took up his feather and began his scratching again and then she edged forward, though she kept her eyes on him all the time. She could not get all her snout through the bars, and the water was not high enough in the bucket for her to be able to lap at it, so she dipped in her paw and licked the moisture from her fur. When she had relieved her thirst enough, she slept again. When she woke he was gone. She lay in the dark, watching the light brighten around the door and in the cracks in the walls. Later her ward came. He scrubbed at her matted fur, where she had not cleaned herself, scraping away her scabs so that she bled again. He threw her food into the cage and left her with the bucket of water he had used to clean her.

She was dozing again when the footsteps roused her. She scented that it was him even before the door opened. He was carrying his lamp, and his other things, which he set on the table. But he did not start with his scratching immediately. He came over and bent down in front of the cage, speaking to her as he did so. She felt a strange pleasure at this, which disturbed her, and she growled at him. Speaking all the time in a low soft voice he reached forward and tossed something through the bars of her cage. She sniffed at it, but she would not touch it until he had gone back to his table. Then she stretched forward and snuffled up the apple, licking its juices afterwards from her nose and lips.

The following day she waited for him, but he did not come, nor the next day. She had begun to forget him, as she had forgotten so many other things, when she heard his footfalls. She waited for him to bring her another apple, or at least to talk to her. But he went straight to the table and began his dipping and scratching. After a time he picked up the sheet on which he scratched and spoke to it, at first quickly and quietly, and then more loudly. Then he set it down and began making big, harsh scratches on it, which disquieted her and made her draw back into the cage. He had calmed again, and had renewed his small scratching, when abruptly he gave out a cry, as if he was in pain, and swept his hand across the table, knocking the pot to the floor in front of her, where it spilled dark blood.

She growled at him when he approached her but he spoke so kindly now, squatting down in front of the cage, that she ceased to be afraid and felt the pleasure of his attention again. She twitched her nose and peered at him. His skin was smooth and pale compared to the angry red welts on the face of her ward. He fumbled in his pockets and brought out something that smelled good, which he held out to her. She waited for him to toss it into the cage, but instead he set it down just inside the bars. She hesitated, but then reached forward. For a moment her claws were only a few inches from his hand, his fingers pale and fragile compared to the thick fist of her paw, and then she was pulling the food towards her. He talked to her while she ate and she looked up into his face, but she could not hold his gaze. He spoke for a long time, at first to her, but soon he was standing up and circling the shadows of the stables, his hands moving as he spoke, speaking as men did to other men, though only she was there to hear him.

She did not see him again before her day came. She knew always when it was her day and she lay in her cage, apprehension coursing through her, though anticipation, too. When it was time her ward came and let her out of the cage and she sat impatiently while he brushed her. Then he took up her chain and led her through the stable door and out into the daylight. She turned her head away, blinded by the brightness, but he pulled her on and she had to follow him. She could hear the roar of the men waiting for her and the fear and excitement rose in her.

At first the roar was above her and in front of her but as she came out into the open it was all around her. Smells filled her nose and her throat. Something struck her on her head and she forced her eyes open though she knew they would not set the dogs on her yet. First she would be walked round and round between the men rising up on all sides and then her ward would fasten her chain to the stake. She shook her head and followed him. She could smell the dogs now and hear their barking and squealing. And now she saw them straining against their leashes. The noise was terrible, the men shouting and banging, the dogs yowling, and she stood on her back legs and roared and the men roared back.

Then the first dog was let loose and though she was late

to come down from her hind legs and see it, she smelled it and cuffed it away with her paw. The dog rolled over and came at her again, and again she knocked it aside. This time it stood up more gingerly and barked at her but did not come forward.

Before she had time to enjoy her victory another dog was almost upon her and this time when she caught it with her paw the animal fell at her feet and in a moment she had picked it up in her mouth and half ripped its leg from its shoulder, tasting its hot blood. Her ward and the other men were upon her at once, beating at her with their sticks, pulling the dog from her jaws, but she barely noticed their blows, though she was not so mad that she struck any of the men. She had learned never to do that.

The dogs came thick and fast now. One she slapped away, another caught hold of a fold of her skin and she had to shake it off, while a third dug its fangs into her haunches before she battered it away and it cartwheeled across the ground. She pulled at her chain, clawing at the dogs, wanting only to taste their blood, urged on by the roaring of the men all around her.

Then it was over, and her chain was unfastened from the stake, and she was led away into the shadows, where her ward paused for a few minutes, while she sat, panting, so that he could watch the men breathe fire from their mouths.

When she woke it was night. There was someone beside the cage and she shrunk back, growling. Her nose was swollen from the blow of one of the men's sticks so that it took her a while to know it was him, and to quiet enough to hear that he was speaking to her. He was holding out something to her and she sniffed at the piece of apple until he dropped it in front of her. When she had swallowed it she lifted her head. He had another piece in his hand but this time he did not drop it but moved backwards away from her, still holding the apple, and only when she shuffled her own aching body forwards did she realize that the door to her cage was open and the keys were dangling from his other hand. He dropped the piece of apple outside the cage and she came out and took it. Again he had another piece of apple and again he moved away from her. He was talking to her all the time. She came forward and took the apple by the stable door, which was open also. He talked to her and went through the doorway and she followed him, taking the piece of apple that he dropped though it was as much his voice that drew her, and the smell of him, as the sweetness of the apple. When they were out of the stable building he turned not towards the yard, but in the other direction, to the back gate, which was open.

He called to her and she followed him. They went along a path between buildings. At first the only smells were those of men but as they went on she began to taste other scents in the air, which stirred her. She padded after him, forgetting her weariness and stiffness. They came out on to a wider path. She could see the lights of buildings but ahead was only darkness. Soon on one side was darkness, too, and then all around and as she grew used to it she began to be able to make out the shape of the land and what rose from it. She stopped and lifted her head and sniffed, and the smells intoxicated her, so that it was no longer even him drawing her on, but herself. She began to move more quickly, and soon she was loping. She passed him on the track and she heard him calling to her, but whether he was calling her back or urging her on did not matter, for she had the scent now and she could not have stopped herself.

Curry Paradise

34 Brick Lane

A pale shape rose out of the blackness and he whipped his arm down, the spear making barely a splash in the water, and when he lifted it again there was a quiver of silver on its point. He pulled off the fish and smacked its head against the rock, and satisfying himself it was dead set it down and lowered himself again into his half squat in the shallows, oblivious to the moths and other insects drawn by the lamp and fluttering about him.

He caught two more fish and after the second one he stood and leaned on his spear. The only noises were the belch of frogs and the sawing of crickets, though further away in the darkness he could see here and there the flicker of other lamps, like stars fallen to earth. Then he coiled himself again, and was absorbed by his task, and after a time by thoughts that rose up in his head, like the fish in the black water, so that he did not notice it had started raining again until the drops were falling too thickly for him to be able to carry on fishing. He counted the fish he had lain on the rock: nine, not a bad catch, though only one was longer than the spread of his hand or wider than three of his fingers. The larger ones had been fished out weeks ago, or had grown wary of the lamps. Unwinding a piece of twine from his wrist he threaded the bone needle at its end through the mouths of the fish and draped them over his spear, which he balanced across his shoulder.

The rain was falling so heavily now that he could see no more than half a dozen paces ahead of him, even with the glow of the lamp, and though he waded in water up to his shins, and sometimes lapping over his knees, he did not once hesitate or miss his step. He sensed the wall ahead of him before he saw it but when he lifted the lamp, the colours and shapes appeared as if by magic. He walked slowly along the path, the lamp illuminating first the tail of the aeroplane and then its wings and nose, and as he moved along the wall, the buildings it was flying towards, the tall one with the clock, the one with the rounded roof and spire, at the end the brightly painted one with the square window, beneath a row of letters he could not read though he knew what they spelled out. He remained there looking until he became aware that he was shivering and he set off again along the drowned paths.

In the morning the rain had stopped. The waters were still only a few steps from the hut, but they had not risen any more in the night. He ate a handful of leftover rice and when he was finished he took up his knife and wading out into the water began to cut back the water hyacinths that stole the light from his rice plants, carrying the thick stems and leaves he had cut to the edge of the water and throwing them on to the mud. He was careful as he walked through the paddy not to damage his rice plants. He had sown each one himself in the seedbeds behind his hut, fertilizing them with decomposed water hyacinth and his own and his family's waste. While the seedlings were growing he had ploughed his field six times, working from first light until he could no longer see to drive the bullocks forward, for each day he rented the plough and the pair of beasts had to be paid for with two days of his own labour. Then he had transferred the young plants into the paddy fields, one by one.

When he was sure that not a single hyacinth was left on the surface of the water, he gathered the cut plants into bundles. He had more than enough already for his own needs, so hefting the first bundle on to his back he carried it to the homestead below which he had paused the previous evening, where there was always need for food for animals. Boats paddled across the deeper waters, but he kept to the drowned pathways. After the third journey he received his payment, a small bag of rice. When he reached home the women were squatting in front of the hut, descaling the fish he had caught the previous night, the two older girls helping their mother and grandmother, the baby sleeping beside them.

In the afternoon, he slept for a while, too, and when he woke, stiff from the night and his morning's work, he called for his eldest daughter to massage his back. He lay on his stomach while Soraya knelt over him, her small hands kneading the flesh on his shoulders and down his spine. Five times Najma had given birth and of the five it was the two boys who had not lived. Motosir Ali was not blind to the pleasures of living in a household of women, but one day his daughters would marry and go to live with their husbands, whereas a son would work alongside him in his field and when he married would bring his wife here. He thought with pleasure and hope of the swelling in his wife's belly.

Later he busied himself as best he could about the island that his small homestead became during the floods, frustrated that there was so little that could be done at this time of year. He might have waded across to one or other of the larger homesteads to ask if there was any work, but he had done this many times already during the rains, and he knew there would be no day labour now until the rice had ripened. Instead he told Najma to bring him his meal early, so that he could take advantage of the dry evening. He ate alone, as usual, the women watching him in silence, waiting for him to finish so they could settle down to eat their meal together. Licking the last grains of rice and flecks of fish from his fingers, he wiped his hands on his lungi, and taking up his spear and lamp, went out into the night.

The rain returned the next day but for less than an hour, and the day after that was dry, as were the days that followed. By the end of the week the paths had begun to emerge from the waters and people were walking again between the homesteads. Under the sun the rice plants turned from green to yellow and Motosir Ali weeded them and fertilized them, moving carefully among them to aerate the soil with a forked stick. One evening Najma informed him that they were close to the bottom of their last bag of rice, but Motosir Ali would not countenance buying any more. Each year at harvest he had to sell more of the rice he had grown on his land to pay off his debts from the previous year, and so had to start borrowing further before the next harvest to buy rice from the bazaar, which pained him beyond the debts he was accumulating, for no rice tasted as good as that grown on one's own land, nor nourished so well. They would just have to make this bag last, he said. But oil was needed, and a few vegetables, now that their only source of fish was those trapped in their small pond, and he took the basket Najma gave him and set off for the bazaar.

It was more than two miles across the fields and he was thirsty by the time he reached the first of the stalls crowded along either side of the dusty street. He bought a glass of tea and drank it down in three gulps. His throat was scalded but the hot sweetness was delicious; it was seldom he could afford to buy sugar for home. He took out his money from the waist roll of his lungi. There was not enough for all the things Najma had asked him to buy, and he would have to go to Sharif anyway, so he bought another glass of tea, drinking it more slowly this time, savouring it, and when he had finished that he walked a little further down the road and bought some pan, which he chewed slowly as he made his way through the crowds. The larger shops were interspersed with smaller stalls selling sweetmeats and bidis, and old men sitting crosslegged on the ground in front of odd items spread on a piece of ragged cloth: a torn book, a comb missing half its teeth. Sewing machines whirred and barbers whetted their razors with a flourish. The moneylender was sitting behind his counter fiddling with the knobs on a television, wired up to a car battery, which was giving out crackling sounds and the occasional squeak.

Bloody transmitter's on the blink again, Sharif said.

Motosir Ali said nothing. He had seen televisions often enough, but he had never actually made one work.

You have come to pay what you owe me? Sharif said.

I need to borrow a little more.

More, more. Sharif sighed. Everybody always wants more. He waggled his bald head. He was the richest man in the whole district, it was said, and could have retired long ago and lived in luxury, but every day he was here sitting at his stall. Sell me your land and you'll have all the money you want.

Two hundred taka, Motosir Ali said. That is all. Until harvest. Then I will repay everything I owe you.

Whatever you wish, the moneylender said. Who am I to give advice? Nobody listens to me anyway.

His hand disappeared beneath the counter and came up with a stack of small notes. He set them on the counter and began to count them, licking his thumb after every second one.

Two hundred, he said. He held up the notes but made no move to give them to Motosir Ali.

I will get your land in the end, he said. It is your choice only how it happens. Piece by piece until it costs me only a last few taka, or now while there is still enough to do something with it.

Motosir Ali said nothing and the old moneylender shrugged and handed over the notes. As he walked away, Motosir Ali heard the television begin to crackle again.

The paddy turned golden and Motosir Ali laboured under the hot sun to cut the rice and carry it up to the earth beside the hut, where the women laid it out to dry. When every last plant had been cut he left the women to glean the field and start on the threshing, and went to sell his labour in the fields below the homestead with the painted wall. The pay was small, but he was given a midday meal of rice and vegetables at noon, which saved him from needing more than a snack in the evening. The other workers sat in the narrow band of shade beneath the homestead, their backs against the wall, but Motosir Ali didn't mind the sun as long as he could look on the painting. It was paler and less beautiful than in the glow of a lamp at night, the colours bleached by the sunlight, and he could see the imperfections where the paint had peeled away and the cement was cracked. But he had looked at it so many times that he saw less the scene in front of him than the image his mind had come to make of it.

In a short time the harvest was over. The fields lay bare and brown in the sun. Most of Motosir Ali's rice was now in sacks in the back of the hut. Out front, Najma was husking what they would need soon, pushing down on the dheki with her foot, though it was clear from the swelling beneath her sari that her time was near. They had not eaten any of the new rice yet. They had kept to what Motosir Ali had brought home from his labour. He picked up some of the newly husked rice and let it fall through his fingers. It was good quality. He walked into the back and counted the sacks again. Somehow he had thought there would be more, but he could not complain. It had been a fine harvest. The rains had neither come too early nor stayed too long. The sun had been allowed to ripen the rice for just the right amount of time. There had been no plague of insects, no disease. He set aside the sacks he would take to market to sell. He could wait a few days, the price would not fall and he would get a bullock more cheaply.

When Najma's pains began, his mother took her into the back room and closed the shutters. The girls looked after the baby and brought messages to Motosir Ali, where he waited outside. When he could bear the screams no longer, he walked down on to the hard brown earth of his field and squatted there picking at his teeth with a twig until his mother appeared from the hut to tell him that he had been blessed with a son.

Two days later Motosir Ali took the bags of rice to the bazaar to sell. Returning home he led the bullock back along the path between the dry fields to the Londoni homestead, and when he had handed over the beast, he walked around the cement house until he came to the painted wall.

He had been working here when it had been done. An artist had come from town, staying in the house, eating and smoking as much as he liked. The other men labouring in the fields derided what he was doing as ungodly and decadent, but Motosir Ali had been fascinated by the images taking shape.

The painting had been commissioned for the owner of

the house by his sons as a surprise gift. They had sent photographs and instructions as well as money, and it had been finished shortly before the old man arrived for a rare visit. He had been accompanied by two of his grandchildren, and with the painting now part of the landscape, it was they who became the object of gossip and disapproval in the fields. The girl kept indoors most of the time, like their own women, except when she had to be taken into town so she could make her ablutions on the white marble lavatory in the Sylhet Hotel, but the boy was often to be seen walking about or sitting in the shade listening to his music on his Sony, staring back defiantly at anyone who came to look at him more closely. Motosir Ali agreed with the others that he showed a lack of respect, but there was something else about the boy, a spirit, a refusal to bow down, that Motosir Ali could not but help admire, and which, lying in the dark of his hut, he had wondered whether he might ever know himself what it was like to possess.

A few days after he had sold his rice, Motosir Ali went back to the bazaar. That afternoon he set about preparing an extra large vegetable patch. All day he carried water in a bucket from the shrinking pond to soften the earth, which he turned over with a spade. When everything was ready he planted lentil, onion and cauliflower seeds, which he continued to irrigate every hour for the next three weeks, squatting directly over them every time he needed to defecate, so as not to waste a single scrap of the precious goodness. When he was not carrying water, he fixed things around the hut, a broken shutter at the back, a hole in the roof. He opened and resealed the rice sacks to make sure no weevils had got inside them and that they were secure from rats and mice.

One morning, as the call to prayers was drifting through the village, the family emerged from the hut. Motosir Ali was holding a small suitcase bought in the bazaar, and was dressed in grey trousers, which came to a flared stop several inches above his ankles, a pair of blue plastic shoes and a yellow shirt. It was the first time he had worn trousers or shoes, and he felt constricted by both. His hair was plastered to his head with oil. While the women about him moaned and the baby began to cry, Motosir Ali looked out. Even in the morning mist his land looked more beautiful than ever. But it was no longer his land, and eventually he peeled his wife and children from him, and said his last farewells, and walked away down the path.

Trails of mist floated about him, offering cover to any lurking bandits, and his hand kept slipping nervously inside his shirt, where the thick roll of money was wrapped in a little bag on a string around his neck.

As he walked, the sun burned away the mist. Halfway to the town he stopped and looked back for a last time. He could not see his own hut, but the larger mound of the Londoni homestead was still visible, rising above the fields.

Several times during his visit the old man had come down to the fields before Motosir Ali had found the courage to walk up to him and speak to him. He could still feel the pleasure he had experienced at the old man's consideration towards him. When the foreman had rushed forward, shouting at Motosir Ali to go back to work, the old man had waved him away and patiently answered the younger man's questions: telling him how many tables there were in the restaurant, what the kitchen was like, that in one evening a waiter might make 500 taka in tips. That was when he had said that if Motosir Ali could make his way to London there would be a job there for him. Not serving food at first, of course. Working in the kitchen, cleaning plates, chopping vegetables – women's work, the old man had apologized. But in time, if Motosir Ali worked hard, it was quite possible that he would become a waiter. The old man had used the English word and Motosir Ali repeated it aloud now as he walked, his mouth tasting its music.

There was a crowd waiting for the bus and Motosir Ali did not get on the first one. But by pushing and jostling forward, and holding up his money, he managed to attract the attention of the wallah on the second bus, who took his suitcase and fastened it on to the roof, and shoved Motosir Ali inside. The seats were all taken and he was pressed sweatily between other bodies. When the bus started he lurched forward and after that he held on to the back of the seat. The bus rattled and creaked, the driver hooted, a duck inside someone's shirt quacked.

Dhaka, a man beside him was saying to his neighbour. I am buying and selling. Do you have business in Dhaka?

No, I am going to Saudi, the other man said.

First time?

I have been there five years. I work in a factory. I will stay five more years and then I will come home.

The bus swerved and they all rocked forward together.

I am going foreign too, Motosir Ali said.

Heads turned to look at him.

Saudi?

London.

Oh well, it is easy for you Londoni people. In London you can walk about picking up money.

I am not Londoni, Motosir Ali said.

Then how are you going?

I am going to see a broker in Dhaka. I have his address. Sharif had given it to him when he had collected his money.

The businessman going to Dhaka looked at him and Motosir Ali was glad now that he was wearing his new shirt and trousers and shoes. You must be very rich, the businessman said.

I sold my land, Motosir Ali said. After my debts were paid I received thirty thousand taka. Immediately he said this, he cursed himself silently for his foolishness. Who knew what thieves might be lurking on the bus?

Thirty thousand? the businessman said.

I will stay two years, three years, Motosir Ali said, unable to stop himself. I am not greedy. Only long enough so that I can buy a little more land for my son, to make him a better future.

Motosir Ali smiled at this thought, but the businessman was looking at him with a strange face.

Thirty thousand? he said. That would not buy a ticket to

Saudi, let alone get you unlegal to London.

Three hundred thousand you would need, a voice said from somewhere in the bus.

More even.

You hear that? This fellow in the yellow shirt thinks he is going to London unlegal for thirty thousand taka.

Going nowhere fast, more like it.

What are you saying? Motosir Ali said, straining his neck to follow the conversation, to make sense of what was being said, panic rising like a snake on his chest. What are you saying?

Brother, someone has tricked you, the businessman said softly.

It cannot be true, Motosir Ali said, looking into the businessman's face, beseeching him, but his words were drowned by a prolonged hoot of the horn, and when the hoot stopped the conversation had moved on to the price of a sack of rice in Dhaka, the government's promise to build a new road.

The bus swerved to avoid a pothole, and Motosir Ali was thrown into the passenger in front of him, who cursed him over his shoulder. Motosir Ali grasped for the back of the seat and clung to it while the bus careered on, his feet cramping in his plastic shoes, his yellow shirt sticking to his moist skin.

The lost years

37 Brick Lane

In the days after her husband's death, Mistress Brown's life was thrown into turmoil. Master Brown was soon buried, for it was a warm July, but while his affairs were, as would have been expected, in good order, the one thing he had not anticipated was the abruptness of his end, and as well as his will to be read and acted upon, there were decisions to be made about his business, whether to sell it or keep it, and how to deal with it in the meantime, and a host of other matters which he had managed without Mistress Brown noticing, but for which she was now responsible, and all this on top of a steady stream of well-wishers dropping in on her, all of whom had to be provided with ale and victuals and time to pay their condolences. Fortunately Mistress Brown could call on good advice, and it was not long before the business was sold, the money invested, and other matters arranged so that she did not have to concern herself with them. In time, too, the number of visitors lessened until the day finally arrived when not a single neighbour, or friend, or niece, came to call.

It was the height of summer. Bees buzzed about the lavender and hyssop in the garden. Mistress Brown walked around the house, pointing out to Audrey and the undermaids the cobwebs that had spread across the ceilings, the stains on the pewter. At noon she sat down to a hot dinner. A few days before her bereavement she had begun a new embroidery, and in the afternoon she took it up again, retreating with her stool and sewing box to the shadiest part of the house, her brows knitted in concentration. Later, when the sinking sun glared through the window, she went out into the garden and walked among the tomatoes and the vines with Tom, the gardener. At six she ate a supper of cold meat, bread and mustard, as she and her husband had for as many of the evenings of the thirty-three years of their marriage as she could remember.

Although Mistress Brown had watched Master Brown's body being carried out of the house and had seen his casket lowered into the earth of the churchyard, his presence was not so easily removed from the routine of the household, which had been shaped according to his needs, or the mind of its mistress. Mistress Brown still slipped quietly out of bed in the morning and spoke to the maids in a lowered voice until the time at which Master Brown would normally have appeared for breakfast. She still ordered his favourite meals and praised the cook for making the coney stew, or the roasted starling, just as the master liked them. She still had the ale brewed strong, though she would not drink it until it had been watered down, and reminded Tom to pick the apples early, for Master Brown preferred them crisp and tart. And when she went to bed at night she lay facing the wall, for her husband had not liked to feel her breath on his face or his neck while he slept.

Although by no means as frequently as in the days after her husband's death, Mistress Brown still from time to time received visitors or went out herself. She had grown up in the town and was acquainted with many of its gentlefolk, and related to more than a few, if she could not have claimed any of them as good friends. As a child she had been close to her family, especially to her brothers and sisters, and her mother, and, once her eldest brother was wedded, to her sister-in-law, but after her own marriage, her husband had discouraged her from spending time at Henley Street, or inviting her family to his house, for it did his trade no good to be associated too closely with her father's disgraces, as he called them. Nor did her brother's success, when it came, change Master Brown's opinion. Her husband was one of the members of the town council who had passed the measure banning the players from the Guild Hall and other town property. But all that was long ago. Her brother was dead, as were all her closest relatives. The family she saw now were cousins and nieces, with their own lives. They would talk politely about inconsequential things until sooner or later, if it did not do so naturally, Mistress Brown would steer the conversation round to the subject of Master Brown: what an upright and honourable man he had been, how well he had served the town, how fortunate Mistress Brown had been to have enjoyed so long and profitable a marriage. She told herself the same things. Master Brown had been a good husband. He had provided for her. He had never once struck her. Her only regret was that they had not managed to raise any of their children.

With all that had to be done, and all that had been neglected while that was being attended to, it was not until after Master Brown's stone, a large solemn monument, fitting a man of his high stature, was set, some six weeks after his death, that Mistress Brown turned her attention to sorting through his possessions. She began with the bed chamber, throwing the window wide open, though it was no longer so warm, and keeping a handkerchief at hand, for dust always made her eyes run and her nose itch. Several times she had to use the handkerchief to dab away a tear from her eye. His jerkins and doublets, hanging in the press, still smelled of him. His shirts, for all they had been washed and scrubbed, still bore the stain of his sweat under the arms. Putting her hand into his boots she felt the imprint of his large, broad feet, the girth of his heavy calves. She had his clothes all over the room, spread on the bed, hanging over a chair, when she lifted some old netherstocks out of his trunk and uncovered a letter which bore a familiar hand, though it was not her husband's. It was addressed to her father at Henley Street. Thinking it might be something of importance, she opened it. Now she recognized the hand and looked at the date. As she read, her head grew hot, and she could feel her heart thumping beneath her bodice. When she was finished she sat for a long time, among her husband's clothes and papers, holding the letter in her hand, and when she stirred it was to replace it where she had found it, and put the netherstocks back on top of it.

That night she could not sleep. She had told Audrey to put away her husband's clothes, and to close up the press and trunk, but her eyes and nose still itched. She lay on her back, but that only made her sneeze so she turned on to her side, facing into the bed, but still she could not sleep. Rising, she took a candle and sat in front of the glass, and began to brush her white hair. It was how she had used to calm herself at night in the years during which her children had been born and died. Most women of her age had lost their hair or kept what remained short so as to fit beneath their wigs, but though her hair was now completely white it was still long and thick. She made gentle strokes with the brush. In the glass the candle flickered and she leaned forward slightly, peering at her face. A fairy face, her brother had called it once, long ago. She blushed at the memory and reached up to touch herself, trying to imagine her skin pale and smooth again, her lips red, her hair black, dark eyebrows arching over eyelids not rumpled like the skin of a rotten apple, but heavy with expectation.

It was almost dawn when she fell asleep, and she woke late. Hurrying to dress, she surprised the maids sitting in the kitchen with the cook. Brusquely she told them to make ready the fat and the moulds, and she spent the morning pouring candles, the wax burning her fingers and collecting in thick wedges on her apron. After lunch, she told Audrey to have the bed turned and sat down with her needlework. A cousin was to be married later in the month and she had

decided the embroidery would make a good wedding pres-
ent. Her fingers were numb from the hot wax and it was not
until she saw blood on the cloth that she realized she had
pricked herself. Within an hour her thumb was throbbing
painfully. That night she developed a fever.

For three days she lay in the grip of the ague. The doctor
visited twice a day, instructing Audrey to bathe her swollen
thumb, and her brow, in cold water every hour. Several
times Mistress Brown cried out and once she wept, tears
streaming down her face. Sometimes she spoke, and amid
her outpourings Audrey, who had been with her through
many years, recognized the names of Mistress Brown's late
family, and of the children she had lost. On the fourth day
the fever broke and the following afternoon the doctor said
she could sit by the window, as long as it was kept closed.

Mistress Brown sat in the chair, a blanket on her lap,
gazing out of the window. It had begun on a September day
like this, though it had been another garden she had looked
out on then.

When her father had told her the news, she had thought
he must be joking, and when she had seen the expression on
his face, and realized he was serious, she had said, Never,
and he had reached across the table and struck her with the
back of his hand. She had wept fiercely and he had come
round the table to comfort her, tears in his eyes too, plead-
ing with her, offering her a silver chain, the softest fur.
When still she had said no, he had dragged her up the stairs
to the bed chamber and after he had locked her in she had
stood at the window, looking out at the flowers and trees,

feeling that never again would she be part of that sunlit world.

Later, her mother had brought her food and drink, and though she heard her mother locking the door when she left, she did not hear her taking the key from the lock. She made her mind up in that moment. When the house fell quiet, she used a trick her brother had taught her: pushing some paper under the door and poking at the key until it fell out on to the paper, and pulling it back under the door.

Creeping about the sleeping house, she made a parcel of a few clothes, an apple, half a loaf of bread, and some money she took from her mother's purse. She left while it was still dark, gently closing the front door behind her, not once looking back. By dawn, she was a mile outside Stratford.

She walked, or rode on farmer's carts, luxuriating on hay, bruised by seats of potatoes. Birds sang in the hedgerows. A travelling gentleman bade her ride on his horse and she sat in front of him, smelling the sweat in the animal's mane.

Mistress Brown, at her chair at the window, searched the remembered thickets for robbers and murderers, and worried at the intentions of that gentleman, a child pressed between his thighs, but the girl she had been had felt only the intense wonder of setting out on an adventure.

It took four days to reach London and half a day to cross the city and find her brother, surrounded by baying crowds in what had once been the yard of an inn. Her first sight of him was a sword piercing his chest. His eyes gaped open and he fell to the floor, his own sword clattering on the ground. She clapped and cheered with the crowd, and when it was over, she found him in the tiring house and he took her out drinking with his friends, who insisted on stroking her black hair, first one and then all of them calling her beautiful, at which her brother laughed and said she was a little fairy escaped from the Forest of Arden.

For two weeks she went with him everywhere, watching him rehearse, watching the plays, sitting in taverns with him and his friends, falling asleep to the sound of his scratching, and waking with her head snug against his back. He let others buy him drinks, but he barely touched them himself, so she drunk his too, and the second evening she told the man who had first said she was beautiful that she loved him, and he had laughed and draped his arm languorously around her brother's shoulders.

She had been there ten days when her father's letter came. She didn't want to know what it said, wouldn't listen to her brother reading it, lay on the bed with her hands over her ears.

He sat down beside her and put his hand on her head.

I won't go, she said. I'll kill myself first.

I don't want you to go either, he said. But you are only a child.

I am not.

You are sixteen.

Then why do I have to marry?

Father—

He's not my father if he wants me to marry that man.

I forbid you to speak like that.

I'll say what I will, she cried. If I do not speak my heart will break in two.

If you do not go back it is Father who will be broken.

That's what he told you and it did not stop you, she said. I am not so young that I do not remember that.

I mean it will bankrupt him, he said. If you would uncover your ears you would learn that your betrothed—

He is not my betrothed.

—has brought an action on breach of contract for a hundred pounds. Father does not have that kind of money. If he loses this action it will ruin him.

He made the contract, not me.

But only you can keep it.

It's not fair, she cried. I want to stay with you.

And live how? he said abruptly, leaping to his feet, his face dark and fierce. You think I can support you? I can hardly support myself, let alone send anything home to my family. What are you going to do? Serve in an inn? Sell yourself like me?

She stared up at him and his voice grew quiet.

That is what I do here, he said. Do you not see? I sell my soul, jumping in and out of old jerkins and breeches, killed ten times a day by rusty swords with broken hilts, sharing the stage with tumblers and jugglers and performing apes, rewriting plays other fools have failed to fill enough with severed hands and plucked tongues. I am no better than a bear chained to a stake.

She was crying now as much from his anger, and in sympathy with his pain, than over her own life, for she was still a child, and what was most immediate caught her heart most strongly.

He bent down and lifted up her chin with the tips of his fingers.

Look at you, he said. Not such a beauty now. I must stay here, parted from my wife, my children, but you are free to go home. Your betrothed is a good man, a wealthy man.

I would not marry him for a mine of gold.

You will marry him, he said, throwing his hands into the air, startling her so that her tears came afresh.

Not looking at him, she said in a last act of defiance, If I was a boy you would keep me.

What came next Mistress Brown had buried so deeply that recalling it she felt the shock of it as if she had been struck at that moment. It was barely a cuff, nothing to how her father had hit her, but the hurt was tenfold. She curled up on the bed and would not move or say a word to him and in the morning he led her mute to the inn from where the coach left.

They stood in the yard. He had been so tender with her all morning that it was a struggle not to speak to him.

Is this not well? he said gently.

Only now, half a lifetime later, could Mistress Brown hear that he was trying to reassure not her but himself. The letter she had found was dated the very night she had arrived. He must have written it as she lay in his bed, while she had thought he was scratching out his poetry. Come, my sweet sister, he said. Give your brother one kiss. She had thought it was because he did not want her to go away with her conscience heavy, so she had kissed him, and once her stubbornness was broken, she had clung to him, kissing him a thousand times, weeping into his breast, until all the other travellers were on board.

She was married within the week, the wedding brought forward as if she had been with child, though no man had ever touched her before her husband on her wedding night. After he had rolled off her, Master Brown told her she was fortunate he had still been willing to marry her. Then he said she should turn the other way to sleep, so as not to breathe on him.

The first time her brother came home she managed to steal him for an hour and walk with him along the river, begging for news of London, his friends, what plays he was labouring over.

The second time, he had had his first success, and she had lost her first child. She did not ask for time from him, and he did not offer. Every visit home after that he was more celebrated, his time more precious, his stays shorter. She lost another child and then had John, who died at two months.

Some years after that, a guest in their house, a man passing through Stratford, leaned across to her, and whispered, Your brother has seen the face of God.

By then Mary was dead and the surgeon had warned her she must not become with child again.

The last day of that week was Mistress Brown's fiftieth birthday. Her cousin came to see her, the one who was to be married in a fortnight's time. She sat holding Mistress Brown's hand, chattering sweetly, until she had stayed long enough for it to be polite to leave. Mistress Brown let herself be kissed goodbye and sunk back into her chair, relieved to be alone again.

She was still weak but she knew she would live. She had outlived them all, her brother, his wife, her parents, Master Brown, John, Mary, probably her brother's friends as well, and now she would continue on again. But for what purpose? If Master Brown had died ten or twenty years earlier, if she had found the letter then, perhaps she could have walked out of the house another time, climbed on a wagon, bought herself a seat in a coach. She had the money and no ties to hold her back. At thirty she could have done it, perhaps even at forty, but at fifty it was too late.

A weaver's daughter

38 Brick Lane

Boswell first began to take an interest in his penis when he was twelve years old. 'In climbing trees, pleasure,' he wrote some years later. 'Thought of heaven. Returned often, climbed, felt, allowed myself to fall from high trees in ecstasy.' He tried asking the gardener about it but he, 'rigid, did not explain it'. Soon, though, a 'playmate' taught him how to carry out 'the fatal act' without the need of trees. Brought up in a strict Calvinist Edinburgh household, the young Boswell was horrified by the fear he would 'sin and be damned' but was unable to resist his 'youthful passions'. The dilemma brought on a moral and religious crisis, and he considered castrating himself, but eventually he decided that what he was doing was a pardonable sin. It was fornication rather that was 'horrible' and damnable.

His first experience of fornication came six years later, when he was nineteen, in 1760. He had fallen in love with a Catholic actress and run away to London where he was secretly admitted into the Roman Catholic Church, apparently with the intention either of proving his love or becoming a monk. London, however, distracted him from either plan and before long he had lost his virginity to a woman named Sally Forrester in a room in the Blue Periwig in Southampton Street. Over the following weeks, in the company of Lord Eglinton and the Duke of York, Boswell savoured the delights of a good number of London's minor actresses and prostitutes until he contracted from one of them his first dose of gonorrhoea, for which he was treated by a former naval surgeon, Andrew Douglas, who had a medical practice on Pall Mall. The experience cannot have been too devastating, though, for when, after his cure was complete, his father ordered him back to Edinburgh to study the law, Boswell consoled himself with a visit to a local brothel, where he was infected again.

This attack – 'a Tartar, with a vengeance' – lasted four months and Boswell determined 'to have nothing to do with whores, as my health was of great consequence to me'. Keeping away from women entirely was another matter. In rejecting the Calvinist strictures of his upbringing he had liberated what Lawrence Stone, in his 1977 study, *The Family, Sex and Marriage*, describes as 'an overwhelmingly powerful sex drive – crude, unrefined, urgent – and a very large member'. Or as Boswell himself put it, 'I am of a warm constitution; a complexion, as the physicians say, exceedingly amorous.' His large member apart, he was not particularly physically prepossessing. He was 'a swarthy young man, a little shorter and plumper than most, with a prominent, curving nose,' according to a recent biographer, Adam Sisman, but he had 'a hungry appetite for experience and an engaging cheerfulness' which 'men found endearing and women attractive.' He was also 'a shameless flirt'.

Over the next two years, while studying law in Edinburgh, he had affairs with at least four women and fathered an illegitimate child with a servant girl. When he returned to London in 1762, he was soon pursuing a new mistress, an actress he called Louisa. His efforts to woo her, recorded in detail in a journal he posted in weekly instalments to an Edinburgh friend, finally climaxed in a night of 'supreme rapture' in which he performed five times. Boswell was swollen with pride at his 'godlike vigour'. Louisa, he wrote, declared him a 'prodigy'. Invited a day or two later to a gathering at Lady Northumberland's, he was no more the unconfident provincial, standing in the corner, but 'strutted up and down, considering myself as a valiant man who could gratify a lady's loving desires five times a night'. If his diary can be believed, he told one of the ladies, 'You must know, Madam, I run up and down this town just like a wild colt', to which she replied: 'Why, Sir, then, don't you stray into my stable?'

Soon, however, Boswell began to feel a familiar 'heat in the members of my body sacred to Cupid'. It was 'Signor Gonorrhoea' again. Boswell was outraged. He had been 'expecting at least a winter's safe copulation' and now he had to retire to his rooms and take the painful cure again. He had been sleeping only with the 'treacherous Louisa' and decided she 'deserved to suffer for her depravity'. He wrote to her demanding back the sum of two guineas which he had lent her. 'You cannot have forgot upon what footing

I let you have it. I neither paid it for prostitution nor gave it in charity. It was fairly borrowed, and you promised to return it. I give you notice that I expect to have it before Saturday night.' Confined to his rooms for five weeks, Boswell wrote in his journal, received friends when he felt well enough and turned them away when overcome by melancholia. One such rejected visitor, William Cochrane, Judge Advocate of Scotland, and a cousin of his mother, left a note upbraiding Boswell for depriving himself 'of the comforts of friendly confabulation. Who in the performance of a manly part would not wish to get claps? The brave only are wounded in front, and heroes are not ashamed of such scars.'

Confinement gave Boswell time to think. Third time infected, he had learned his lesson, and as soon as his cure was complete, he went down to Mrs Phillips's shop on Half Moon Street and purchased some 'armour', as he called condoms. Made from the intestines of goats and sheep, these were thick and hard, and his first experience of sheathed copulation, with a street prostitute, provided 'but a dull satisfaction'. Needs were needs, though, and that spring – of 1763 – he was a familiar loiterer about the darker alleys and corners of central London. One night he 'took the first whore I met into the park and without many words copulated with her free from danger. She was ugly and lean and her breath smelt of spirits.' Another time, he picked up a 'damsel' at the bottom of Haymarket and 'conducted her to Westminster Bridge, and then in armour complete did I engage her upon this noble edifice. The whim of doing it there with the Thames rolling below us amused me much.' On a third occasion he 'took a streetwalker into Privy Garden, and indulged sensuality. The wretch picked my pocket of my handkerchief and then swore she had not.'

Boswell's conversion to Catholicism had proved a brief dalliance and he eventually settled for a sceptical and luke-warm Anglican Episcopalianism. But while he had liberated his body from the teachings of Calvinism he could not so easily free his mind. As perilous to him as pickpockets or venereal disease were the feelings of guilt and the 'lacerating self-reproach', in Stone's words, that beset him once he had spent his desire. 'After the brutish appetite was sated,' he wrote of his coupling on Westminster Bridge, 'I could not but despise myself for being so closely united with such a low wretch.' Returning home from the pickpocketing incident, 'I was shocked to think that I had been intimately united with a low, abandoned, perjured, pilfering creature.' Again and again in his journals he agonized over his slum-ming and resolved to do no more of it, but it was never long before he yielded to temptation. In May 1763, he made the most important acquaintance of his life, with Samuel Johnson. He was immediately impressed with Johnson's character and determined to be more like him. 'Since my being honoured with the friendship of Mr Johnson, I have more seriously considered the duties of morality and religion and the dignity of human nature. I have considered that promiscuous concubinage is certainly wrong . . . If all the men and women in Britain were merely to consult animal gratification, society would be a most shocking scene. Nay, it would soon cease altogether.' Two weeks later he wrote, 'I should have mentioned that on Monday night, coming up the Strand, I was tapped on the shoulder by a fine fresh lass. I went home with her.' Later that year, before setting out on a European tour, he drew up an 'Inviolable Plan' for moral reform. 'For some years past, you have been idle, dissipated, absurd and unhappy,' he lectured himself. From now on he would be 'as chaste as an anchorite'. In Dresden, without condoms, he was obliged to ejaculate between the thighs of prostitutes to avoid infection. In Italy he 'ran after girls without restraint. My blood was inflamed by the burning climate, and my passions were violent.' Soon he was copulating without the security of 'armour', and inevitably he contracted another bout of gonorrhoea. Once again he vowed to be more careful and once again he broke his vows. 'The wounds of my Roman wars were scarcely healed before I received fresh ones at Venice.' Reaching Paris in January 1766, he received news that his mother had died. 'Quite stunned,' he wrote. To 'dissipate grief' he went straight off to a bordello. Back in Edinburgh, he gave a bachelor party to pay a debt of honour to friends whom he had bet, several years earlier, that he would stay free of the clap, after which he went whoring and was reinfected once more with the disease.

'Why,' writes William B. Ober, an American pathologist, in *Boswell's Clap and Other Essays: Medical Analyses of Literary Men's Afflictions*, 'should a man of good family, considerable education, adequate professional status, and prominent social connections, deliberately expose himself to the risks of gonorrhoea?' Boswell's own view seemed to be simply that he had a high sex drive and low will power, and he devoted his intellect to rationalizing, rather than explaining, his behaviour. If, reading the New Testament, he found it against 'concubinage', he would turn instead to the Old Testament for the examples of the patriarchs who 'went to harlots' but 'were devout'. Yet Boswell did not merely go to harlots, he went to them repeatedly without protection, even though he knew well enough both where to purchase it, and the consequences of going without it. Each bout of gonorrhoea meant pain, withdrawal from the world, the likelihood of the return of his melancholia, and the necessity for expensive, and often agonizing, treatments, such as bloodletting, incisions in the foreskin, and the irrigation of the urethra by way of a primitive syringe with dilute solutions of vitriol or nitrous acid. 'One can only imagine,' Ober writes, 'the discomfort caused by instilling acid into an already inflamed, pus-producing urethra.'

In a chapter on Boswell in *Great Men: Psychoanalytical Studies*, Eduard Hitschmann, a close collaborator of Freud, draws attention to the history of mental illness in Boswell's family. One of his uncles, his brother, and his daughter Euphemia all suffered from various 'maladies of the mind', and Hitschmann claims Boswell exhibited signs of manic depression. 'I was born with a melancholy temperament,' Boswell wrote, and certainly he was more inclined to get drunk and go out whoring when suffering from melancholia, as a way of temporarily relieving his mood. But Hitschmann also diagnoses Boswell as having a 'psychopathic personality', defined by 'intact intelligence, a defective superego, self-destructive tendencies, social mal-adaptation, unpredictable behaviour, intense narcissism, and a weak ego'. And the cause of this, Hitschmann concludes, was not a hereditary weakness, but Boswell's relationship with his father.

Alexander Boswell, eighth laird of Auchinleck, was a wealthy landowner and one of the six judges of the High Court of Justiciary, the supreme court of Scotland. Aloof, arrogant and manly, Lord Auchinleck was disappointed from the start by his weak, girlish son, who grew into a man who would avoid a duel by apologizing, and the father seemed to take pleasure in humiliating Boswell and calling him an idiot. 'Psychoanalysis has shown that a man's con-science originates in an identification with his parents, chiefly his father,' Hitschmann writes, and 'where a father merits only his son's hatred, the healthy development of a son's masculine character is impaired'. Imbued with a sense of inferiority and doubts about his masculinity, Boswell's promiscuity was an attempt to 'prove that he was virile'. A stern, remote, fear-inspiring father can also foster the devel-opment of homosexuality, Hitschmann continues, and Boswell's 'whoring' may have been 'a defence against uncon-scious homosexual trends'.

A libertine in behaviour, Boswell had never managed to be a libertine in conscience. His 'gonadal urges', as Ober calls them, were a response to his father's oppressive yoke, yet in indulging them he exposed himself to lacerating feelings of guilt and self-disgust. 'By pursuing only the cheapest whores, with the consequent near certainty of disease,' Stone writes, 'it almost looks as if he were deliberately seeking to punish himself for his sensuality.' Time and again he had intercourse 'with women who were repulsive to him,' writes Ober. 'One penalty for sexual guilt is castration, and to contract venereal disease is equivalent to castration, as it involved mutilation and impairment of the sexual organs.' Burdened with inherited mental illness, his masculinity impaired by his overbearing father, without the benefit of modern knowledge and psychoanalytical treatment, Boswell was, Ober writes, tormented by 'forces beyond his conscious knowledge and control'. 'Eager, inquisitive and naive,' Sisman writes, he was 'an enthusiastic participant in the game of love.' For all 'his philandering, Boswell was an innocent.'

In 1769, Boswell was married. His wife was a cousin, Margaret Montgomerie. She was a gentle, kind, intelligent woman who 'loved him deeply, understood him, and was patient with all his weaknesses and follies', according to Stone. In his own way Boswell loved her, too. He kept a notebook titled 'Uxoriana, or my Wife's excellent Sayings' and after her death preserved her purse, a lock of her hair, and 'two stalks of lily of the valley which my dear wife had in her hand the day before she died'. While she was alive, Stone writes, he 'paid her the compliment of always being frank and honest with her'. For three years after their marriage, his diaries record no episodes either of infidelity or gonorrhoea. But in the spring of 1772, after a period during which his wife first had a miscarriage, and then became pregnant again, Boswell 'went with bad women a little'. By now he was drinking heavily. His wife always seemed to be either pregnant or recovering from giving birth, and while he liked making love to pregnant women, for it removed one of the fears of sex, Margaret, with her tendency to miscarry, was not so keen. Soon he was back to the pattern of his bachelor days, with one addition: he would confess to his wife and she would forgive him. Bouts of gonorrhoea followed. Cures were taken. More than once he tried 'the experiment of cooling myself when ill', by which he meant having sex with a prostitute while infected, but this did not work, and he returned to his doctor. Whoring now also meant committing adultery, and he suffered even more from guilt. He consulted anyone he could about his dilemma: friends, female mentors, Dr Johnson – but while their advice was usually the same he did not take it, though he prided himself that he never passed on the clap to his wife.

Boswell's wedding to Margaret had not been attended by his father. On the same day, Lord Auchinleck, then a 62-year-old widower, had scheduled his own remarriage: 'a more obvious attempt at the sexual castration of his son could hardly be imagined,' according to Stone. Lord Auchinleck died in 1782 but Boswell's behaviour did not alter. In 1789 Margaret died of tuberculosis, and a year later, at the age of 50, with eighteen episodes of gonorrhoea behind him, Boswell still managed to visit a newly discovered prostitute three times in the course of a single day. 'To whet his now jaded palate,' Stone records, 'he tried "an experiment on three".' By now his own health was in serious decline. Ober lists the consequences of repeated attacks of gonorrhoea: chronic urinary tract infection, intermittent low-grade fever, impaired renal function, general malaise. In 1795, Boswell collapsed at a dinner of the Literary Club. Four medical advisers attended him, including a physician, a surgeon and an apothecary. He had chills, fever, violent headache and nausea. Within days he was dead: the cause, Ober writes, 'the complications of his many episodes of gonorrhoea'.

Lull's wyrth

41 Brick Lane

The breeze bent the hay into the swing of the scythe and Otha mowed empty of everything but the rhythm of his arm rising and falling, so that when he heard the clang of metal and felt the judder of pain in his shoulder he cursed himself for letting down his guard and dropped the scythe and swivelled all in one moment. But there was only the mown hay flat on the ground before him, and beyond the ripening barley, and beyond that the beast tethered to a post and a faint curl of smoke drifting up from the roof of the hut. Understanding was slow to come to him. He bent to retrieve the scythe and saw it was broken in two, and saw then the rock it had struck, only it was not a rock, but another of the pots, cracked open, its dust spilling out, and rising out of the dust the dull gleam of a scaled coil.

He glanced towards the hut and reached into the dust. There were two snakes, he saw, when he wiped them, their tails entwined, their heads facing each other across the gap that broke the circle. He held them in his hand, feeling their weight. His arm was thick and strong even by English standards but when he slipped them on to his wrist they hung loose on him like on a woman. His eyes lifting again towards the hut, he tucked them into his trousers, hidden beneath his tunic, and picked up the broken scythe.

You must fire it here, his wife said, when he had carried the pieces of blade back to the hut.

You are an idiot, he said. Without the proper heat it will only break again.

Brunna scowled, her eyes turning to the north. You cannot show your face there again.

There is the other settlement down river, he said. The one they spoke of at Gyffa's wyrth. There will be a smith there.

She turned her back on him, but in the morning when he woke she was up in the grey light, the skins already wrapped in cloth with the pieces of scythe. He slung the parcel over his shoulder and picked up his spear.

I will be back tomorrow by dark, he said.

If there are skins left over get some salt, his wife said. And some good beans for planting.

The boy was at her side, Otha shrinking from the accusation in his blonde hair and soft face. At least the baby had his darkness. He admired her in her mother's arms, noting as he did so the clawed hands that held her, the knuckles red and swollen. He turned away and did not look back.

From the stump of oak tree at the corner of the field the path was overgrown with brambles and nettles, for only he used it with any regularity, and when he came out on to the giants' way he was careful to put back the branches, so that unless a man was looking for it he would walk past without realizing there was a path. Not that many men came by here. The way further to the north, which went round the giants' works, was still used by travellers, but the path he now took, eastwards into the sun, along the ridge of the way, was trodden down by deer and boar.

Several times he passed the ruins of small giants' works, grass growing out of the cracked and fallen stones, but he was used to such things, living as he did in the shadow of the walls.

The first river he came to he had reached before, exploring the land in his first spring here, but he had never crossed it, and after he waded the ford, he walked more carefully, his ear bent to the breeze, his eyes casting back and forth. More than once he stooped to examine a blade of grass, or a snapped twig, sniffing the air. After he picked out the musky scent of a boar he sung as he walked, to make his presence known, but when the air was clear again he lapsed into silence.

At a second river, barely wider than a stream, he stopped to drink and sitting on a rock took out the snakes. He dipped them into the water and rubbed them against his arm until he had cleaned a patch of shining silver scale. He had not brought them with any intent, but nor had he wanted to leave them. The other things he had unearthed, the comb, and the goblet, and the brooches, his wife had thrown in the river, cursing him that he had brought enough bad luck on them already without raising the spirits of the giants' dead. He rubbed the coils some more. He was not afraid of any spirits. The dead could not harm the dead.

The way now entered the shadows of an oak wood. Squirrels scampered across the trail and up the trees. Birds sung above him. It was many months since he had seen any oak other than the hollow stump that marked the edge of his land and he breathed in the strong, damp smell. When he was a boy he had often hunted with his father in the deep oak woods about their homestead and in the evenings afterwards the men would talk of hunts in greater woods, in the land they had left behind, the trees taller, the beasts fiercer.

He was still adrift in his thoughts when he came round a corner and saw the stag barely ten steps ahead. They stared at each other until the stag crashed away through the trees, while he stood, his spear held up, a hot, sour taste in his throat.

After that he kept his senses sharp.

By afternoon, he was seeing tracks, of dogs and men. Reading the signs he turned off the giants' way on to a trail that led southwards, into more open country. Eventually he saw smoke and a short time later stock grazing in a field. He took the horn from his belt and blew it, and kept blowing as he walked across the fields to the homestead.

Once he had made his intentions known, and left his spear, he was free to walk about within the fences. He found the smith and agreed a price in skins for the work. The rest of the skins he traded with the smith's wife for salt and a bag of beans.

Otha was not the only stranger in the homestead. A pedlar had come that morning and he was sitting outside the hall, knives, beads, needles, twine, bags of herbs and medicines spread out in front of him. Otha watched him haggle with a woman over a necklace of glass beads.

When she had gone, the pedlar looked up at him. What can I interest you in? he said.

I have nothing left to trade, Otha said, though after a time he asked, What are these medicines?

I have many kinds.

Do you have one for hands clawed and red like a chicken?

This would cure that, the pedlar said, indicating a small bag. But I do not trade for nothing.

Otha felt the weight of the snakes at his waist. He reached under his tunic and caressed the coils. He took them out and held them out to the pedlar

Where did you get this? the pedlar said, turning them over.

Otha shrugged. From the earth.

The pedlar looked at him, eyes narrowed as if trying to see beneath Otha's skin. Where is your homestead?

Over there, Otha said, waving vaguely. We are only few, I have brought all we have to trade.

He was glad when the pedlar ceased his questioning. He wished he had not brought out the snakes, but it was too late, the pedlar was tucking them into his pack and measuring out the medicine. He handed a small package to Otha, telling him to boil the leaves to a paste and rub it into the joints.

Walking to the smith, it occurred to Otha that he might have traded more for the snakes, but he did not go back to the pedlar.

The smith was dipping the blade in water. The mended part was discoloured and the seam thicker, but sturdy. Otha waited while the smith sharpened the edge for him.

The men were coming in from the fields, and soon the horn bade them to the hall. The women brought meat and bread and poured ale into the men's drinking horns. Smoke rose from the fire and gathered in billows beneath the roof. The ale warmed Otha's belly. He remembered another hall, larger than this, the ale stronger, the talk louder, the men more companionable. He had a good memory for the rhymes, but when a man called for the stranger to tell a tale he said he knew none. He felt he had drawn enough attention to himself already. Once he saw the pedlar eyeing him through the flames from the other side of the hall and he lowered his look and chewed at his meat.

There were mats of reeds to lie on, but unused to the ale, he did not sleep well, and he was up with the first pale light. He took his parcel and spear and slipped away while the others slept.

He walked swiftly, sure of his way now, and by mid-morning he had reached the first of the rivers. He drank deeply, quenching the thirst made by the ale and the salty meat. He was home well before night. He gave Brunna the beans and salt, and the medicine, telling her what the pedlar had told him.

You should have traded for something more useful, she said. But later, he saw her boiling the leaves, and when he lay with her, he smelled the bitter paste on her hands.

He was up early again, wanting to get on with the

mowing. He took his spear with him and when she looked at him, he told her he had seen wolves close by. He heard her telling the boy. He planted the spear and set about the work. He had lost two days, but he mowed quickly with the sharpened blade, bringing in the last of the hay as the first raindrops began to fall.

Fine weather returned for the harvest, and Brunna and the boy helped gather the barley. He still could not look on his son without seeing the one whom he so resembled, but the boy was proving to have Otha's stolid endurance, and he laboured without complaint. Brunna worked more easily, too. Her joints were less fiery, her hands more open.

When all the barley had been gathered, Otha stood among the stubble and looked over towards the dark shape of the giants' walls. It had been the sight of the works from the river that had distracted him so that the boat had snagged on what he later discovered was a line of wooden stakes which showed only at low tide. He had kept the boat afloat until they were past the works. Coming into shore he had thought this the worst place in the world they could be stranded. He promised Brunna they would stay only as long as it took to mend the hole. But that night, lying under the stars, it occurred to him that they could not have chanced on a better spot. Who would look for them here? Once he had made up his mind there was no changing it, even more so after they stumbled on the old stump of oak, which he took to be an omen, here, where no other oaks grew, and when shortly afterwards little Snecka, wandering off on his own, found the fresh water of the spring bubbling up from the earth.

They were far enough from the giants' way, as overgrown as it was, but still close enough to the river to escape on the boat, which he had mended and kept hidden in the reeds, checking it regularly. They were lucky in the season. It was not so cold they could not sleep outside but early enough to give him time to clear a little land and plant on it. He was thankful many times that he had grabbed what he could before they left, and at the last minute, as they were about to push off, that he had gone back and fetched the beast and dragged it into the boat, for the boy would not have survived those first months without its milk. Only when the seeds were in the ground did he build the hut.

It was not until later that he discovered that men lived among the ruins. Natives, not English, and on the other side. Once he had ventured far enough into the works, clambering through ruined halls and between the trunkless legs of a stone giant, to see where they squatted among the rubble. If he had had even a couple of half-grown sons he might have gone with arms and seized a few of them to work the land for him, but as it was he was grateful they did not come to disturb him. In all the time they had been here, not a single man had stepped on the land he tilled.

Autumn drew in and one day he saw that a branch on the stump of oak he had thought was dead had sprouted a clump of green acorns. When they ripened he pulled off a handful and dropped them in his pocket.

The first snow fell and he brought the beast into the hut, humans and animal lying together. Brunna had made mead with some honey from a bees' nest he had found in a tree, and he drank it in the cold nights until it ran out, dreaming of riding wave horses with a war party of comrades. He had never seen the sea himself. He had been born in these lands, it was his father who had come over the whale ways, but he had grown up listening to stories of the homes left behind, the seas crossed, the raiding, the bloodshed, those rising in glory to the halls of the Gods.

The days grew shorter and he used what light there was to hunt deer that strayed within range of his arrows and snare rabbits and wild fowl in the frozen reeds along the edge of the river. He shot foxes, too, when he saw them, for their fur, and because they stole from his traps. He welcomed the snow for making everything that happened open to his eyes, though he worried about his own tracks, keeping when he could to hard snow, going to check his snares down by the river only when new snow was falling.

For a week the sun shone out of a cold blue sky. The river froze and one morning he saw three men on the ice. They saw him at the same time and he turned and ran back to the hut, calling to Brunna to put out the fire and gather what she could, blankets, food. They spent the night huddled together in the woods, shivering, listening to the wolves howl.

In the morning he crept back to the hut. There was no sign of the men. When he went down to the river, he saw the scrape of their boot marks heading back to the far bank: they must have thought he was running to bring other men. Still, it was a week before he went back to the river, to find all his snares raided by foxes and badgers, blood staining the snow.

Several times that winter he saw wolves in the distance but they did not come on to his land. He saw no more sign of men.

When the thaw came he took out the plough and rubbed the straps with fat, to soften them. Snecka went with him out to the fields and Otha showed him how to lean into the handle and shout at the beast to direct it. The sun warmed them as they ploughed together, turning black furrows in the sod.

Snecka was growing, changing. For the first time Otha looked at him and saw the shadow of his own people.

It was while fetching the seeds from the corner of the hut that Otha found the acorns he had plucked from the oak stump. When the seeding was done he and Snecka began to walk along the edge of the fields, planting the acorns every fifty or so steps to mark the boundary of his land. This year he might even start putting up a stockade around the field to keep out the deer and boar, make a proper wyrth of this place.

They were covering up the last of the acorns on the eastern boundary when the boy pointed into the sun.

There were five of them, carrying swords and spears. One among them came forward, his hair golden like Brunna's, like the boy whom he resembled. As he approached, Otha saw the glint of a polished coil loose at his wrist, above where he held his sword.

I have been expecting you, Lull, he said.

Diana Leathers

51 Brick Lane

Since his own business had closed, some eighteen months earlier, it had become Mr Basu's habit on weekday afternoons to walk down Brick Lane and spend an hour or so in his son's shop drinking tea and watching the comings and goings, before picking up his grandsons from school. The shop was not actually Shahid's. He managed it for the owner who paid Shahid almost nothing on the assumption that he would make his own deals on the side, which Shahid did. The owner had chosen the name, but Shahid thought it a good one: it brought in the public, though the main business was trade rather than retail. Using leather supplied by the owner, Shahid made up coats and jackets which he sold wholesale to shops outside the East End, or to middle men. The manufacturing was not done in the shop: the heavy machine work was contracted out to one or other of various nearby workshops, while the linings were sewn by women working in their own flats. But the materials were cut in the small back room, and the shop was always strewn with rolls of leather, piles of cut pieces, and half-finished items, as well as completed coats and jackets hung on rails or flung on the floor or over the backs of chairs. When Mr Basu made his afternoon appearance, Shahid would call for a chair to be cleared, and a cup of tea to be fetched from the Sylhet Café two doors down. If there was a copy of the *Surma*, Mr Basu might put on his reading glasses and run his eyes down a column or two. If not, he would sit quietly in the corner, keeping his nose to himself. Although he had been the owner of a business – or at least the sixth part of one – he did not question his son about the shop, or offer him advice. For more than fifty years, except for the few months when he had been on the dole, Mr Basu had worked: first on the family land in what had then been East Pakistan, then at various jobs in London, and finally in his own business; and at the age of sixty-four years and eleven months he was content that the burden of making a living had passed to the next generation. In a little over four weeks he would be entitled to his old age pension. As soon as it came through he would arrange for the payments to be made in Bangladesh. When that was done he would take the money he had put aside and purchase two air tickets, for himself and his wife, to return home: not for a visit this time, but to stay, until the end.

Mr Basu usually set out for the shop at two o'clock, following his afternoon nap, a habit he had begun during the years when he had owned the sixth part of a restaurant and would often not come home until after midnight; though these days it was his early rising, rather than any lateness to bed, that necessitated a daytime sleep. In his retirement, Mr

Basu had taken up again the religious practice he had let lapse in his early years in London. He attended the mosque on Brick Lane and prayed five times a day, and he liked to make his first prayers before his grandchildren were up and running about the flat. At this time he could also perform his ablutions without anxious calls through the door that Zakir, his younger son, had to be at work, or the children would be late for school. Shahid and his family had their own place in the same block, but good council accommodation was hard to come by these days, and Zakir and his wife, Kulchuma, and their three children, a baby girl and two boys, aged eight and six, still shared the two-bedroom flat with Mr and Mrs Basu.

It was these two boys whom Mr Basu collected in the afternoon and also walked to school in the morning. Zakir, who was employed in a workshop to which Shahid often sub-contracted work, had to be at his machine by eight o'clock, and though, through the long years that Mr Basu had worked, Mrs Basu and her daughters-in-law had performed such tasks, now that he was free to do so, it pleased Mr Basu to relieve the women of their outside duties. After he had left the boys at school, he usually carried out the daily household shop as well. If the weather was bad, or his bowels were playing up, or his scarred hand was troubling him, he made do with one of the Bengali shops on Brick Lane, but he preferred to continue down to the market that spilled across the broad pavement of Whitechapel Road. Here, for a few pennies in the pound less than in the shops on Brick Lane, he could purchase English-grown tomatoes, onions and potatoes, as well as produce imported if not always from Bangladesh, then from other tropical countries, such as jack fruit, cooking lime, jinga and water pumpkin. Other men of his age also shopped here and afterwards he would linger for a time, sharing news over the roar of the buses and lorries, before turning for home, a bulging plastic bag dangling from each hand.

On this particular afternoon, Mr Basu had come home from his shopping in good time to make his prayers, eat the meal Kulchuma had prepared for him and have his nap. But the previous night he had not slept well: his mind had been travelling ahead of him once again across the oceans and down the rivers and along the paths to his land and the concrete house he had built there; and when he had lain down shortly after noon he had been overcome by exhaustion and fallen into an unusually deep slumber. By the time Mrs Basu thought to wake him it was already nearly two, and when he walked out from the estate on to Brick Lane, an umbrella in his hand, for the skies were heavy with dark clouds, it was approaching half past the hour. Even so, Mr Basu did not hurry. It was not as if he had any particular purpose at the shop and to have hastened would have marred his enjoyment of the walk. If anyone had told him, when he had first arrived in London, that he would ever consider it a pleasure to stroll down Brick Lane he would have thought it a sour joke. Then he did not stroll but scuttled, head bowed against the inclement weather and the possibility of meeting any unfriendly eyes. But that was almost forty years ago and he had by now spent almost twice as long living around Brick Lane as he had in the land of his birth.

Of course, the Brick Lane he had first encountered, when he had stepped out of the tube at Aldgate East in the spring of 1962, was scarcely recognizable in the Brick Lane of today. There had been no Bengali supermarkets then, no Sylhet Café, no Sonali bank, no International Curry Festival as had been held the previous week, with tables out on the streets, and the mayor of Tower Hamlets cutting the ribbon, television cameras capturing the event for the local news. The mosque had still been the Jewish temple where Mr Basu's first employer, Mr Lewis, had attended services on Friday evenings. The only Asian premises on Brick Lane then, among the Jewish shops and tailors, the Italian and Maltese cafés, the English newsagents, and the still untouched bomb sites, strewn with rubble and rubbish, had been the Bombay Curry House, Oriental Journeys, a travel agent specializing in tickets to the subcontinent, and two general shops, one run by a Hindu, the other by a Muslim, which stood on either side of an empty lot across which the shopkeepers would hurl insults and sometimes a pork samosa or a cow's hoof.

Mr Basu had come in the rush to beat the new immigration regulations of that year. His uncle, who had served the king as an engine-room wallah in the merchant navy during the war, had spent eight years in London afterwards, and he had lent Mr Basu the money for his plane ticket and given him a letter of introduction to Mr Lewis, for whom he had himself worked for his last five years in England. On his arrival, Mr Basu had joined a workforce comprising another Jew almost as old as Mr Lewis, a Tamil, and two Bengalis from the Sylhet district of East Pakistan, as Mr Basu was; both bearing the name Mohommed, as Mr Basu also did: the three Mohommeds, Mr Lewis called them. His first months in London Mr Basu spent pushing a delivery cart about the streets and slowly learning the art of a machinist. The pay was miraculous by the standards of home, but prices were equally high. Mr Basu's accommodation, in the same house in which he worked, was free, but when winter came he had to purchase himself a coat and gloves and long underwear and heavy shoes, and he also had to buy his own food. A single chicken cost more in London than a day labourer would earn in a month at home, but at the corner of Brick Lane and Heneage Street was a Jewish egg merchant's, and there he and the other two Mohommeds, with whom he shared the attic room, bought eggs in bulk and made egg curries every night for three years, until Mr Basu's bowels rebelled, a rebellion from which he had never properly recovered. Through those long winter nights, curled up under layers of heavy, itchy blankets, ice forming on the inside of the window, egg curry rumbling in his belly, Mr Basu dreamed of the wife with whom he had spent only a few weeks of marriage, the son he had never seen, the warm sun on his back. In his letters home he hinted at the pain of his exile; the letters he received back sung of the transformation his monthly remittances were making to the lives of those he had left behind.

After four years he returned home for a visit. He was

shown the additions built on to the old clay house and the new land that had been acquired with his earnings. In the evening a feast was held in his honour. His son, dressed in new clothes for the occasion, sat on one side of him, his father on the other. The choicest pieces of meat were put on his plate. That night, when he and his wife retired to a room specially prepared for them in the new extension, Shahid wailed that the stranger was supplanting him in his mother's bed, and Mr Basu spilled his seed before he could enter his wife. But when it came for him to leave, three months later, his son cried to see his father go, and Mrs Basu was pregnant again.

When he arrived back it was autumn. Rain drizzled from a grey sky. A big order had come in and before Mr Basu even had time to take his suitcase upstairs he was sitting at his sewing machine. When he went to bed, despite his exhaustion from his journey and the day's work, he lay awake long into the night, listening to the snores and farts of his roommates.

One morning, a few weeks after Mr Basu's return, Mr Lewis did not come down to work. After half an hour, the other old Jew went up to Mr Lewis's rooms and found him lying on the floor in his pyjamas. The last Mr Basu saw of Mr Lewis was on a stretcher being carried out to the ambulance. Two days later a young man in a pin-striped suit came to the house. He was the son of one the two daughters Mr Lewis had used to visit in turn on Sundays, riding the bus up to north London where both families lived. He gave them his card – he was a lawyer – and told them they had to be out of the house by the end of the week, though the old Jew could stay on as a caretaker until the house was sold. Mr Basu and the other two Mohommeds bought a get-well card and sent it to the address on the grandson's business card, but they received no reply, nor ever heard of old Mr Lewis's fate.

In time Mr Basu found work in another tailoring shop, and a bed in a room with three West Pakistanis, in a house shared with several Irishmen and a West Indian family.

The plan, agreed before he had returned to London, was for Mr Basu to stay in England for five more years. In that time he moved jobs twice and accommodation four times. Every month he sent home half his earnings: from what remained, after he had paid his rent and bought food, there was sometimes enough left over for a meal at the Bombay or a visit to the cinema. He did not choose the films he went to see; he did not understand what was spoken anyway. The little English he had learned, sprinkled with Yiddish, Urdu and Caribbean words, bore no resemblance to the English spoken on the screen. But he liked to sit in the dark, on the luxurious seats, and watch the flickering pictures.

The five years had almost passed, and he had begun to enquire about the price of a one-way air passage home, when war broke out between West and East Pakistan. All flights were cancelled and the post stopped. The West Indian family had a television, and he and his West Pakistani room-mates would crowd into their kitchen and watch the terrible scenes unfolding on the news. After six weeks a letter arrived. His family were all alive, though conditions were not good and one of his cousins had been taken by the soldiers. From other East Pakistanis, who gathered in a café on Commercial Street, he heard what the West Pakistani soldiers did to their prisoners: hanging them by their penises, peeling off their skins, putting pencils in their ears and driving them into the brain with the slap of a hand. Though nothing was said, he moved out of the room he shared with the three West Pakistanis.

One afternoon, crossing Bethnal Green Road after making a delivery, he was set upon by three shaven-headed youths. Why they attacked him, rather than merely cursed him as had happened on other occasions, he did not understand, though for a long time afterwards he was haunted by the absurd idea that one of them – the one who had run after him and knocked him to the ground and given him the first kick – had possessed his own father's face. He never mentioned this to anyone and he told the doctor who sewed up his head and bandaged his ribs and gave him some pills for the pain that he had fallen down some stairs.

Eventually the war ended. East Pakistan had gained its independence as Bangladesh. Mr Basu gave up his job, bought presents, and flew home to join in the celebrations. But the end of the war had not brought peace. Sylhet district, like other parts of the new country, was plagued by lawlessness. Ten days after Mr Basu arrived, the village was raided by the new Bangladeshi army. Mr Basu's father went out to speak to the soldiers and was knocked down with a rifle butt. In trying to protect him, Mr Basu had his own hand sliced open by a bayonet. Two days later the old man was dead. On the radio they heard that hundreds of thousands of Bangladeshis were now trying to go to Britain and that new strict laws were about to be passed. Mr Basu returned immediately to London and applied for entry for his wife and two sons.

By the time Mrs Basu arrived with Shahid and Zakir, Mr Basu was working in the plastics factory in Wapping, making hosepipes. The bayonet had damaged the tendons in his hand and he could not operate a sewing machine. As it turned out, the factory work was lighter, and the wages better, even after paying national insurance and tax, much of which he got back in family allowances. For the first two months the family lived in a single room, until the council provided them with a two-bedroom flat on an estate at the top of Brick Lane. With his father dead and his family in London, Mr Basu cut back on the remittances he sent home, and instead began to put money aside in a post office savings account. At first his sons were unhappy and cried for home, but they attended English school and learned the language and in time they began to forget their previous lives. Mrs Basu took longer to adapt, but over the months and years so many Sylhetis moved into their block that it came to seem like a corner of Sylhet itself and earned the nickname Sylhet House. After seven years Mr Basu was made a foreman and was given a raise. He bought a new carpet for the living room, a dresser, a television. When the factory closed, he went on the dole. He was now well past fifty, with a clawed hand, and it seemed likely he might never be able to find another job. Then one day he ran into an old Sylheti workmate from his tailoring days, who was opening a restaurant. A premises had already been leased on Brick Lane and was being converted at that very moment. There was room for one more partner willing to put in his fair share of money and of work in the restaurant.

A first drop of rain landed on Mr Basu's face. He opened his umbrella and held it over his head as he waited to cross Bethnal Green Road. The rain was coming down steadily by the time he passed the new row of shops, where the two Asian general stores had once stood on either side of the empty lot, and walked on beneath the walls of the old brewery. Beer was no longer brewed here, the chimneys had ceased pouring out smoke and steam a good few years back, and all sorts of strange and modern things went on in the buildings now, but Mr Basu could still remember how, when the weather was warm, or the wind blew in a certain direction, the air would seem to taste of beer. Beyond the brewery, he came to the first of the 'Indian' restaurants, as people called them, though, of course, they were all owned by Bangladeshis. Normally there would have been men in white jackets standing at the doors of the Preem, the Bengali Balti, the Taj Mahal and the others, soliciting custom, for lunch hour did not end until 3 p.m., and Mr Basu might have paused for a moment to ask how business was, or at least nodded in greeting as he walked past; but with the rain coming down heavily now the lane was almost empty, and he pulled his umbrella low over his head and hurried on.

Shahid stood up as soon as he came in and took the umbrella from him, shaking it out in the doorway.

113

I was worried you weren't coming, he said.

Your mother did not wake me.

I sent for tea half an hour ago. Come, sit down. There are some sweetmeats for you. Hey, he called into the back. Go and fetch my father another tea, this one is hardly warm.

Don't waste your money, Mr Basu said. Cold is good enough for me.

I can't afford a hot cup of tea for my own father? Shahid said. Take a sweetmeat. He pushed the box across the desk. Eat as many as you like.

Perhaps just one, Mr Basu said. He put his hand on his belly. You know my troubles.

Shahid grinned at him foolishly, and Mr Basu had the feeling that his son had not heard what he had said.

I want to talk to you about something, Abba, Shahid said. But I have to run out for a moment. Don't go anywhere. Hey, he called over his shoulder. Look after my father. Turning back to Mr Basu, he gestured at the sweets. Eat as many as you want.

When his son had gone, Mr Basu leaned forward and took another sweetmeat.

While he savoured it, he picked up a newspaper he saw poking out from beneath a pile of papers. It was a week or two old, but he didn't mind. The main story on the front page was about power cuts in Dhaka but he soon grew bored with this, as he did with the story next to it, which concerned yet another political scandal in Bangladesh. What went on in Dhaka or Bangladesh in general held little interest for him. When he was born the country was part of

India, while he grew up it was East Pakistan, and now it was Bangladesh, but in all that time his district had kept the same name, as had his village, and it was there that his concerns lay, with his village and the land he owned and the concrete house he had built there. He had not seen it in three years, since his visit with his two oldest grandchildren, the time he had arrived to find to his embarrassment that his sons had arranged for an entire wall to be painted with images of aeroplanes and London buildings and his own restaurant. He left the painting and did not tell his sons how they had shamed him: they had grown up in England, they did not understand the ways of the people at home.

He might have stayed then, if he could have arranged the finances, but Mrs Basu, having wept for home every night for her first five years in London, now wept at the thought of leaving her sons and daughters-in-law and grandchildren here and he had agreed to wait until he was sixty-five, but no longer than that. He was attached to his family too, but the pull of his house and his land, of the red earth where his father was buried, and where he would one day be buried, was stronger. He did not intend to wait until he had to be transported home in a box.

He popped another sweet into his mouth, and turned the page, his eyes passing over an article about a youth cricket team, beneath a picture of a smiling boy holding a bat, and another about a Bengali councillor in Tower Hamlets, whom he knew from personal experience had bad body odour.

He read, instead, about a man, presumed to be

Bangladeshi, though he had no papers on him, whose body had landed in a Sainsbury's car park. A witness had seen him fall from the sky as a Biman airline aircraft flew overhead and it was suggested he had hidden himself in the undercarriage of the aircraft in Dhaka, in an attempt to smuggle himself into Britain, and fallen out when the wheels had been put down before landing. The witness said he had thought it was a great yellow bird swooping down on him, for the dead man had been wearing a bright yellow shirt.

Mr Basu was reaching for another sweet when Shahid came back in to the shop.

Eat, eat, Shahid said, nodding at the nearly empty box.

I've had enough, Mr Basu said.

Then take the rest home with you.

Shahid sat down on the other side of the desk. His hair was wet with rain and a trickle ran down his cheek.

Abba, I need to talk to you about something.

I see.

About the business.

It's going badly?

Not badly, well, I'm working day and night.

Good, said Mr Basu, relieved.

Good for this bloody fellow who owns the place, Shahid said. Not good for me.

Mr Basu's eyes fell on a pink and green sweet.

I've got this deal set up, Shahid was saying. Everything is in place. All for me, nothing for him.

Mr Basu bent forward slowly and took the sweet.

Only I need a little capital, Shahid said. He leaned across

the table towards his father. Just fifteen hundred pounds and I can make this deal work.

It sounds good, Mr Basu said, pushing with his tongue at a bit of sweetmeat that had stuck to his tooth.

Abba, Shahid said. Fifteen hundred pounds. If you could lend me even twelve hundred.

But I don't have it, Mr Basu said. You know all my money was lost in the business.

It was the truth. The restaurant had made good profits for its owners for several years, amounting to considerably more than they had put into it, but Mr Basu's share had been spent on the family here and on the house at home, and when the restaurant had gone bust none of the capital had been recovered.

I know you have money in the post office, Abba.

That is for our aeroplane tickets.

I need it Abba.

Shahid, you are my son, but—

You'll get it back, Abba. In six weeks. In four weeks. You will have it all back. More, if you want.

Shahid—

This one thing, Abba. To get me out from under this fellow. So I can start my own business. You had your own business.

Not at your age.

It's not for me, Abba. For me I don't mind. But for the children. If we are to find a suitable husband for Kalpona the wedding costs will not be small and then— he leaned towards his father, lowering his voice to a whisper— there is

Johar. With my own business I would have something sub-stantial to offer him.

He gave Mr Basu a beseeching look.

Before it is too late.

Mr Basu could feel his gut beginning to bloat. Tomorrow, he knew, his bowel movements would not be regular.

Oke Cottage

51½ Brick Lane

Father, she called. Is that you?

She had sat down only a few minutes earlier, her legs so tired they pained her, but she pushed herself to her feet and went to the door. He was standing at the sty, stroking the hog's ears. The animal was pressed against the fence, grunting softly.

There'll be no acorns this year, he said, nodding his head up into the branches above. I don't know what we'll fatten her on.

Maybe they are late, she said.

Some seasons a tree doesn't give, he said. It happened the winter your mother passed.

She watched him pulling at the hog's ears and scratching between them. He had not spoken to her this much in days.

I'll fetch sow thistles and dandelions, she said. I'll bring her snails. I'll be able to go about by then.

He turned to her.

I told you to keep in, he said. And don't go calling out like that. What if it were one of them busybodies?

When he came in she had the food ready on the table. She sat with him, though she hardly ate herself. She watched him chew and swallow, her hands on her belly below the table.

When he was done he took the scraps out. She heard the hog snort and snuffle, and after, the murmur of his voice. She thought of his thick strong fingers gentle on the hog's hide.

She had taken to bed by the time he came in again. He threw his blanket on the floor without a word and wrapping himself in it was soon asleep. She lay on her side, sleep not a thing she could rely on any more. The moving had been less these past days and now her belly was quiet but she could not find a way to lie that did not squeeze the breath from her.

She woke needing to relieve herself, and afterwards she lay listening to the sounds of the night: scratchings, hoots and lowings, and from further away, whether the tower or the town or some other place she did not know, sounds that might have been the cries of animals or men or spirits for all she could conceive.

Glad of the morning, she cut him a hunk of bread. Keep in, mind, he said, closing the door after him.

She stoked the fire and sat at the table peeling potatoes and carrots. All she did was slow. Without taking the bucket to the well and tending the vegetables and all the tasks that were usually hers there was not enough to fill the day, but she felt she was moving in mud anyway. When she had finished she put her head on the table and slept. Later she opened the door. The great trunk of the oak, and the hedge beyond, hid her from the lane and there were only cows in the pasture. She threw out some grain for the chickens and walked across to the sty with the peelings.

Grunting like a half-wit the hog trod the peelings into the mud, and then had to root in its own ordure for what it had buried. When it could find no more it looked up at her, muck dripping from its snout and caked on its eyelashes.

Look at you, she said haughtily. As if he would love you.

She was picking up eggs when she heard a voice calling out, not to her, but close enough by. It was not obvious on her, squat and thick-haunched as she was anyway, and in her mother's smock that even now was big on her. She had not known it herself before her father had divined it, she not believing him until he mentioned the quickening she had thought was the gripes. A woman's eye might have told, but he had made it clear to all them meddling busy-bodies to keep away. Mrs Samford and Goody Hawke had come to the door the first Sunday she had stayed from church, to see to the poor motherless child, they said, and he had told them she wasn't fatherless too and he would thank them to keep their snouts out of what was his. It had brought on a warm feeling in her when he had said that, and she felt some of that warmth even now, at the memory. But she was supposed to be ailing, not up and about, so she went inside.

The labour's up the Hyde these coming weeks, her father said, when he returned. Digging ditches and filling them in.

He looked at her.

You won't be long now I reckon, he said.

He seemed pleased by that, or by the Hyde, one or the other, and she was cheered too. When her time was passed they could get back to how it was before. That what she was carrying might have some say in things she did not consider.

While he was out, she picked up the new layings, warm in her hand, and packed the basket for him. Eggs brought them all the money they earned. Her father's labour for the bishop, and hers too at harvest time, was boonwork for their cottaging rights, and what they tilled on their own patch, grain and vegetables, was no more than enough for the table, and the chickens and the hog.

She waited for him, and when he had come and taken the basket and set out for the town, she stood at the door and looked across the fields to the walls, dark against the evening sun. She had been up to them but never within them. The town was no place for a girl, her father said, and she could not argue by what came out of it into the fields on Sundays and holidays, lads who shamed the Lord with trampling the grain and scaring the livestock and looking over hedges at folk's daughters, and what she heard drifting from it on the night air. At harvest her father had to sit up in the fields with the bishop's other boonmen to keep thieves from the town from stealing the grain.

She sat at the table. After a time she fell asleep. It was deep into the night when he clattered through the door.

She lit the candle and counted the coins he threw on the table. Two halfpennies and a farthing: short by nigh on a penny. She could smell the liquor on his breath and when she came round to him she saw the split skin on his cheek.

What have you been getting into? she said.

Nothing.

Let me clean you, she said.

Leave me be. He swatted at her and she saw there was blood on his fingers too.

She fetched some water and a cloth, and though he swore at her, he let her wash his cheek, and afterwards his grazed knuckles, his hand resting in hers.

When she was finished she bent down and unlaced his boots, and he let her pull them off.

It was more intimacy than she had had from him in weeks.

Father, she said.

He grunted at her but he did not lift his head.

I am so lonely in the bed at night.

He swayed back, as if considering her words, and rocking forward again struck her in the face with his fist.

The lump rose up and closed her eye. It was still closed when it started two nights later.

He came to her with a candle and held it between them. She saw with her one good eye that he was scared, too.

Was it like this when I came, she said.

It's always bad, he said.

The pain came and went again.

Maybe you should fetch a woman, she said. That Goody Hawke's seen many a babe into this world.

It was her killed your mother, he said.

When the pain came she thought she was going to die too, but slowly it went. Then it came again.

Shortly before daybreak the waters flooded from her, soaking her clothes. She took them off, pulling a blanket about her.

Her father went out, though he left the door open.

When the pain came again, she cried, I hope you are not stroking that damned hog.

The pain made her crazed.

What have you done to me, Father? she cried

He came in and put his hand over her mouth and told her to be quiet, did she want the world to know?

She didn't care, but his grip was hard on her, hurting her where he had hit her.

When the need to push came, she squatted, holding on to the bed and moaning.

Her father was outside again.

It seemed to go on for ever and she was calling out that she wished she was dead when it fell from her all in one slippery go.

Father, she called, I think it's come.

She looked down at its slimy back and head, dark hair wet with blood and other muck.

She tried to pick it up but it slipped from her hand.

Her father came, helping her by the arm until she sat on the bed. He took the baby and wrapped it in a piece of cloth.

Let me see its face, she said.

He turned it over and she saw it wasn't a monster. Its eyes were shut and its face wrinkled like the baby rats she had cleared out of a nest a few months back. Her father let her hold it while he took his knife and cut the cord and tied it off at both ends. It lay still and peaceful in her arms and the idea came to her for the first time that it was a thing in itself, that it could be loved and could love her in return.

Look how well it sleeps, she said.

She had the blanket about her but she started shivering and then the pain came again.

What is happening? she said.

It's the afters.

She hadn't the strength to squat, so she lay on the bed, the baby sleeping beside her, pushing again until more came out. Then she slept herself.

She woke in the dark. She reached for the baby, but it was not beside her. Father, she called, but he was gone too.

She slept again, and when she woke, he was there in the early morning light.

Where is it? she said. I want to see what it is.

Gone, he said.

Gone where? she said, afraid he had given it away.

To our maker, he said.

It was sleeping.

There was no life in it, Peg.

She let out a cry like an animal and tried to get out of the bed, but she was too weak and hurt. She fell back.

A little later, she said, What was it?

A girl.

Where is she?

Put in the earth.

Could we not at least give her a Christian burial?

I saw to it good enough don't you mind, he said.

He stayed at home through the day, sleeping the night on the floor. The next morning he went to work.

When he had gone she pushed herself to her feet. It was strange not to have her belly so big in front of her. She walked slowly to the door, holding on to the bed and then with her hand on the wall. The daylight blinded her and she had to wait for her eyes to stay open. She felt weak but she had to know at least where he had put her. The idea she had was under the tree. She walked over and looked about but there was no earth disturbed. She could not think where else he would have put her.

The hog was grunting and squealing at her.

Let me be, damned beast, she said.

She looked about the yard but there was no dug earth. The hog started up again and she turned to curse it. Its face was covered in mud except for its little hog eyes. It had only been two days but she could swear it had fattened up.

Band of brothers

58 Brick Lane

By the spring of 1973 most of what remained of the large stone Roman fortress at Vindolanda had been uncovered and the archaeologists were excavating the civilian settlement, or vicus, next to it, when the work was interrupted by flooding. To divert the waters, the team began to dig a ditch across ground leading away from the south-west corner of the site. Some three feet down they came across pottery, leather and pieces of textile. They continued to dig and at thirteen feet they found posts, oak beams, planking and wattle-and-daub walling. It was the remains of an earlier timber fort, floored with straw and bracken, and it was tangled up in this flooring, in the mud at the bottom of the ditch, that the first two fragments of wood were found and handed to Robin Birley, the excavation leader.

Birley's father, Eric, had begun the diggings at Vindolanda in 1930, and Birley had been working there on and off since he was a schoolboy in 1947. His first thought was that the fragments were simply 'oily plane shavings', but when he looked at them more closely he saw what appeared to be writing in ink on them. 'If I have to spend the rest of my life working in dirty, wet trenches,' he wrote soon after, 'I doubt whether I shall ever again experience the shock and excitement I felt at my first glimpse of ink hieroglyphics on tiny scraps of wood.' The 'hieroglyphics' were, in fact, Latin handwriting. The pieces of wood were part of a letter to a soldier stationed in the fort. Its subject could scarcely have been more mundane – informing the soldier that underpants and socks had been sent to him and asking for greetings to be passed on to his messmates – but to Birley, used to piecing together the past from shards of pottery, scraps of petrified leather and stone foundations, it was almost as if a Roman soldier had stood up from the muddy ditch and spoken to him.

Over the years that followed, hundreds more tablets, or parts of tablets, were uncovered from the earlier layers of the site. Many were in fragments, but when whole they were about the size of postcards, between 1–3 mm thick, and made of birch, alder or oak. In some cases, holes had been punched in the corners and several tablets tied together with string to make a longer document. The Romans more usually wrote on papyrus or parchment, but the former was grown in Egypt, a long way from northern Britain, and the latter was expensive. The wooden tablets were clearly a local answer to the need for cheap writing material, and fragments since identified at other sites in Britain suggest they were widely used, though elsewhere most perished, as would be expected of such delicate organic matter. That so many survived at Vindolanda was due to a combination of the particular environment and, ironically, the fact that as cheap writing material, used often for drafts or quick notes and letters, they were readily discarded. Built in a wet valley, the floor of the fort was prone to damp and rising waters, and to keep it as dry as possible the Romans regularly threw down straw and bracken. In time this coagulated with the moisture into layers of peat-like material, sealing and so preserving anything trapped with them – such as lost or discarded tablets – in an oxygen-free environment.

The extraction of the tablets was a long and delicate process. Blocks were cut out from the layers of flooring and disentangled, bracken frond by bracken frond, so that no fragments were missed or damaged. Each fragment then had to be cleaned and photographed under infra-red light to bring out the writing, which then had to be deciphered and interpreted. Every word was valuable. A rich library of writing has survived from Roman times but little of it concerns Britain. There is Caesar's account of his invasion, Tacitus' history of Agricola, the governor of Britain from AD 78–84, but other than that only a few bits and pieces in Suetonius, Dio Cassius and Ammianus Marcellinus, and of all these authors, only Caesar actually saw Britain for himself. Many historians have extrapolated a picture of Roman life in Britain from writings about other parts of the Empire, but even these mostly address what Roman writers considered important: politics, wars, the lives of the high and mighty. This is not what the Vindolanda writing tablets record. They are memos, invoices, work rosters, interim reports, applications for leave, birthday invitations, children's homework tablets, shopping lists, letters and notes about the most ordinary concerns and interests. They speak to us, across 2000 years, as no other Roman find has, about ordinary Roman life, about the day to day life of an ordinary Roman garrison, of the ordinary Roman grunt.

The fort of Vindolanda stands on the lip of an escarpment in a Northumberland valley, almost exactly halfway between the North Sea and the Solway Firth. It was established around AD 85, in the aftermath of Agricola's campaign in Caledonia, which had concluded with the crushing defeat of the Scots at the battle of Mons Graupius, but also with the realization that the mountainous northern regions of Britain would be more sensibly contained rather than ruled over: a realization that would eventually lead to the building of Hadrian's Wall, but in the meantime saw a series of forts put up along the frontier. The men who built and garrisoned the first fort were not in fact Romans. The units stationed at Vindolanda during the time of the tablets were Tungrians, from the east of present-day Belgium, and Batavians, who came from the lower Rhineland in what is now the Netherlands. The Roman military had long ceased to be a citizen army. It was a professional force, made up of Greeks, Syrians, Egyptians, Moors, Gauls and other European races, all of whom would at some time or another come to Britain. But these soldiers were not mere mercenaries. By joining the Roman army they hoped to gain something more valuable than money, for those who managed to survive twenty-five years of service would earn themselves Roman citizenship. This did not mean they would necessarily live in Rome itself. Most Roman citizens never set foot in the eternal city: Rome was an empire and its citizens were drawn from and lived all over the Roman territories. But to become a Roman citizen was effectively to cross the borders into another country, a promised land. To be a Roman citizen was to gain access to Roman culture, Roman wine, Roman bathhouses, Roman brothels, Roman prosperity and Roman opportunities. Roman rule was absolute. Carthage, the only other superpower in Roman times, had been vanquished in 146 BC and Rome's power had been unchallenged ever since. But Roman rule was meritocratic as well as autocratic. Anyone, from whatever race, or class, could, in theory, become a Roman citizen, and the surest way of achieving this was by joining the Roman army.

That is not to say that any man could become a Roman soldier. Recruits had to pass strict physical examinations and interviews. A likely recruit, wrote Vetegius, 'should have shining eyes, an erect carriage, a broad chest, muscular shoulders, strong arms, long fingers, a modest belly, sinewy feet and calves'. Once accepted, the recruits were sent to bootcamps for basic training in route marches, calisthenics, running, jumping and swimming. They were taught to fight, first with wickerwork shields and heavy wooden staves and swords, and when they had mastered these, with the real things, the throwing spear, or pilum, and the short sword, or gladius, for close combat. They went on night marches carrying heavy packs and water they were not allowed to drink; at the end of the march their commander would check their canteens. They were drilled in battle formations: single line, double line, square, wedge, circle; repeating them until they could change from one formation to another mid battle. The tougher they became the more their commander would expect of them. Julius Caesar often made his men 'turn out when there was no need at all, especially in wet weather or on public holidays', according to Suetonius. 'Sometimes he would say, "Keep a close eye on me!" and then steal away from camp at any hour of the day or night, expecting them to follow.' The drop-out rate was high but those who made it through had been honed into an elite fighting force. They were experts in the use of their weapons, skilled in tactics, and ready to carry out orders unquestioningly. They knew how to dig a camp, build a bridge across a river. They could live in the field, sleep in a foxhole, march all day and through the night. They knew and trusted each other. They were prepared to die for each other; more important, they were prepared to kill for each other.

The Batavian and Tungrian cohorts garrisoning Vindolanda in its earlier years were especially crack troops, veterans of Mons Graupius. Caledonia was then the furthest frontier of the Roman Empire: the 'very limit of the natural world', as Tacitus put it. For several years before Mons Graupius, Agricola had been making advances into the northern territories, and in AD 83 he had finally got the battle he had been seeking: 30,000 British warriors ranged on the slopes of the hill against 8000 Roman infantrymen and 3000 cavalry. British chariots displayed back and forth in front of the Romans. The battle began at long range. A 'great rain of spears' fell on the Roman shields. Finally the two armies came together in hand-to-hand combat. It was what the Batavians and Tungrians 'had been trained for in their long service'. Their short swords, designed for thrusting, were far more effective than the Britons' heavy slashing swords with their blunt ends. 'Consequently,' Tacitus wrote, 'as the Batavians went to it in a flurry of blows, slamming into the enemy with the bosses of their shields and stabbing at their faces, they overcame the warriors stationed at the bottom of the slope and began to advance uphill.' By the end of the battle, 'everywhere you looked were corpses, mangled limbs and bloodsoaked ground'. Tacitus recorded 10,000 British fatalities, and 360 Roman dead.

Vindolanda was established some two years later. The first fort, put up by the Tungrians, was a hasty affair, but when the Batavians took over around AD 87 they rebuilt and extended it, as the excavations were to discover, across a seven-acre site. Although made from wood it was still an impressive structure, with barracks, granaries, stables, a hospital, kitchens, a temple and workshops. Around AD 101 a stone bathhouse was put up, nearly 100 feet long, with vestibule, changing rooms, cold, warm and hot rooms (plastered to keep in the heat), a cold plunge and latrines. The Batavian soldiers may not yet have been Roman citizens but they lived a Roman lifestyle. Among the writing tablets are records of olive oil and wine imported from the Mediterranean, a set of dining bowls ordered from London, clothes sent from Gaul and mirrors brought from the Rhineland. Most had taken Roman names, translating their original German names or finding Roman approximations

(Agilis from Agilo, Audax from Audagas). They were also rewarded for their service with Roman military decorations: crowns, medals, torques – rings worn in pairs on the chest below each collar bone – or armlets – heavy, silver, three-quarter circles worn about the bulging bicep.

More than anything what comes across in the letters and memos is the confidence of the writers. 'I am writing,' one letter goes, 'so that you may know I am in good health, which I hope you are in turn, you most irreligious fellow, who haven't even sent me a single letter – but I think I am behaving in a more civilized way by writing to you.' A memo to an officer reads, 'My fellow soldiers have no beer. Please order some to be sent.' Others are requests for leave or invoices for the many goods they purchased: glasses, plates, cooking kettles, boots, even in one case a horse. They were members of an elite brotherhood and in letters they addressed each other as brothers: 'I pray that you have good health brother'; 'Farewell, dearest brother'; 'If you love me, brother.' Reinforcing this was their attitude towards the people over whom they ruled. One tablet mocks the Britons for fighting 'naked'. Another refers to them as Brittunculi: literally little Britons, but implying that they were feeble, uncivilized, of little reckoning. Several tablets refer to the British slaves of officers, and even ordinary soldiers may have owned them. One of the last tablets, probably written in AD 122, when the Emperor Hadrian visited Vindolanda, was a letter from a merchant complaining of harsh treatment from soldiers and imploring 'Your Clemency not to suffer a man from overseas to have been made to bleed by a beating.'

A 'man from overseas': the implication being that if he had been a Briton the beating would have been acceptable.

Elsewhere in writing and art the Romans recorded their brutality in battle and in 'pacification'. Columns in Rome celebrating the triumph of Trajan in the Carpathians show Roman soldiers fighting with severed heads between their teeth, setting fire to villages, separating women and children from their menfolk. That the Batavians and Tungrians would have treated the peoples of northern Britain in a similar way can scarcely be doubted. The Romans conquered by stick and carrot; or sword and vine. If the natives resisted, they were crushed without mercy; if they submitted, their leaders were rewarded with the fruits of Romanization: 'advanced education for their sons,' as Tacitus wrote, 'the corrupting charms of colonnades, baths and elegant dinners'. In war, Rome shocked its enemies into capitulation; in peace, it awed them with its grandeur. The historian John Morris describes how great forts and towns of 'huge buildings' were built by the Romans 'in a countryside that had hitherto known no structures more elaborate than a large timber hall, or a high bank and deep ditch about the hutments of a royal centre. They spoke plainly to the native population. Rome was too great to challenge.'

The Roman justification for this, for the arrival of their armies in foreign lands, and the imposition of their rule, they considered equally unchallengeable. The benefits of the peace they brought, of the Pax Romana, were stability where there had been turmoil, civilization where there had been barbarity, and economic prosperity where there had been poverty. Whether this was actually true, at least in northern England, is another matter. Certainly the records from Vindolanda do not support it. The fort and the soldiers employed in it undoubtedly brought money and jobs to the area: the Vindolanda tablets record the presence in the vicus of shopkeepers, traders, potters, cobblers and other artisans and craftsmen. But in almost every case, their names are foreign, not British; they were contractors from the more Romanized parts of the Empire. Then there was the food consumed in the fort, most of which came from the local areas, but which was on the whole not bought – so that money might reach the local economy – but levied as tax. The fort, the tablets suggest, was an island of Roman prosperity in an ocean of British poverty, an impression that is supported by the other archaeological evidence. Comparing artefact discard rates – the quality of rubbish – of fort and vicus sites with ordinary farm sites in northern England, archaeologist Nick Higham has found a difference as great as between a modern Western city and a 'Third World village community'. Coin finds, equally, are 'extremely rare from rural settlements to the point where it seems unlikely that coins ever penetrated to the farming community with any degree of regularity'. The only finds even relatively common in land outside the forts from this period are 'coarse pottery and cheap glass bangles'.

The Vindolanda writing tablets are a window into a brief moment in the past. They date from a handful of years either side of AD 100, up to the construction of the stone fort, with its stone floors to keep out the damp. Other evidence suggests that the Tungrians at least were still at Vindolanda into the 140s, though these Tungrians would have been replacements for the soldiers who wrote the tablets. Those who had lived and seen out their duty would have earned their Roman citizenship. Some, no doubt, would have returned to Tungria, to be reunited with families long left behind. Others would have stayed in Britain, perhaps even settling in the vicus outside the fort, though more probably they would have headed south to Verulamium, a city full of veterans, or most likely of all Londinium. This by now had grown into a miniature eternal city, complete with forums, libraries, bathhouses and colosseums, and extensive cemeteries outside the walls to the north and the east. Here they could open a shop or start a business or simply enjoy their prosperous retirement, like the writer of the tablet who promised his correspondent how he would show him his 'silver armlet of two entwined snakes' when he 'arrived in Londinium to embark on my new life as a citizen of Rome'.

L'Église Neuve

59 Brick Lane

1674 Born in Caen to Jonas Racine, silk weaver and
Protestant deacon, and Susanne Vaillant.

Baptized Abraham Racine in the Protestant church
of Caen, famous for its octagonal shape and
suspended ceiling.

1679 Starts school.

1683 Wins medal for an essay written on the occasion of
Louis XIV's fortieth year on the throne.

1685 Edict of Nantes, by which Protestants granted
freedom of worship in France, revoked by Louis
XIV.

Father refuses to abjure his Protestantism and is
imprisoned. The rest of the family abandon their

home and take refuge in the house of Catholic neighbours.

Protestant church of Caen razed.

1686 The family covertly visited by a former prisoner, who reports that Jonas is in good health and is still resisting all efforts to make him take the Mass.

Looks out from window as the corpse of a member of the Protestant congregation of Caen is dragged through the streets behind a horse.

1687 Father released. He has lost the hearing in one ear and is racked by constant fits of coughing.

The family flee Caen carrying what small amount of money they can raise and the family Bible baked in a loaf of bread. The money pays for their passage across the Channel in a fishing boat.

Arrive in London penniless. Father applies for relief from the French Protestant church in Threadneedle Street.

1688 With his father unable to work due to ill health, Abraham is apprenticed to a French weaver of Lamb Street, Spitalfields. The family rent a room nearby. His mother and sisters take in washing.

The family join the congregation of the newly opened Church de l'Hôpital in Black Eagle Street, Spitalfields.

Overhears his father, weeping, telling his mother how the prison guards beat him until he danced to a fiddle played by another prisoner.

1690 French defeat English at battle of Beachy Head and burn Teignmouth. Abraham and a fellow French apprentice attacked in the street for being 'dirty Papist buggers'.

1691 Father dies.

1692 Dreams he is walking through the fields outside Caen with his father, the birds singing, the sun on the corn fields, reciting the Catechism.

1693 Weaves for two days and two nights to complete an order for his master. On the third morning is found asleep at the loom, the work finished.

1696 Completes his apprenticeship. With assistance from the consistory of the Church de l'Hôpital sets up his own business in a rented room with a leased silk loom.

1699 Produces the first batch of 'Blue Flowers of the

Meadow' design, which will keep one and often two looms busy for the next twenty years.

1702 Rents larger premises on White Lion Street, Spitalfields, where he operates four looms and also lives, along with his mother and remaining unmarried sister.

1703 Plants a mulberry tree in the garden.

1705 Marries Madeleine Albert, daughter of Nicolas Albert, cheesemonger of Brick Lane and elder of the Church de l'Hopital.

1706 A daughter, Esther, born.

1707 Moves the business to a workshop on land east of Brick Lane, where he runs ten looms.

1708 A son, Jonas, born.

1709 Made a deacon of the Church de l'Hôpital.

1711 Builds a three-storey house on Masson Street, Spitalfields.

1712 Meets an onion seller who used to sell onions in Caen and remembers his father. Invites onion seller home for a drink and a meal. Afterwards,

instructs his wife to buy onions only from this
onion seller.

1713 Returning home with his family from Sunday
morning service at the Church de l'Hôpital, the
sermon still ringing in his ears, he reaches down and
lays his hand on his son's shoulder as they walk.

1714 Mother dies.

1715 Jonas nearly dies from the ague. Madeleine blames
Abraham for taking him for walks through the
stinking miasmas produced by the foul fuming
clamps of the brick fields.

1716 Purchases a further two looms and takes an interest
in a haberdashery shop on Brick Lane.

1719 Flood of cheap materials from India causes first of
periodic crises in the Spitalfields silk industry.
Weavers are laid off, women wearing printed
calicos are attacked in the streets. Abraham donates
£20 to help set up La Soupe to provide free food for
needy weavers.

1721 Jonas begins his apprenticeship.

1722 Elected an elder of the consistory of Church de
l'Hopital.

1724   Takes his belt to his son after Jonas is seen coming out of a public house on Brick Lane.

       Hears from Madeleine that Jonas only went into the public house to see objects of scientific interest displayed there.

       Spends a day working at the loom beside his son, the first day's weaving he has done in eight years.

1725   Meets his son coming out of a public house with ale on his breath. Beats him. Next day tells Jonas how his father was beaten in prison until he danced to a fiddle.

1727   Esther marries Paul Lemaître, a tapestry weaver of Dean Street, Soho.

1728   A daughter, Catherine, born to Esther.

1730   Speaks out at a meeting of master weavers against employing migrant Irish workers at under rate when there are local weavers who cannot find work.

1731   Jonas marries Marie Maldron, daughter of Jacques Maldron, master weaver of Fournier Street, Spitalfields.

1732   A son, Abraham, born to Jonas and Marie.

1733   At a visit to his daughter's house hears Catherine speaking to her mother in English. Tells Esther how his father was beaten in prison until he danced to a fiddle. Esther replies that it is a good thing she is bringing up her daughter in England.

1734   Makes Jonas a partner in the business.

1736   Discussions begin between the consistory of the Church de l'Hôpital and the landlord over renewing the lease of the building.

1737   A daughter, Susanne, born to Jonas and Marie.

1738   Pays a visit, in his role as elder of the consistory, to the home of Pierre Bachard, a member of the congregation who has been accused for a third time of drinking and singing all night with women. Tells Bachard how his father was beaten in prison until he danced to a fiddle. Bachard tells him he is a little dog stirring up other little dogs.

1739   Having failed to secure a satisfactory lease for the church building the elders of the consistory vote to build a new church. A fund is set up immediately. Abraham donates £50 and the copyright to the famous 'Blue Flowers of the Meadow' silk design.

1740   A plot is found on Brick Lane but shortly before

papers are signed it is claimed that a witch once murdered a child on this spot.

Another plot is purchased further up Brick Lane.

1741   Proposals for an octagonal church are rejected in favour of a four-sided building by a vote of eleven to one, though the suggestion that the ceiling should be suspended so that all pews have good views of the pulpit is unanimously accepted.

Plans are approved for a church with seating for 1500 people and an attached school where 200 children of the poorer members of the congregation will be able to learn to read and write in French and recite the Catechism. The running costs are to be paid by leasing vaults which are to be dug beneath the church and school.

1742   A thirty-year lease signed with Benjamin Truman, brewer, of Brick Lane, for the use of the vaults under the new church and school for storage.

1743   Construction begins.

Stands on the muddy floor of the half-finished church, the roof still open to the sky, the bare brick walls darkened by rain, imagining the pews full, the church ringing with French voices.

Construction delayed for a month after a member of the Consistory reports that bad bricks are being used. The bricklayers are reinstated after they have given a written undertaking to use only the best stock.

A proposal from a member is taken up by the Consistory to leave a place for the Ten Commandments to be painted on the wall of the church.

alluever.com

91 Brick Lane

ADAM AND RICHIE'S DOTCOM START UP, STARTED UP A FEW CRUCIAL MONTHS TOO LATE, HAS ARRIVED AT ITS NEED FOR SECOND ROUND FUNDING...

JUST AS THE BUBBLE IS BURSTING.

GOD, WE'RE GOING TO MAKE MILLIONS OUT OF THIS!

WHAT ABOUT ALL THAT MONEY YOU RAISED?

WE HAVE EXPENSES DAD. GOOD SITE DESIGNERS DON'T COME CHEAP AND YOU NEED THE RIGHT PRESENCE TO ATTRACT EYEBALLS.

149

150

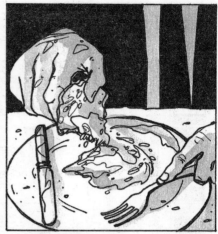

WE'VE GOT FIRST MOVER ADVANTAGE, WITH THE FRONT END RIGHT WE COULD BE LOOKING AT AN I.P.O. IN A MATTER OF MONTHS.

WELL, WHAT DO YOU THINK DAD?

WHAT I THINK....

IS THAT I HAVEN'T UNDERSTOOD A WORD YOU'VE SAID.

WHY DON'T WE EAT BACON?

WHAT KIND OF A QUESTION IS THAT?

FOR THIS WE STRUGGLED IN EXILE FOR TWO THOUSAND YEARS?

WHEN HE'D RENTED THE PREMISES IN THE OLD BREWERY HE HADN'T KNOWN THIS WAS WHERE HIS GRANDMOTHER HAD GROWN UP, HIS GREAT GRANDFATHER HAD RUN HIS TAILORING BUSINESS.

BRICK LANE!?!

HE OUGHT TO FIND OUT WHICH HOUSE IT WAS.

HIS GREAT GRANDFATHER— ZEYDE THEY CALLED HIM,

YIDDISH FOR GRANDFATHER— HAD STILL BEEN ALIVE WHEN ADAM WAS YOUNG....

THOUGH HE WAS NO LONGER LIVING IN BRICK LANE THEN.

ADAM HATED VISITING HIM.

HIS SISTER WOULD STROKE ZEYDE'S HAND

AND FEED HIM CHOCOLATE BUTTONS.

157

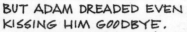

BUT ADAM DREADED EVEN KISSING HIM GOODBYE.

ZEYDE DIDN'T LIKE ADAM EITHER

THOUGH IN TRUTH

ZEYDE HADN'T LIKED ANYONE MUCH....

...EXCEPT HIS BLACK NURSE.

MUHAMMAD, THAT WAS HIS NAME. HE WASN'T REALLY BLACK. THEY WOULDN'T HAVE EMPLOYED A BLACK MAN IN A JEWISH NURSING HOME. HE MUST HAVE BEEN A YEMENI JEW OR SOMETHING.

HIS NAME WASN'T REALLY MUHAMMAD EITHER. THAT WAS WHAT ZEYDE CALLED HIM. AFTER MUHAMMAD ALI, THEY PRESUMED.

HE LOVED THAT NURSE, ZEYDE DID.

THERE YOU GO, MR. LEWIS.

159

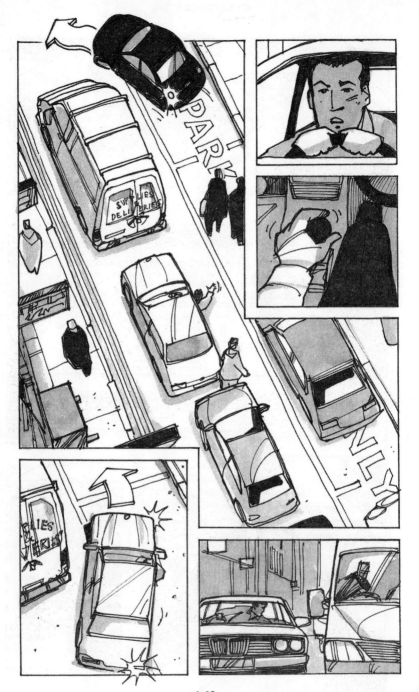

162

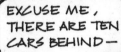

167

People's Restaurant

98 Brick Lane

Apart from to Yud, perhaps, she never spoke about her family, or her early years. Whether Zippy Levov was even her real name no one knew: names were bourgeois labels, to be changed when necessary, to escape the law, or the cloying past. What mattered was not what had gone before, but what lay ahead, the glorious future they were building together, and the only family they needed were the brother and sister comrades who met each Friday evening in the Sugar Loaf pub on Hanbury Street.

When exactly she had first started coming to the meetings, no one could say either. She had made no grand entrance, like Yud, or Rudolph Rocker, or the Witkop sisters with their flaming red hair. As much as anyone could remember was that before a certain time she wasn't there, and afterwards she was: a small girl with a broad, Slavic face, not exactly pretty or noticeable in any particular way, but with a seriousness in her slanted eyes that made even the most exalted among them think twice before behaving in a boastful or self-indulgent way. She was usually with Minka in those days, so it was probably Minka who brought her: the one tall and mannish, the other scarcely more than a child, though Zippy was already working twelve hours a day by then in some grimy sweatshop, as most of them were. She must still have been living at home, for one evening she attended a meeting barefoot, and hiding shoes was a common way for parents to try to keep their children in. Before long she took to staying at Minka's after meetings, perhaps because her parents were locking the door on her. In time she moved in to live with Minka, until Minka shipped out to join her brother in America.

This was 1896 or so. The back room of the Sugar Loaf on a Friday night was the only home the movement had. The Berner Street club had been knocked down a couple of years earlier, and the *Worker's Friend* was being produced out of wherever the current editor was lodging that week, and composited in a loft reached by a ladder in a warehouse on Romford Street. To get to the meetings the comrades had to walk through a public bar crowded with drinkers, but once the door closed behind them that dimly lit room with its peeling walls and rows of hard benches seemed to them like the pulsating heart of the world. Here the future of society was being shaped and the arguments were daring and furious. One evening, in a lecture on religion, the speaker, a fellow named Luntz, took out his pocket watch and held it up in the air. If there is a God, he said, let him prove his existence by striking me dead in the next minute. For those sixty seconds the silence was so deep that every one of them could hear the ticking of the watch and when the minute was up the cheering brought the land-lord in from the public bar to see what was happening. Another time, during a debate on evolution, one of the comrades leaped to his feet and tore his coat as if he was in mourning, before disappearing into the night; though after-wards no one could quite remember whether his disgust had been at the suggestion that he was descended from monkeys or with the doubts of some of his comrades that this could be true.

Zippy's voice was seldom heard during these evenings, unless it was to hush hecklers, or at the end, when she carried round the collection box and urged the comrades to give all they could to the *Worker's Friend*. The organ of the movement operated at a loss and every week a pound or two had to be found to pay the printer or to stop the editor from being thrown out of his lodgings, as there was rarely any money for his wages. Zippy did not write for the *Worker's Friend*, but she never failed to drop more than she could afford into the box and many hours of her brief week-ends were spent delivering copies of the newspaper to the bookshops that sold them or hawking them at any likely gathering. At that time, sales were seldom more than 200, and half of those were to the regulars at the Friday night meetings. The great days of the movement lay ahead, though the Sugar Loaf was already known as a refuge for radicals arriving in London from Russia, or passing through on their way to America. In 1897 alone, speakers at the pub included Walexia, Isas, T. Aronski and Cellokov. One evening, towards the end of that year, the lecture was given by a new arrival by the name of Yud Kosminski. Few had heard of him and when he stood up he looked so frail and haggard that a voice was heard to wonder whether he would survive his own address. As it was, he spoke for nearly four hours. By this time Minka had gone to join her brother in America and Zippy was living alone. Within a week, Yud had moved in with her.

He was ten years older than Zippy, though he looked double that. He had been a travelling preacher in his younger days, before his conversion to freethinking, and had spent some years in prison, though whether the conditions there could have been any worse than those he imposed upon himself was questionable. He never ate, unless Zippy made him, having apparently survived for years on a diet of tea and sugar. He hardly slept either. There was no time. During the day he worked as a presser and in the evenings there were meetings to attend, articles to write for the *Worker's Friend*, books to be read, plans to be made. Even when he lay down at night, Zippy confessed to Millie Witkop, his body was seldom still, twitching and thrashing while he slept, and after three hours he would be up again, his fires burning.

If the *Worker's Friend* survived from week to week, sometimes failing to appear for a month or two before hitting the streets again in a special edition, crammed with accumulated articles, under a new editor, then Yud's and Zippy's own existence was scarcely less peripatetic. Yud cared nothing for money. Many a Friday night he put his entire week's wages into the collecting box, and if he did manage to bring home a few shillings he flung them on top of the chest of drawers for any visitor to take. Some weeks he and Zippy had not a penny left by Wednesday, but somehow they never starved. When summer came the comrades pooled their resources and headed out to Epping Forest for the annual Sunday afternoon anarchist picnic, riding the bus to the end of the line and walking from there into the trees, singing revolutionary songs, until they found some suitable glade where they could sit on tree stumps or sprawl in the damp grass, eating black bread and brown herring, and continuing the arguments of Friday night. A couple of the girls had babies by now and they brought them along and let them crawl about, their fingers sticky with herring, but Yud did not think it right to introduce children into the world until it had been remade, and he and Zippy practised his own method of contraception.

Yud was now one of the brightest lights of the movement. He wrote a weekly column for the newspaper on subjects such as free love, the ownership of property and the use of violence. By now, though, Rocker had entered the scene. A German gentile who had taught himself Yiddish, he was as brilliant a speaker as Yud and a masterful planner and organizer. When the editorship of the *Worker's Friend* became vacant Rocker took it on and its circulation was soon soaring. The years either side of the turn of the century witnessed a rising tide of labour activism in the East End and the pragmatic Rocker seized the opportunity to broaden the reach of the movement and fashion the newspaper into the voice of Jewish trade unionism. This provoked furious arguments at the Sugar Loaf, in the compositing loft, and even out in the streets. One evening Yud and Rocker came to blows, or more correctly to embraces, for Rocker was twice Yud's size and he held him in a bear hug while Yud beat his fists against the larger man's chest and Zippy tried to insert herself between them. She had given herself to Yud, but she had been serving the *Worker's Friend* for longer and it was now selling by the thousand.

While the ideological debates raged, often on the pages of the *Worker's Friend*, Rocker got on with his programme. To raise money and spread the word, he organized dances at which, before the band began to play, dazzling speeches would be made to the gathered. He also attended union meetings and invited union leaders to the movement's own assemblies. In 1904, when the Jewish Bakers' Union went on strike, it was with the encouragement and aid of the anarchists. Previous strikes in the East End had suffered from failures of solidarity, but in this case someone – Rocker, some said, though others suggested it was one of the women – came up with the idea of getting those bakeries that had agreed to the union demands to stamp their loaves. The *Worker's Friend* carried the call to buy only stamped bread on its front page and Zippy and the other sisters spread the message from street to street and door to door. At first only a few bakers made the stamped bread, but when the grocery shops found that the unstamped loaves did not sell, they refused to take any more and the bakers were quickly forced to give in.

It was a famous victory, winning conditions the envy of bakers across England. But it also brought the movement to a wider notice, and that spring saw the beginning of concerted attacks against it. While editorials in the *Jewish Chronicle* thundered against 'a certain turbulent element in the East End who use strikes as a stalking horse for propaganda in the cause of a systematic subversion of law and order', gangs of thugs broke up anarchist meetings, beat up individual comrades and disrupted the production and distribution of the *Worker's Friend*. Newspaper sellers were robbed, newsprint mysteriously failed to turn up at the printers and one week an entire edition of the paper was printed with the words 'Destroy the *Worker's Friend*' in bold letters on the back page, in place of the usual advertisement to 'Support the *Worker's Friend*'. By the time this was discovered the compositor responsible had vanished: gone, it was said, to America, by way of the ticket with which he had been bribed.

The comrades could not prove who had bribed him, or was paying the Bessarabian Fighters, as the thugs liked to style themselves, but they could fight back. Rocker, though he always argued against violence, was good with his fists, and even Yud made up with ferocity what he lacked in size. The real battle, though, was not waged with punches, but was for the minds and souls of the immigrants of the East End, and in 1904 the officers of the Great Synagogue on Brick Lane unleashed their most powerful weapon: Chaim Zundel Maccoby, the Kammenitzer maggid, one of the most famous orators of Eastern Europe. Throughout that summer Maccoby's Saturday sermons drew crowds of 3000 people or more into the synagogue and as the high holy days approached the talk was of what he would say in his oration on Yom Kippur, the Day of Atonement, the most holy day in the Jewish calendar. This was also the day when the comrades held their annual ball. That year, moreover, some of the comrades had decided to hold their ball across the street from the synagogue, in the recently opened People's Restaurant, where a bowl of soup and a chunk of bread could be had for half the price of a normal restaurant.

Rocker had little liking for these provocative Yom Kippur balls and he was particularly against holding one so near to the synagogue. But he had not grown up keeping Yom Kippur, and though none of the comrades fasted any more – at least not for religious reasons – or attended prayers, their childhoods had been steeped in the ancient rituals and meanings. The mockery they saw the service making of a day that was supposed to be about penitence for the sins of the year – the rich sitting in their furs and jewels on the expensive seats at the front, their stomachs gurgling in expectation of the feasts awaiting them at home, while the poor and hungry crowded on to the hard benches at the back, their clothes pathetically patched up for the occasion – embodied all the comrades most hated in religion and capitalism.

Voted down, Rocker organized a second ball in Bow. Advertisements were run for both in the *Worker's Friend* and tickets were sold in bookshops and cafés, and at meet-

ings and dances – though it was only to the bal
People's Restaurant that invitations were sent out
officers of the synagogue.

Yud was one of the fiercest supporters of the Brick Lane
ball and there was no doubting which one he would attend.
But when the evening arrived and the Bow ball began,
Rocker and his followers were surprised to see Zippy there,
alone. The speeches were made and the band started to play,
but the dancing had barely begun when word arrived of
trouble up on Brick Lane. A dozen or so of the dancers
immediately grabbed their coats and ran out, Zippy among
them. They jumped on a tram and jumped off again at the
bottom of Osborn Street and ran up on to Brick Lane. The
trouble had apparently started when the service had ended
and the congregation had flowed out, the words of the
Kammenitzer maggid still ringing in their ears, to the sounds
of the revelling from the People's Restaurant and the sight of
ham sandwiches flying through the air at them from an
upper storey window. Or so one version of the story went.
Another was that a brick was put through the window of
the restaurant. Whatever the cause, the restaurant was
besieged by a huge crowd. Zippy and Polly Witkop, clinging
to each other's hand, tried to force their way through, Zippy
petrified that Yud would come out to fight and be torn to
pieces. As Polly later told it, they were swept one way and
then another by the crowd until they were pushed into the
back of an old man, his prayer shawl still draped over the
shoulders of his coat. He turned and seeing their dancing
clothes cursed at them. Then he stopped. It could not have

been more than a second or two, Polly said, that the old man and Zippy stood there staring at each other, but it was enough for the blood to drain from Zippy's face and a tear to well up in the old man's eye, before the crowds surged again, and they were drawn apart.

In the end the police had to break up the mobs and the event was to prove, if not the end of the trouble, then its apogee. Several arrests were made on both sides, with resulting publicity that did neither cause any good. It may be that Sir Samuel Montagu, the Jewish MP for Whitechapel, brokered a secret meeting, or visited Rocker himself, for though the comrades continued to hold their Yom Kippur balls, they never again booked rooms so close to the synagogue, and that autumn the Bessarabian Fighters were back to thieving and gambling, and beating up people without any heed to their political affiliation. If the People's Restaurant ball had been a challenge to Rocker then he emerged from it stronger, and he cemented his leadership by taking the circulation of the *Worker's Friend* over 5000 during the next two years, raising enough money for the movement to open its own club.

Yud wrote a column in the newspaper arguing against the establishment of so bourgeois an institution. But a building had already been found, an old Methodist church that had more recently been a Salvation Army home on Jubilee Street, and once the lease had been secured the comrades, Zippy prominent among them, threw themselves into the work of refurbishing it. They scrubbed and painted and collected scrap wood to make shelves for the library and the

178

benches for the theatre. Within two months the club was ready for its opening. The guest of honour was Kropotkin, the Russian prince turned anarchist, and Zippy had the honour of taking his wife to the lavatory.

Around this time, Zippy and Yud moved into new lodgings in Dunstan House, on Stepney Green, where Rocker also lived, but neither of them spent much time there. Zippy was caught up in the excitement of the club. Every evening after work and on her days off she was there, volunteering in the kitchens, serving tea and coffee, reading in the library, attending lectures or plays, listening to Berman, the anarchist pianist. Another visitor to the club was a small Russian with red hair and a little beard, with whom Rocker often sat and spoke. One evening he asked Zippy if she would accompany him to a music hall. Through most of the show he sat impassively, his pale eyes unblinking, but when two clowns came on stage and began to fall in and out of each other's trousers, he laughed, Zippy reported back, until he wept.

Yud, too, was seldom at home, but he was even less often at the club, and when he was there it invariably ended in a slanging match or a fight. The place was full of Bundists and socialists, he complained. He still wrote for the *Worker's Friend*, but his copy was often late and sometimes did not arrive at all. He had taken to using his wages to print up leaflets of his own devising, which he left on tram seats, or in the pages of library books, or between the sheets of paper in public lavatories. Sometimes it was almost morning before he climbed into bed, while other nights he did not come home at all. Zippy never asked where he went, but she must have known that he could not spend whole winter nights walking the streets. One December morning he came home without his coat: he had given it to someone. Another time he took Zippy's only good dress, compensating her for the loss with a penny he had in his pocket.

They had been together now for a decade and a half. Yud was approaching middle age while Zippy was entering her thirties. They could neither live happily together nor bring themselves to separate, though perhaps it might have come to that if it had not been for what took place in 1912. There had been strikes since 1904 but none as successful as that of the bakers. Then, in the spring of 1912, 13,000 Jewish garment workers walked out of their East End workshops. The *Worker's Friend* was immediately issued as a four-page daily, with Yud taking up his column again. The club was turned into a campaign office and a canteen opened there, under Zippy's direction, to feed the strikers and their families. In the excitement, political, and other, differences were forgotten. Out of each twenty-four hours, Yud and Zippy were busy for nineteen or twenty, but the other four or five hours they spent making love or lying in bed talking or sleeping entwined rather than with their backs to each other. After three weeks the employers gave in to the tailors' demands. The Jews of the East End poured out on to the streets in celebration. Strangers kissed strangers. At last, it seemed, the dream of a new world, free of persecution and hunger, was within reach.

For Yud and Zippy it was as if they had met anew. Yud's

column in the *Worker's Friend* was made permanent again. That summer they went to the picnic in Epping Forest. For the first time in ten years, Zippy spoke about having a child, and though Yud said nothing, the next time they made love it was as nature intended. When the threat of war arose they went together to marches and sat long into the night with the other comrades talking about how the international camaraderie of the working man would defeat the forces of capitalism and secure peace. They were at an anti-war rally in Trafalgar Square when one of the speakers, his face pale, announced that war had been declared.

The comrades were stunned – and worse was to follow. The *Worker's Friend* was shut down. Rocker, as a German national, was arrested and interned. The tailoring shops where most of them worked were switched from manufacturing coats and dresses to producing khaki. Yud refused to press military wear and resigned his job, living off Zippy's earnings, which he spent on printing up leaflets on an underground press, calling for the tailors to walk out of their sweatshops. Once again he began staying out all night. In February 1915, he was arrested for making public speeches opposing the war and was sent to prison for eight weeks. A few days after he came out Zippy returned home from work to find him in their bed with another woman.

A year later Zippy turned up distraught at Millie Witkop's door. She had seen in the newspaper that her little brother – Millie had not even known she had any brothers – had been killed on the Western Front.

The following year, prompted by complaints that the East

End Jews were failing to do their duty, the government issued an edict that all Russian nationals living in Britain must either join the British army or go back to Russia to enlist. Yud declared he would not fight in any capitalist war and began to mutter about taking the war to the oppressors in their own land. Then, a miracle occurred. The Tsar was overthrown. Out of despair rose hope. Yud ran down to the recruiting offices and signed up to be returned home, to help build the new Russia. Six weeks later he was gone. Left behind, Zippy put away her earnings, saving for the first time in her life. It was several months after the end of the war before it was possible to travel again across Europe and it took her another six weeks to reach Moscow. When she arrived she found that Yud was in prison, along with hundreds of other anarchists and thousands more whose doctrines differed from the Bolsheviks'. For two years she waited in Moscow, surviving any way she could, unable even to visit Yud. Then, Kropotkin, who had also returned to Moscow, died, and the Bolsheviks, in a last gesture of open-handedness, let out the anarchists for the day to attend his funeral. Yud had lost the last of his hair and though it did not seem possible he was even thinner. Afterwards an hour was made for Zippy and Yud to be alone in an apartment. Yud's body was covered with the raw wounds of scabs he had picked off for the occasion. They lay in bed together, Zippy pressing her body to his, trying to give him some of her warmth, her strength. She begged him not to return to prison, to escape with her to England, to Palestine, anywhere. But he had given his word to the prison authorities that he would go back, and like all but seven of the hundreds of anarchists let out that day he returned to prison. Zippy never saw him again.

For three more months she waited in Moscow until she received information that he had been sent to Siberia. She borrowed what money she could and set off after him, though her friends begged her not to, for her belly had already begun to swell. It was not for another two years that it was learned that Yud had never arrived at the prison camps: he had died on the journey. Of Zippy herself nothing more was heard. Whether she had reached Siberia or died herself trying to get there, no one knew. She had been swallowed up by the vastness of the Russian hinterland and none of the surviving comrades ever heard from her again; though shortly before she died, in 1961, a story reached Millie Witkop about a Jewish trade unionist on an official visit to the Soviet Union.

This had taken him to a town in western Siberia, where breaking off from a tour to go to the lavatory he had been approached by an old woman, who had heard him using a Yiddish word. Snatching a few moments' conversation, they discovered that they had both grown up in the East End. The woman asked if he remembered Rocker, which he did. Then she asked if the name Yud Kosminski meant anything to him and it so happened that as a teenage boy he had read Yud's column. When he said this a look of unutterable happiness passed across the old woman's broad Slavic face, and she begged the man to wait. She hurried away and a few minutes later returned with a dumpy Russian woman of

183

about thirty-five years, with features like a potato, as the trade unionist put it, who spoke no Yiddish, but whom the old woman proudly introduced to him as Yud Kosminski's daughter.

Le bryk place

104 Brick Lane

North of Whitechapel, by way of Bethnal Green,
a gentleman, once brewer, fishmonger,
and other things, 'tis true, not quite so clean,
a fair field dug up to sate the hunger
of Londoners for building out of bricks.
His name was Brampston, Hugh – no local, he:
when young he'd legged it up here from the sticks;
nor freeman of the city, nor yet unfree.
He owned no man for his master,
he was the lord of all that muddy pasture.

A Fleming, 'twas, who told him that this clay
was good for making bricks, over an ale
one evening down the Horse & Dray,
and so, outsiders each, outside the pale,
Hugh putting up the brass, the Flem the art,
they leased a field, turned o'er the lugs,
puddled the dirt with shovel and foot,
threw it into moulds, threw out the slugs,
skintled them in hacks against the damp
and set them to fire in a Dutch clamp.

That Hugh, at seventeen, had left his blood,
his home, had set out for the city
to escape a life of days steeped in such mud,
he had forgot, or caused him no self-pity.
He was a self-made man. Dirt is not dirt
when it's thy dirt and earns thou money.
Nor could a foul fuming clamp disconcert
one used to the stink of haddock and tunny.
He had left home, the squire of these lands,
with nothing but his head and his two hands,

and in his pocket an epistle
from his priest to a brotherly brother
at the priory of St Mary Spital,
where, by his good service, he earned another
from no lesser person than the prior,
attesting that it was his fondest wish
to see said young Hugh soon in good hire.
Which was how he came to monger fish,
and fishmonger become, when, having wed the
    daughter,
one slippery night the master slipped into the water.

The prince of mackerel, the king of eels,
was how this good man was known in Whitechapel,
of whom the last thing seen were two pale heels
sinking beneath the inky ripple.
Hugh inherited his crown, and barrow,
his reputation for the freshest sturgeon,
oysters that wriggled against the swallow,
flesh flayed from bones as neat as any surgeon,
the cheapest fish this side of Cheapside,
tipped off the back of boats on the night tide.

Chartered in twelve hundred and seventy-eight,
the Fishmongers' Worshipful Company
did the fish trade control and regulate
within the bounds of London city,
which suited Hugh, who had rather peddle
the rude suburbs without the walls
than have those liveried fishmeters meddle
in his affairs. As for their feasts and halls,
their robes and airs, he cared not a turd.
A night down the Horse & Dray's what he
    preferred.

One barrow became two, then three, then he
opened up a shop on Aldgate Street.
Brampston's, and going swimmingly,
fish shifted nightly off the fleet
on its way up Fish Wharf by London Bridge,
eels bought still wriggling from the basket,
low overheads, no quarterage,
until the king – not Hugh, Hal – quoth, Ask it.
The Company's reach was extended by decree
to all fishy business within two miles of the city.

Rather than pay his dues, he shut up shop,
switched his money out of fishes into beer,
made a killing brewing with the Flemish hop,
and a few marks on small deaths in the rear.
'Twas some years after, in the Horse & Dray,
Jan told him what the rich would pay for brick.
That so much could be made from simple clay,
he'd never dreamed. And what poetic
justice to charge those liveried fuck-
ers the earth to build their houses out of muck.

One fine spring morning he was up his place,
checking the clamp fires kept a constant heat
(the secret is to have enough air space
between the stocks) when he received a visitation from the past. An architect
working for some warm fellow worth a few groat
needed a ton of bricks, and would Hugh inspect
the site and plans, and give him a quote.
Any chance you could come now, quoth he, it'll
only take an hour, it's the old spital.

Like some old dissolute man, the remains
of the priory hospital lurched among
the tangled worts. On ruined walls were stains
of bonfires lit to melt the lead tiles sprung
from the chapel roof. Where the monks had knelt
before the looted rood a cow now grazed.
This rubble was where the prior had dwelled,
that flutter once a page. The architect waved
his hand. There's building stone enough, quoth he,
but the lord wants nothing popish in his see.

Hugh had never cared much for such houses,
monks in their robes were one more company.
But standing among these ruins a sadness
gripped him, and as he stood there he
saw peering at him from the undergrowth
an old woman, wizened, like some old dry root.
Oh don't mind her, the architect quoth.
They left her behind, she's mad and mute.
We let her tend the weeds, she does no harm.
What's wrong? Why do you clutch your arm?

Seamen's Café

120 Brick Lane

It had been the last night of his shore leave. He and his shipmates had spent most of their four days in London lying
about the lodging house, content to sleep and fill their bellies
after the long weeks of unchanging rations and hard labour
stoking the engines at sea. But for their last evening they
decided to take the bus into town. Charlie might have gone
with them but another fellow who was staying there had
told him about a café not far away owned by a man from a
village near Charlie's own. Charlie didn't much like this
other fellow, but it was almost a year since he had left home
and when he heard the name of this village, he felt a sudden
yearning to make contact with something familiar. Charlie
and the other fellow, who had offered to take him there, set
out from the lodging house with the rest of his shipmates in
the warm light of the early evening, shirts and trousers
freshly washed and pressed, hair oiled. When they reached
the church, the others went one way and Charlie and his
companion the other. They crossed the big road and after a
few steps turned into a narrower street where the other

189

fellow told him most of the shops were owned by Jews and he peered curiously in through the open doors at the women and old men behind the counters. The café was towards the other end of the street. It was a tiny place, half a shopfront huddled between an equally small newsagent and a bakery. Inside there were four small tables and a stove behind a makeshift counter. As it happened, the owner was away and the man looking after the place in his absence was not even from Charlie's district. They were there now, though, so they sat down and ordered their food. They were the only customers and they ate without saying much to each other. The food wasn't bad, not as good as the other fellow had promised, but then it wasn't the owner cooking it. When they had wiped their plates clean the other fellow leaned across the table and suggested that they go to drink some beer.

Charlie glanced around. The temporary cook-manager was leaning over the stove with his eyes closed.

He thought of the things he had done since he had left home: the prayers he had neglected; the gambling with dice and cards.

Who knows what will happen at sea, the other fellow said. In the yellow light Charlie could see the pockmarks on his sallow skin. Those U boats are sinking ships every day.

The pub was a short way up the street, past the high walls of what the other fellow said was a beer factory. Inside it was dark and smoky, and Charlie was aware of eyes lifting and talk ceasing as they walked in, but the other fellow strode confidently up to the bar and ordered two pints of beer.

To reach the brown liquid beneath, Charlie had to put his

190

lips to a white foam that looked – and tasted, he imagined – like the scum that gathered round the ship in the harbour. The beer was hardly more palatable, but after he had forced down a few gulps, he began to feel more at ease. The pub became more amenable, less threatening. The other fellow made a joke and Charlie laughed out loud. It was this that brought over the two girls.

I'm Annie, one of them said. Her top lip curled under her nose like a snail's foot. What's your name then?

Charag Uddin.

Well, Charlie Hood, she said. Are you going to buy me a drink or do I have to go thirsty?

He bought her the gin she asked for, and, when she had drunk that, another, and another after that. His pint was more than enough for him. By the time the beer was two-thirds gone he had discovered in himself a garrulousness, an eloquence, he had not imagined he possessed in his own language, let alone in English. While she drank her gins, he told her about stealing away from home at the news of the war, about waiting in Calcutta to be chosen to serve the king, about the heat of the furnace and the grease that had to be constantly fed to the engines to keep them from seizing up. Words were still coming out of his mouth when she reached up and put her finger to his lips and said, Well, Charlie Hood, are you going to carry on talking all night?

He looked for the other fellow, and his girl, but they were nowhere to be seen. Annie took his arm and led him out through the doors.

The evening had deepened but it was still light enough to see. Annie turned her face up to his and he felt her breath on his chin, warm and sweet.

They walked up the narrow street, through the shadows beneath a bridge. Ahead of them two boys were playing around a lamp-post, swinging from a rope attached high up on the pole. As they drew near the boys stopped and stared at them. One of them said something and Annie took a step towards them. They ran off, calling out over their shoulder. Annie shouted back and then pushed open a door a few feet from the lamp. Charlie followed her up the stairs, averting his eyes from her pale calves.

The room was small, but tidy. When she had secured the curtains across the window she switched on a lamp, which cast a feeble light on a wallpaper of pink and yellow flowers. She took off her coat and walked across the room to hang it on a nail on the door, brushing his shoulder as she came back past him.

I'll have the money first if you don't mind, she said, holding out her hand. That's five bob.

He stared at her. He had spent five months on the docks of Calcutta before he had found a ship, but it still took him a few moments to appreciate her meaning. He dug into his pocket and took out what was there and held it out to her.

I'll count it then, shall I? she said, stepping forward. Her fingers made trails on the skin of his outstretched palm. Three and eight and a half. Is that all you got?

He nodded.

She sighed. Well, as they say, there's a war on.

She put the money away and turning her back to him reached across herself with her hands and with one movement pulled her dress over her head. She folded it and laid it neatly over the chair. Then she sat down on the bed and looked up at him.

In her dress she had seemed small and thin like a boy. Now he saw the spread of her thighs on the bed and the fleshy surprise of her breasts in their grey cups.

Come along, she said, patting the bedcover beside her. I've got to be at work in the morning.

His eloquence had deserted him. He parted his lips but all that came out of them was a soft burp. Sorry, he whispered. Very sorry. Then he turned and fumbled for the door handle and when he was through the door he lurched down the stairs, knocking against the wall as he went. It was a relief to reach the cold night air. He took several deep breaths and then he bent double and emptied the contents of his stomach over his polished shoes.

He felt better once he had been sick, and he had little trouble navigating through the unlit night back to the lodging house. It was almost easier without the distractions of buildings: he was used to finding his way across invisible landscapes.

He was shaken awake at seven. They had to be on board by nine. The next four days they spent loading coal and greasing and priming the engines. Two more days of light work and they were under way. They were given no information as to where they were going but they did not need to be told they were heading south. The air grew steadily warmer. Flying fish leaped out of the path of the ship. Birds hovered in the watery air above the funnels. The engine-room shifts were four hours on, eight hours off, and when he wasn't working Charlie slept on his bunk or squatted on deck with the other engine-room wallahs, cooking rice and curry and playing cards. Sometimes he stood at the edge of the ship and stared out at the water. Unlike the Hindus and Sikhs and some of the other Muslims, who wouldn't go near the rails, he was not afraid of the sea. He had grown up surrounded by water for half of every year and he could swim and manoeuvre a boat.

The ship's first stop was in Freetown. They walked around the town, looking at the Africans with their purple skins and brightly coloured clothes, gorging themselves on the fresh fish and the mangoes, as sweet as the ones at home, though not so delicate in flavour. Some of the engine-room wallahs went off with the girls who tugged at their sleeves and called out to them at every street corner, to taste another kind of fruit, and came back grinning and clutching their loins, but Charlie was not attracted to these jiggling girls with their cawing laughter. When he closed his eyes at night it was another woman he saw, her flesh paler, a kink in her top lip.

From Freetown the ship sailed to Durban and from there they made the long haul to Australia. To speed their passage they increased the amount of coal they loaded into the furnace and the ship left a dark trail behind it. At the end of his shifts, Charlie went out on deck and let his sweat dry in the wind. The sea changed in colour from dark red to turquoise to black. Twice the alarm sounded, but each time it was only whales rising up to blow.

In Australia they loaded up with wheat and turned back for the Mediterranean. They had two days leave at Port Said and a week at Jaffa. Then it was on to the North Atlantic. These were dangerous waters and the ship travelled in a great convoy. From the deck Charlie looked out at the other boats, grey shapes moving through the mists and dark waves. They stopped in America only long enough to load up and turn round again. Huge waves and cold winds battered the ship and the engine-room wallahs cooked their meals against the bulkhead and played cards on their bunks until the wind died and they steamed through flat seas under a white sun.

If the good weather was bad luck for the ship – the U-boats liking the calm waters – it was good luck for Charlie, for had he been below deck when the torpedo struck he would have had no chance. The engine-room wallahs who were on duty or sleeping in their quarters he never saw again. The ship went down in little more than ten minutes. The water was so cold when he entered it that Charlie thought the air was being squeezed out of his lungs, but then he saw a plank of wood and he swam for it and pulled himself on to it, only his feet dangling off the edge.

Through the night he saw lights and heard voices in the distance, but it was not until morning that he was rescued. The ship that found him was going to Trinidad and he spent six weeks there, warming up in the sunshine, until he and two other engine-room wallahs were taken on by a ship heading for London. Again he crossed the Atlantic and after a week in port he was given a three-day shore leave. He caught the bus up the East India Dock Road, gazing out of the window at the shattered buildings and the craters filled with rubble. Leaving his bag at the lodging house, he went out again and walked up Commercial Road, looking for the church, though that too had taken a bomb. He crossed the big road and turned up the narrow street, past more empty lots and boarded-up windows.

The building where the café had been was untouched, but the window was dusty, and peering through he saw that the tables and chairs had been removed. He stood there for a moment before continuing on, past the beer factory, and the pub. The house, he remembered, was on the other side of the street, beyond the bridge. From a distance he could see the row was still standing, but as he drew closer he saw that one of them was not there. It was gone like a tooth extracted from a mouth. He looked at the doors, searching for something that would tell him which one had been hers. Then he saw the lamp-post beside him. Dangling from the top were the frayed ends of a piece of rope. He turned back to the bomb site. Thick wooden beams had been fixed at an angle into the rubble to prop up the houses on either side, their brickwork ragged where the walls of the missing house had been ripped away. Looking up to the top floor, Charlie saw a few scraps of wallpaper still sticking to the bare plaster, and though faded and weathered, it was possible to make out the pattern of pink and yellow flowers.

He was still standing there when an old woman stopped beside him and began talking.

One of them five hundred pounders it was, she said. I was down under the Jewish temple, safest place in the East End them vaults. I may be old but I still enjoy my life. I'm not letting Mr Hitler take it away from me. Didn't go off, otherwise it would have knocked down the whole lot of them. Did enough damage though. Killed two and poor Annie was more dead than alive when they pulled her out.

Annie? he said. Did you say Annie?

Harelip Annie, poor girl. Got more to worry about than her lip now I imagine.

He turned to look at her.

Where is she now? he said.

Still in the London as far as I heard.

Where?

The London, I told you. The London Hospital. She said it loudly, as if he was deaf. Down the Whitechapel Road.

Thank you, he said, and began to walk in the direction she had indicated.

Oy, you.

He stopped and looked back.

There's some flowers here if you're going to visit her.

He walked back and looked where she was pointing. On the remains of a wall a small clump of dusty weeds was growing and on them a few buds had begun to open into pale reddish flowers.

He hesitated, but the woman gestured him forward, so he clambered under the beams to the wall and pulled out a handful of the plants. The woman gave him a toothless grin.

He turned again and hurried down the lane, until he came to the big road. A few minutes later he was in front of the hospital.

The grand exterior loomed imposingly above him, and he faltered for a moment. Then he walked up the steps.

I want to visit a patient, he said at the desk.

Name?

Charag Uddin.

The patient's name.

Oh, Annie.

Annie what?

Charlie looked at her helplessly.

Only family are allowed to visit, she said firmly, and she turned away from him and began to busy herself with something else.

He began to walk away. Then he stopped. I am serving the king for two years, he said. My ship went down in the North Atlantic. I went to her house but it is no longer there.

The woman looked at him, and then at the flowers in his hand.

Annie, did you say it was? she said. There's only one Annie here if I remember rightly. Annie Wilson.

She gave him instructions where to go and he followed them until he came to the doors of the ward and pushed them open. Beds were lined down either wall, patients covered by sheets and bandages.

Who you looking for?

It was a young woman sitting on the edge of the second bed on the right.

Annie Wilson, he said.

Over there, she said. Bed number nine, with the leg up. Annie, she called, you got a visitor.

She was lying on her back, one of her legs raised up with ropes and pulleys above her.

She looked up when he approached.

You come to see me? she said.

He nodded. Her lip was more deformed than he remembered, but the bomb had not done any further damage to her face.

Then he saw her squinting up at him and it occurred to him that she did not know who he was.

I am Charag Uddin, he said.

Oh yes.

From the pub, he said quietly, and when she still peered at him, he said, Charlie Hood.

Now a faint light came into her eyes.

He held out the flowers to her.

For me? she said.

He nodded.

She gestured at the chair beside her bed, and said, Well, Charlie Hood, you'd better sit down then, hadn't you?

Ide Park

129 Brick Lane

The first invaders began to arrive within days or even hours of the bombs, floating down by silky parachute on to the shattered buildings and still smoking piles of rubble. Few can have survived these initial conditions, but among the early infiltrators were the windblown seeds of the rosebay willowherb (*Epilobium angustifolium*) and the Oxford ragwort (*Senecio squalidus*), plants tolerant of the high levels of nitrates produced in ground that has been exposed to fire or sudden bright sunlight. Originally an inhabitant of open and burned ground in Scotland and northern England, the rosebay migrated southwards in the nineteenth century along the growing road and railway networks. A single rosebay produces up to 200 pods, each of which contains 400 seeds, a millimetre in length, with some 70 long silky hairs which open out to form a parachute in dry air. The first seeds probably reached the bomb sites from the nearby embankments of the Great Eastern Railway, germinating in pockets on the truncated walls where settled ash and dust formed a nitrate-rich soil. The majority of the bomb sites in the East End were made between November 1940 and May 1941. Rosebay plants were well established on walls before the end of 1941 and, as the sites were cleared, began to spread across the rubble piles and bare ground by means of underground shoots, or rhizomes, to form dense, exclusive stands.

Where the rosebay settled, the Oxford ragwort was usually not far behind. An immigrant from southern Europe, the first ragwort specimens were brought from the slopes of Mount Etna to the Oxford physic garden in the late 1700s, from where the plant dispersed on to the old walls about the town. When the railway arrived the ragwort took a liking to the furnace slag, or clinker, used as gravel between the tracks, and spread up the Great Western Railway line to Reading, Maidenhead and eventually London. Larger and heavier than the rosebay's, its seeds benefited from being pulled along in the slipstream of the trains, even wafting in the windows of trains and wafting out again some miles later. Like the rosebay, it favoured bomb sites devastated by fire, which produced habitats resembling its native lava soils.

As the sites were cleared and the burned ground became more hospitable and mosses and liverworts tolerant of high levels of nitrates, such as *Ceratodon purpureus* and *Marchantia polymorpha*, bound into the rubble and helped to lay down a subsoil, a second wave of wind-blown interlopers arrived. One of these was the Canadian fleabane (*Erigeron conyza*), the first seeds of which were said to have crossed the Atlantic in the stuffing of a bird specimen in the seventeenth century. Another was the coltsfoot (*Tussilago farfara*), also known as son-before-father because it puts out its flowers and fruits before its leaves, often as early in the year as February, giving its seeds an advantage over less thrusting plants. Common on rough and waste ground, the coltsfoot was found on poorly drained bomb sites where calcium had been leached from the mortar into the soils.

The clearing of the sites literally brought more itinerant species. Sticky groundsel (*Senecio viscosus*) and pineapple mayweed (*Matricaria disoidea*), a native of north-east Asia that travelled to this country via America in the nineteenth century, were carried to the sites on the wheels of the carts and lorries used to take away the rubble. Sticky groundsel, an alien from the coastal areas of Europe as far north as Belgium, was first recorded in London in the 1930s at Ham Gravel Pits near Richmond, from where its seeds spread eastwards into London in the mud collected in the threads of the tyres of the gravel lorries. It flourished on bomb sites where severe destruction had produced a fine rubble similar to its native habitats of shingle and sandy coastal soils.

Other seeds arrived on the boots of the clearing crews, like those of the ribwort (*Plantago major*), tough and tolerant of trampling and therefore common in pavement cracks, and the chickweed (*Stellaria media*), which was used as a food for caged birds and for the poultry that people had started keeping in their gardens to supply them with eggs. Then there were the burred and mucilaginous seeds that clung to the clothes of the men working on the sites, such as lesser burdock (*Arctium minus*) and the Peruvian native, gallant soldier (*Galinsoga parviflora*), originally brought to Kew Gardens in 1796 and soon after established in nearby gutters and waste places, where it earned the nickname Kew weed.

The spineless saltwort or Russian thistle (*Salsola kali*), a tumbleweed, was another immigrant from Eastern Europe via America. Its introduction into America led to its rapid dispersal across the prairies by its method of growing so dry after flowering that it is uprooted by the wind and blown about, scattering its seeds. The earliest recorded colony in London was in the 1930s on ash tips at the back of the Ford motor works in Dagenham – it seems likely the seeds came in packing material from Ford America – and it spread through London on Ford lorries and by tumbling across the cleared bomb sites.

Fat hen or muckweed (*Chenopodium album*) and red clover (*Trifolium pratense*) were two of several species brought by the horses that pulled the rubble-clearing carts. Common at the edge of fields, the seeds were harvested along with the crops and fed to the horses, which deposited them on the bomb sites in their manure. Other seeds were left in the same way by other species, such as elder bush (*Sambucus nigra*) and woody nightshade (*Solanum dulcamara*) by birds, and tomato (*Lycopersicon esculentum*) by *Homo sapiens*.

Snecockswell

141 Brick Lane

The artwork is in the style of the black and white woodcuts of the period, which is circa 1500. Each panel is bordered by a thick plain line. Some pages are composed of a single scene in a single panel, others contain several panels. There is no ornamentation. The style is simple, flat, the faces almost mask-like.

The first page depicts a walled precinct of fifteen or so buildings in a rough square. They have tiled roofs and arched windows. Towards the middle is a chapel, with a turreted tower at one end and long thin arched windows at the other. There are two walled gardens, both showing signs of cultivation, and a courtyard with cloisters. There seems to be only one entrance to the precinct, through a gate in the wall. In the corner of the page, in a separate panel, is a close view of this gate. It is made of wood, with a metal knocker in the shape of a gargoyle. Carved into the stone above the gate are the words: 'Seynt Maryes Spytell'.

*

The second page takes us into the women's infirmary of the hospital. It is a large stone hall with a network of wooden beams supporting a vaulted ceiling. Down either side are beds of various shapes and sizes, in each of which are between one and three patients. One or two are young, though more are old, as are most of the women nursing them. They are dressed in the plain grey habit of the lay sister, a sort of halfway nun. One lay sister is sweeping the straw on the floor. Another is tending to a patient. Two are standing in front of the fire, while behind them an old patient is reaching out with both arms, her mouth open, seemingly calling for aid. In one corner is what appears to be a body wrapped in a shroud. On the wall are images of saints and of Jesus and Mary. In the middle, in the forefront, a young lay sister, perhaps fourteen or fifteen years old, is washing the feet of a patient.

Page three moves on to another part of the precinct, the kitchen. This is another stone hall, though smaller. The scene is busy. Pots bubble on the stove. Kitchen implements – cooking forks, skimmers, ladles, pipkins – hang from nails on the wall. A cat chases a mouse under a long wooden table, at which stands a cook's boy chopping vegetables. Another boy is turning a pig on a spit in front of the fire. The cook's attention is directed to a third boy of about seventeen or eighteen years. The cook is a big man with a bulbous nose. His sleeves are pulled up and his long tunic is tied under his fat belly. In one hand he has a chopping knife, which he is waving angrily at the boy, who is in the process of spilling a saucepan of fat, some of it over his own arm.

Page four is divided into four quarter panels. The first shows the young lay sister leaving the infirmary. The second shows her walking through cloisters. The third shows her approaching a small arched window in a stone wall at the end of a corridor. The fourth shows the cook's boy being directed by the cook to take a pot to the same window from the other side.

The top half of the fifth page is a single panel. It shows the lay sister on one side of the window, the cook's boy on the other. He is holding the pot, which is resting on the ledge of the window. His head is slightly to one side as he tries to look into her face. She is bowing her head to avoid meeting his look and in doing so her eyes fall on his arm where his sleeve has slipped back to reveal an ugly burn, the skin blistered and raw. The bottom half of the page is divided into two panels. In the first the cook is calling angrily to the boy from further back in the kitchen. In the second the lay sister is scuttling away down the corridor, the pot clasped in her hands.

Page six is laid out in a similar way. The top panel depicts the lay sisters at dinner in their refectory. They sit at a table, on which the pot stands. From the wall above an image of Mary looks down on them. All the sisters are bent over their bowls, concentrating on their food, except the young lay sister, who is gazing into the air. The two panels below

follow her to the herb storeroom. The first shows her standing in the doorway looking in at the rows of shelves on
which sit hundreds of jars and pots and bundles of dried
herbs. The second is a closer view of half a dozen jars on a
shelf. Written on the jars are the contents: 'lycorys', 'gynger-
root', 'notemeg', 'nettel seede' and 'dockes', though it is to
the jar labelled 'malowes, gode for scaldes' that her hand is
reaching out.

The seventh page is a single panel. The scene is the chapel.
Ornate stone pillars support a vaulted ceiling. Holy images
adorn the walls and decorate the long arched windows. Also
hanging on the wall is what appears to be a leg bone of vast
size. At the back, in a separate room, through a gap in a cur-
tain, the young lay sister can be seen, her eyes closed, at
prayer. In the foreground are the monks praying, though
one of them appears to be asleep, and another is surrepti-
tiously eating a chicken leg. Some of the lay staff are sitting
at the side of the chapel, including the cook, who is at
prayer, and the cook's boy who is peering over his shoulder
towards the sisters' room. On his arm is a bandage.

Page eight is another single panel. It takes us into the herb
garden. A tall stone wall runs around the three sides that can
be seen. The garden is laid out in neat rows of rectangular
beds, bordered by lines of stones, and separated by pathways. In each corner is a tree. A bird or two is in the air or
sitting on the wall. A stone-lined channel coming through
the wall supplies a pond in the middle, which is surrounded

by a low stone wall. The young lay sister is kneeling in front of one of the beds, in which grow tidy lines of plants. She appears to have been weeding, as a pile of scraggy weeds lies beside her and she has a hoe in her hand. A bucket of water stands nearby. She is not weeding now, though, for she is staring up, her other hand clutching at the cross about her neck, at the cook's boy, whose head, shoulders and arms are visible over the top of the garden wall, which he has climbed from the other side, and from which he now dangles.

The ninth page is divided into six equal panels. The first shows the young lay sister in the infirmary dropping a lamp. The second shows her gazing up at an image of Mary. The third shows her walking through cloisters at night. The fourth shows her getting into bed in the lay sisters' dormitory. Beside her bed is a chest with the name 'Agnes' on it. The fifth panel shows her lifting her head at a sound from outside, which is depicted by the words 'the songe of the throstlecock' coming through the window. The sixth shows the cook's boy in the garden at night, whistling.

Page ten is a single panel. The moon is shining on the herb garden where Sister Agnes and the cook's boy are sitting on the low wall around the pond in the centre. Their faces are pale in the moonlight. He is looking at her, one hand touching her shoulder. She is concentrating on his other arm, which is bare, the cloth from the bandage lying on the wall beside her. With another piece of cloth she is dabbing at his wound. Poking out from her pocket can be seen some dried leaves of the mallow plant. The view is from the far end of the garden. In the background can be seen the windows of the sisters' dormitory, one of which is lit up, and standing in it is an older lay sister, peering out.

The eleventh page is divided into six panels. The first shows Sister Agnes lifting her head from her pillow as the words 'the songe of the throstlecock' come through the window again. The second shows her climbing out of bed. The third shows the older sister who was looking out of the window calling to her. The fourth shows the cook's boy waiting alone in the garden. The fifth shows Sister Agnes walking down a corridor. The sixth shows her at the kitchen window collecting the pot. The cook's boy is on the other side, his mouth open in speech. Within a banner at the top of the panel are the words 'Mete me at the sprynge.'

The next page is made up of an upper and lower panel. The first shows a low arched doorway through a stone wall leading into a low arched tunnel. It appears to be some kind of culvert or stone-lined underground watercourse, for a stream runs along its bottom. It is dark and gloomy, though part of the tunnel is lit by a candle carried by Sister Agnes. With her other hand she is holding up her habit to reveal bare ankles and feet. She is hunched beneath the low roof. A rat can be seen in the candlelight a few feet ahead of her. The cross she wears about her neck has come loose and is in the process of falling from her. The second panel is a continuation of the first, Sister Agnes still wading through the tunnel. Behind her, her cross and its chain are sinking into the water. Ahead of her can be seen the end of the tunnel and the cook's boy looking down it.

Page thirteen is a single panel showing Sister Agnes and the cook's boy at the spring. It is a bubbling pond, contained by a low wall, which also feeds the water into the culvert. Around the pond is an area of bare ground and around that another, higher wall, with a door in it. Sister Agnes and the cook's boy are sitting on the low wall. He is holding her hand to his lips and she is looking into his eyes. The view is wide enough to show beyond the wall some part of the fields around the spring. A cow is grazing. A track with cartwheel ruts leads by. Approaching the door of the spring along the track, a key in his hand, is a monk.

The penultimate page is divided into four unequal panels. The two above are smaller. In a banner that winds above both of them is written: 'The punyshment for ravyshing a maide of God.' In the first panel a young man who might be the cook's boy is having his eyes poked out. In the second the same boy is having his testicles cut off. The first of the larger panels beneath takes us into the prior's chamber where the cook's boy stands before him, still, apparently, with his eyes and testicles. There are hangings on the wall. The prior is dressed in fine ecclesiastical robes and hat. His face is stern. He is sitting at a desk, writing. Some of the words he has written can be seen on the paper: 'my fondest wysh to see hugh brampston soone in gode hyre'. The fourth

210

panel on the page shows the prior at the gate of the precinct. Hugh stands before him, clutching his letter. The prior is pointing him away from the priory hospital.

The last page is a single scene. It is again in the prior's chamber. This time it is Sister Agnes before him. The prior looms above her. He is gesturing at the carving of Christ on the cross on the wall. In a large banner at the top of the page are the words: 'Ye shall goe with bare feet on Wednesdays and Fridays and not another word shall ye utter untill ye have wyped all trace of thysse false mortal love from thy heart.'

Atlantis Gallery

146 Brick Lane

The corpses started to arrive this morning. Professor Gunther von Hagens will be at the gallery in east London to receive and meticulously arrange them for exhibition, just as he has done already in Japan, Germany, Switzerland and Belgium. All his old favourites will be there. There will be a skinned male body crouching over a chessboard with his cranium split open to show his brain, seemingly contemplating a move he will never make. There will be the Horseman, a rider with his skull chopped in two and his body flayed to show his underlying musculature. He sits with his brain in one hand and a whip in the other, astride the posed and flayed cadaver of a horse, frozen for ever in its leap.

GUARDIAN, 2002

He discovered plastination in 1977 while working as an anatomist in a laboratory at the German University of Heidelberg. He was experimenting with kidney slices and plastic polymers when he came across the technique, whereby blood, fat, water and other fluids are replaced by plastic, enabling corpse tissue to be preserved for centuries. Shunned by German scientists he set up his Institute of Plastination and moved to Asia, where he has been feted as a science pioneer. He has established plastination centres in Bishkek, Kyrgyzstan, and in the Chinese city of Dalian, where he now lives. He has spent almost £5 million creating in Dalian 'Plastination City', a business that employs 200 people to sell plastics and develop new plastination techniques.

OBSERVER, 2002

So far eight million people have seen the exhibition. Among them are the singer Tina Turner ('Thank you for such an examination of the human body,' she wrote), the tennis player Steffi Graf ('I am now able to understand my body in a much better way!') and Andre Agassi ('What an incredible learning experience').

GUARDIAN, 2002

Were I in England now, as once I was, and had but this fish painted, not a holiday fool there but would give a piece of silver: there would this monster make a man; any strange beast there makes a man: when they will not give a doit to relieve a lame beggar, they will lay out ten to see a dead Indian.

WILLIAM SHAKESPEARE, *THE TEMPEST*, 1611

I see myself in the tradition of the artists and scientists of the Renaissance like Leonardo, Vesalius and Dürer. They embodied the last time when art and anatomical science were indistinct and the beauty beneath the skin of the human body was celebrated.

GUNTHER VON HAGENS, 2002

Like a sculptor, the plastinator needs to have the finished pose in his mind before starting work. Von Hagens based his Runner, where the muscles have been splayed out aerodynamically like a fan, on Italian futurist Boccioni's 'Prototypes of Movement in Space'. The Open Drawer model, where the body is prised open in chunks, is based on *Anthropomorphic Cupboard* by Dali; the Muscle Man, with his skin draped over his arm, is based on Bartholomew in the Sistine Chapel; the Chess Player, bent over the board, brain exposed in concentration, on a Cezanne.

OBSERVER, 2001

A man holds up his skin like a jacket, calling to mind the skin suit being sewn by the serial killer in *The Silence of the Lambs*.

NEW YORK TIMES, 2002

Damian Hirst has proven to be a paradigm of a certain kind of modern artist, one that seems in many ways to reflect the nature of our times. He cuts creatures into sections and suspends them in formaldehyde, most famously with a tiger shark entitled 'The Physical Impossibility of Death in the Mind of Someone Living'. His forays into restauranteering might well be encompassed by the concept of the 'total work of art'. He has recorded two pop singles with Fat Les, one of which, 'Vindaloo', reached number two.

CHANNEL 4 WEBSITE, 2004

Actually I am not an artist. I know nothing about art. I am a medical professional, an anatomist, and this is about education, not art.

GUNTHER VON HAGENS, 2002

Physiotherapist Mitchum Hassanali, 27, has recently added a new dimension to his daily battle with pain in his busy NHS clinic, following three fascinating visits to the controversial Body Worlds anatomical exhibition in London. 'It is only now that I fully understand how the neural pathways in the spinal column become dysfunctional following a physical injury and how deep you have to go to palpitate them effectively.'

OBSERVER, 2002

Wittenberg University adopted Vesalian anatomy as a means of imparting morality to Christians. This 'meditation on death' was deemed so useful that the university required all students, not just medical students, to study the art of the healthy body and to think deeply about the beauty and ephemerality of the flesh.

LETTER TO NEW YORK TIMES, 1998

Wrist watch 'Reptile'. Wrist watch with unusual look. The hands are made of little bones revolving round the picture of a human head slice. The strap features an unusual design depicting a spine. Limited edition. 8.00 Euros.

BODY WORLDS SHOP CATALOGUE, 2002

The physician with the scalpel wore bright blue scrubs and a signature black fedora. The cadaver lay on a metal tray below a large copy of Rembrandt's 'Anatomy Lesson of Dr Nicolaes Tulp'. In a former brewery in east London the television cameras turned, a paying audience squirmed, and Britain's first public autopsy in 170 years – since the practice was banned to discourage body snatching – was under way. Two plain clothes police officers accompanied by professors of anatomy sat among the audience. Their mission was 'to see if there was any evidence of criminal activity,' said a spokesman for Scotland Yard.

NEW YORK TIMES, 2002

Channel 4 insists it will be broadcasting the event, saying it is confronting the 'ultimate taboo' of death.

REUTERS, 2002

'Bodyshock: the Man Who Ate His Lover', 9 p.m., Channel 4. It was the case that shocked the world – when German computer engineer Armin Meiwes was found guilty of cooking and eating the body parts of a man he met on the Internet. As the tale progresses, fans of gruesome stories will be in their element, as none of the stomach churning details are left out.

EVENING STANDARD, 2004

It is because it has never been found that it continues to have such a powerful hold on our minds. If it were found, if the remains of a city was uncovered beneath the sands at the bottom of the sea, however wondrous these ruins might be they could never be as wondrous as the city of our imagination.

JORGE RAVAN, *THE ATLANTIS MYTH*, 1973

The viewer must also have clinical detachment. They must see that body as a purely physical specimen, not a person. If I put dead people's names and histories, the exhibition would cease to be what it is. It would become like a holocaust museum, a place of deep sadness.

GUNTHER VON HAGENS, 2002

The daughter of a Siberian hospital patient who says her father's corpse was sold for use in an art exhibition plans legal action to reclaim it. Svetlana Krechetova believes that the body went to German artist and anatomist Gunther von Hagens. 'At first I was told that his body was at the morgue, then that such bodies were usually cremated and I must pay for the ashes.' She buried them, only to be told by officials later that the body went to Germany. 'I really do not know what the fuss is about,' von Hagens said of investigations in Russia. 'I have as much to do with this case as a penguin has to do with Christmas celebrations.'

OBSERVER, 2002

Gunther von Hagens last night agreed to return seven corpses to China after admitting that the bodies used in his exhibitions might have come from executed prisoners. Damning email correspondence from Prof. von Hagens' Chinese manager, Sui Hongjin, boasted that in December 2001 he had obtained the bodies of a 'young man and young woman' who had 'died' that morning. They had both been shot in the head and were 'fresh examples of the highest quality'. The fedora-wearing scientist, known by the sobriquet Dr Frankenstein, employs 200 people to dissect and preserve corpses at a centre in the Chinese city of Dalian, which is close to three prison camps housing political detainees and members of the banned Falun Gong movement.

GUARDIAN, 2004

The bodysnatchers operated from two adjoining cottages in Nova Scotia Gardens, a lonely street on the north-western edge of Bethnal Green. In November 1831 they made friends with an Italian boy, one of London's innumerable waifs. They invited him home to their fireside and gave him a warming drink of rum liberally doctored with laudanum. The child fell into a stupor and when unconscious was taken out and suspended head downwards in a well in the back garden. He was left there for half an hour while the murderers went out to a coffee shop in Old Street, and when they came back they drew him out, a perfect specimen of death by drowning, all the rum and laudanum having flowed out of him during immersion. Next day, having removed the teeth for separate sale to a dentist, they packed up their booty in a hamper and hawked it round the London hospitals.

MILLICENT ROSE, *THE EAST END OF LONDON*, 1951

A court in Heidelberg, Germany, fined Dr Gunther von Hagens, the anatomist behind the 'Body World' exhibitions of preserved corpses, £100,000 for fraudulently using the title 'Professor'.

AGENCE FRANCE PRESSE, 2004

'My mum likes bodies,' said Darren Mudd, 35. 'She's a big documentary watcher. Likes crimes and serial killers, and that sort of thing. So we all go down there, my mum and dad and sister-in-law and me. Let's look at some bodies.' Mudd has since been back four times, discovering new things on every visit ('You start to notice hair. Up their noses, in their ears. The swimmer has eyebrows!') but signed up as a donor after the initial trip. 'I knew immediately. It beats being worm fodder. Or going up the chimney. I don't want people visiting my grave. It's a waste of time. My sister-in-law goes, If you want to do it, get on with it. You're a bit strange anyway.'

GUARDIAN, 2002

Where on earth are you from
We're from England
Where you come from
Do you put the kettle on
nah nah nah nah nah nah nah
We're England
We're gonna score one more than you
Bonjour monsieur
Me and me mum
And me dad and me gran
We're off to Waterloo

Me and me mum and me dad and me gran
And a bucket of vindaloo

LYRICS TO 'VINDALOO', 1998

Gunther von Hagens, the controversial anatomist, has offered to buy ailing giant Alexander Sizonenko, according to German newspaper *Suddeutsche Zeitung*. The Institute of Plastination has written up a contract for the former Russian basketball player, 44, who is 7 ft 10 in. tall and weighs 200 kg due to a tumour that destroyed the part of his brain regulating growth. It offered him a one-off payment as well as a monthly pension for as long as he lives – on condition he leaves his body to the doctor after his death.

PRAVDA, 2004

Vat House

148 Brick Lane

When the ship was docked and they had been paid their last shillings and signed their names to their discharges, or made their marks, some dozen of them who had come through these past months together walked down the gangplank and within a hundred strides back on English soil were taking themselves into one of the alehouses that crowded the waterfront for the very purpose which they now set to fulfilling. When morning came half of them were still drinking, and swearing to keep at it another night, while a few more were gone upstairs with wenches, so it was only three who slipped quietly away, not the sorts any of them for farewells, their sacks slung over their shoulders. They walked through the town without much talk, for their heads were heavy and sluggish, and though hardly conscious of it they fell from long practice in step with each other, the heels of their boots sounding their progress on the stone. Where the houses thinned out and gave way to fields the roads parted and they stopped. The city man of them, who had kept them rapt more than one night as they lay thirsting in the damp and dark with his tales of the great brewery, and its rivers of ale, swore again that if they would keep him company he would see to their hiring alongside him, for those barrels were heavy and the vat house would welcome two such strapping country lads. The brothers let him make his speech but when he fell silent they heard only the whispering of their own road. These past eight years they had swaggered down the cobbled streets of Lisboa and wintered with Wellington in the Pyrenee and marched through more Flemish towns than they could name, but now all they wanted was to stand in the flat fields they thought of as their own, the wide sky flat above them. They shook hands and let their companion pronounce once more the name of the brewery and the street it stood on, and then he turned westwards down the London road and they set off walking into the north.

After an hour their vests were dark with sweat and they were glad of a ride on a hay cart. When it turned off the road they carried on by foot, stopping when the sun was at its highest to sprawl in the shade of a tree and share the loaf of bread they had thought to take from the alehouse, before setting off again. They halted for the night at an inn, for their pockets still clinked with coins, and in the morning their uniform earned them another ride. That currency would soon lose its value, but they were among the first home after the great victory, the year they had served on top of the seven they had signed to seeing to that, and still novelties. The ride took them all of twelve miles and they walked on from there through land that grew more familiar until they were passing between fields they had worked themselves, the clover coming up green in the stubble, and trees they had climbed, and hedgerows coloured red with hips and haws.

The first to meet them was Will Ames, who remarked that they were back and told them the harvest was in. Their progress after that was slowed by folk calling to them or coming out of their doors and it was getting on to dusk by the time they reached the churchyard, where they were left in peace to look on their mother's stone. She had died three years back and she lay now beside their father. They stood over her for a time and then left her to walk in the shadows down the lane to the last but one cottage. The door they had never known locked was nailed shut, but Ned Culley, who had the last cottage, called to them over the hedge and after telling them their mother would have lived to see this day, he went in to fetch his tools so they could pull out the nails. That brought Mrs Culley out too, who wiped a tear from her eye at the sight of the boys returned to an empty house and said she would fry them up some supper if they would come in, but they told her it was a long time since they had sat under their own roof.

Ned lit them a lamp and they carried it inside and stood looking about at the few sticks of furniture, the browned almanac hanging on a nail, the clock that had been their grandmother's sitting on the mantelpiece, though the hands were stopped where the spring had given up after their mother's last winding.

They were still standing there when they heard the snort

of a horse and Mrs Culley's voice saying, You wasted no time.

They went to the door and looked out at the old woman standing on the road with a tray of hot bacon and bread and two mugs of steaming tea below the bailiff atop his piebald mare.

Evening Francis, the bailiff said. Thomas. I heard you were back. Thought I'd come and offer my greetings.

He'll be wanting his two shilling, no doubt, Mrs Culley said.

No hurry with that, the bailiff said. I've had no rent these past three years. The mare shook her head and he leaned forward and patted her on the neck. My considerations over your mother.

We don't need no charity, Frank said, taking a silver coin from his pocket and tossing it up to the bailiff. We'll be paying our rent regular, and earning it too.

The bailiff nodded and slipped the money into a leather pouch at his belly, and tipping his hat again, pulled at the reins and the horse lifted its head and plodded on its way once more.

Before they went to sleep they looked in the chest for their old smocks and hung them over the backs of the chairs to air. They slept that first night on the floor, for they were not used to softness, nor yet ready to lie where their mother had breathed her last. In the morning they put on their smocks and walked through the mist to the farmhouse as if they had never been away.

The grain was still drying out in the barns and they were

put to a ditching crew that day and the next. The day after was Sunday and though they heard the church bells tolling across the fields they did not go. Mrs Culley had come in while they were at labour and dusted the cottage and taken away their uniforms to wash, but their sacks still sat in the corner and they opened them and poured the contents on to the table: the bronze goblet they had taken from a wrecked house; Tommy's button collection; a doll carved out of bone; the skin of a snake Frank had killed in Portugal; the muzzle loader, barrels cut down to eighteen inches, they had used to shoot birds up in the mountains; the finger they had cut off a Frenchman; the small roll of letters their mother had sent while she still lived and the other that Frank took and put in his pocket. The gun they stashed away and the rest they set on the mantelpiece, on either side of the clock. Then Tommy said the sermon should be over and he thought he would go and pay some attention to their parents' graves. Frank reached down and rubbed his leg where he had taken that ball, and though he had not complained of it in months Tommy made no remark.

When he was gone, Frank took up the kettle still warm with the water in it and went outside to shave. He was rinsing the soap from his face when he heard the steps and looked up to see Mary standing there in a blue Sunday frock.

I looked for you in church, she said.

I got out of the habit these past years, he said, wiping his face, his cheeks prickling from more than the shave.

The same with letter writing I suppose.

He studied her. She had filled out a little and there were lines at her eyes but nothing to change what had been in his mind every day of these past eight years.

I put pen to paper more than once, he said softly, looking down. But the right words would not come.

That week the threshing started and it kept the brothers busy through the autumn. On Sundays Mary would come over after church, sometimes with a bit of food spare from the kitchen of the big house, and they would eat together and then she and Frank would go for a walk down the lanes, or Tommy would go to tend the graves or if there was no need stop at the alehouse, to give the lovers some time alone. In the evening Frank would walk Mary back the mile and a half to the manor.

Come November the men laid aside their flails for a fortnight to bring in the turnips and then it was back to the threshing. The last of the corn was done the first week of the new year and after that gangs of them were put to hedging, while the sap was down, and clearing ditches and looking to the fences, but almost as many days as not were lost to rain, or the snow and frost, and by February to lack of work, what employment there was going to the married men. Some turned to the parish but Frank and Tommy still had a few shillings left from their soldiering and days there was no work they went for strolls in the fields and along the hedgerows, coils of wire and whittled sticks in their pockets. Later they would go back to check their snares and if they were lucky come home with something for the pot.

Then it was spring and the labour was more plentiful

again, and after work the brothers planted peas and potatoes and cabbage and beans in the little plot beside the
cottage and tended them until it grew dark in the evenings.
One Sunday at the end of April Tommy walked down to the
next village and came back with a pot of whitewash and
that week their evenings were spent painting the walls and
the woodwork of the cottage, for on the Saturday Frank and
Mary were married, he with a flower in his hat and she in a
dress she had sewn herself in her own evenings. Her former
mistress at the manor gave them a wedding gift of a tea
service, which Mary laid out on the chest of drawers she had
bought with her savings and which arrived in a cart the following Wednesday, tied on top of the new bed she had also
paid for. That was installed upstairs and the old one brought
down for Tommy, who till then had shared with his brother.

Now the men left the house in the morning with chunks
of bread and lard wrapped in a cloth and came home in the
evening to a hot meal of cabbage and potatoes and a piece
of bacon, or hare. Fresh flowers appeared every few days in
a vase in the middle of the table and the Frenchman's shriv-
elled finger that had stood these months on the mantelpiece
disappeared and neither Frank nor Tommy asked where it
had gone. Summer, though, steadfastly refused to partake of
this mood. Day after day it was cold and grey and the corn
remained small and thin in the fields, short in straw, the
ears stunted. When the farmer could wait no longer to bring
it in the talk was of a yield barely half the previous year's
and the men who would normally have competed to be king
of the mowers swung their sickles like luggards, afraid of the

harvest finishing and what would come then. They halted more frequently and drank the beer the bailiff brought them with an urgency not apparent in their mowing, while the bailiff sat atop his mare haranguing them and pointing to the clouds.

When threshing time came only the married men were taken on and not even all of them. That Sunday there was a fight in the alehouse between a man who had been hired and a returned soldier who had not. Tommy, whose practice it still was to be out of the cottage a part of every Sunday, was there to see it, though he said nothing when he came home, waiting until Mary was out of earshot before he told Frank how the two men had let their legs be tied either side of the table and had fought over the top until the wood was slippery with blood and the old soldier had to be pulled off the other to stop him breaking the man's skull.

It was that week or the one after that Tommy met the higgler. He was out on one of his daytime strolls, while Frank was at the threshing, when a figure stepped out from behind a bush. At first Tommy thought he was a keeper and was considering whether he should run or fight, for he had a snare in his hand and more in his pockets, when the fellow assured him he was not spying on him but was admiring Tommy's knowledge of the ways, adding, as if thinking aloud, how so doing had set him to pondering whether any of the folk around here might ever chance across a pheasant or two they had no need for themselves.

Recognizing him for what he was now, though still not entirely free of suspicion, for keepers were not above acting as higglers to snare their prey, Tommy said he wouldn't know himself but if a man came upon such knowledge what might he do with it?

He might bring it to this same spot at dusk in seven days time, the higgler said.

When he had gone Tommy bent down and pushed the stick in his hand into the earth, the loop of wire hanging over the opening in the hedge where he had seen hare tracks, and then continued on his stroll. He and Frank had spent their boyhood scaring crows and stealing eggs and shooting sparrows in the hedgerows with a slingshot and when they were older their own father had taught them the art of snaring, and a trick or two else to catch a bird, but in all his knowledge the old man had never caught a thing he had not brought home for his own pot or taken to the back door of a house troubled by sickness or death. Tommy turned this over in his mind as he made his way home, as he turned over the three weeks it was since he had earned a penny, and the eight years he had served the king, and a future that seemed to stretch ahead into uncertainty and shadow.

Three days later he left the cottage and walked down Hoe Lane and took the path across the fields and into the woods. In his pockets were a dozen snares he had made specially and a knife and a bag of peas. Though he moved with a natural quiet, the pheasants flapped away before he could approach them, but he did not mind. He waited until they were settled again and kneeling to the ground and taking the knife, dug a hole a few inches deep and tapering at its end. Then he poured a handful of peas in and lastly he secured the snare so that the wire circled the top of the hole. Should a bird reach down for a pea, its head would have to pass through the snare, and as it ate more peas it would have to push further into the hole and the snare would tighten around its neck until when it tried to straighten up it would be held and its struggles would only pull the wire tighter. When he had dug one hole, he stopped and listened, for there were keepers in the woods by day as well as night, and then he moved on and dug another, until he had used all his snares.

Four evenings later he met the higgler at the agreed spot, and opened the sack to take out the three birds he had for him.

The higgler lifted them up each by their neck and eyed them and sniffed at them to make sure they were fresh.

That's all? he said.

There was another but that went in the pot.

The higgler put the birds into his own sack, tying up the neck, and then took some money from his purse and handed it to Tommy. It was four shillings and sixpence. Half a week's pay if he had been labouring.

I can take more if you can get them, the higgler said. Same price, three bob a brace.

I put out two dozen snares for that.

The higgler blew his nose into his fingers and wiped his hand on his jacket.

There's other ways to get a bird than snares.

He looked at Tommy and then turned away into the shadows.

A shilling of what he made Tommy kept for himself and the rest he gave to Mary, who looked him in the eye but said nothing and put the coins away. That week he went into the woods and dug another two dozen holes, though when he went back he found all but one of the snares pulled up and the holes filled in and the remaining one that had not been found empty.

The following day, when Frank was gone threshing, and Mary was out too, Tommy went upstairs and pushing aside the bed lifted a floorboard and took out the gun stashed there, wrapped in a piece of oilskin, and the bag of shot and the other of powder, putting his fingers into the last to make sure it was still dry.

It was November time and grown cold when he slipped out of the house, Frank and Mary by now long gone up to bed. He found the gun where he had left it earlier, in the sack, under a hedge, and he took it out, feeling the cold of the metal, before slipping it under his smock. The moon was only a quarter full and hidden half the time by the clouds sliding across the sky, but it was light enough for him to see his way and he headed across the fields to where he had walked at the edge of the trees at dusk time and had heard the calls and whistles of the pheasants as they had risen to roost. As he drew close he slowed his step and circled round so that he came into the woods with the wind in his face, for the pheasants liked to sleep with the wind before them, smoothing down their feathers rather than ruffling them up.

The trees were dark against the sky and moving step by

step he saw after a while a first black tail-feather and the sil-
houette of the hunched body above it, though he did not lift
his gun yet. He planned to fire only once and he carried on
until he came to a tree with a dozen black shapes arranged
along a pair of branches one above the other. As softly as he
could he raised the gun and aimed and pulled the trigger.
Choking black smoke rose from the foreshortened barrels as
the shot rang and echoed through the trees, the birds he
had not felled shrieking and flapping noisily away. As soon
as the smoke cleared he looked about on the floor and found
the first bird, and then another, and another, breaking the
necks of the ones still alive with one snap and moving
quickly on. By the time he had seven birds he thought it
unlikely there could be many more and he slung the sack
over his shoulder and holding the gun in the other hand
stood in silence, listening. Then he turned and walked
swiftly away, heading not straight for home, but to a place
he knew to hide the sack and gun.

Twice more that month Tommy went into the woods at
night. He thought it wise to leave at least five days between
visits, though the nights he did not go he dreamed of walking through the shadows and counting tail-feathers. The
second of these times when he stopped at the edge of the
wood he heard the snapping of a twig that might have been
caused by a boot, but though he waited a good time he
heard no more and he was not disturbed on his way home,
and nor did any keepers come to pay a visit to the cottage,
though if they had they would have found nothing there for
all six birds he took went to the higgler.

Then it snowed and he could not go out while the snow lay on the ground to show his tracks and by the time it thawed Frank was laid off from the last of the threshing. Mary was a good housekeeper, and they had no children to feed or clothe, so money was not too short, but it was not only money that drew a man to the woods, and the next time Tommy left the house he heard steps behind him and turning round with his fists up he saw Frank following after him, his hat pulled low over his brow.

You should go back to your bed.

That gun's as much mine as yours, Frank said. No reason you should have all the fun.

Tommy had seen birds roosting up Long Copse, where he had not yet shot, so when they had retrieved the gun and the sack, Frank carrying the latter, they made for that place, keeping off the road and following the track and then walking across the fields, careful not to set the sheep to making a noise.

The night was still and the moon three-quarters and though still low in the sky it cast a silvery glow on the land and they walked with the ease of men who were not only brothers but had soldiered across half the world together. When they reached Long Copse they stopped and listened. Then they entered the wood, Tommy carrying the gun lightly and taking care of his way, for the last thing he wanted was to trip and set it off.

They had spied the first tail-feather when the keepers stepped out from behind the trees, four at least, though neither Frank nor Tommy were bothering to count. Frank was closest to them and he took a big crack on his leg from a swinging stick before he had a chance to run, and went down. Tommy seeing his brother under a flurry of kicks turned the gun as he had done so many times soldiering, though he thought enough to pull only one trigger.

The shot caught one of the keepers and the others fled. Tommy ran to Frank and dragged him the other way until they were behind an oak tree, Frank on the earth, his leg stretched awkwardly in front of him.

Frank looked wild-eyed at Tommy.

You shot him, he gasped.

They were murdering you.

They heard a groan, the keepers pulling the fallen man away no doubt. Then one of the keepers called out, We know who you are Frank and Tom Wilson.

I still have one barrel, Tommy shouted back.

He listened but there was no reply.

It's the same leg that ball got me, Frank moaned.

Tommy bent down and pulled his brother's trousers up and saw the bone sticking out of the flesh. He looked up at Frank's face, a sheen of sweat glinting on it in the moonlight.

I'll carry you home, Tommy said. Mary can patch you up.

They know it was us.

I won't leave you.

Then they'll hang us both, Frank gasped.

Tommy shook his head.

Looking at him, Frank said, Mary is with child.

Two Brewers

154 Brick Lane

Sidney and Beatrice Webb's account of Joseph Merceron's dominion over the parish of Bethnal Green in the early 1800s, 'The Rule of the Boss', was published in the first volume of their study of English local government in 1906. This was a time of growing interest in London's heritage and history, particularly in the previously neglected eastern parts of the city. The *East London Advertiser* had for several years been running a nostalgic column, 'East London Antiquities'. The successful campaign to save the Trinity Almshouses on the Mile End Road in the 1890s had given birth to the *Survey of London*, the first volume of which, on Bromley-by-Bow, was published in 1900. New developments were being used as opportunities to commemorate prominent local figures from the past, and among them was Joseph Merceron. In 1901 a block of social housing put up by the East End Dwellings Company in Bethnal Green was called Merceron House, while two years later a new road was named Merceron Street.

The Webbs' concern with local history had nothing to do

with nostalgia, however. Campaigning social reformers, they were prominent members of the Fabian Society and had founded the London School of Economics (they would later help to relaunch the Labour Party, Sidney becoming Labour's first President of the Board of Trade). By 1906 they had published pioneering works of 'social science' on the history of trade unionism and industrial democracy, and in *English Local Government* (which would run to nine volumes) they had set out to expose, through a rigorous exploration of previously ignored sources, how the lives of ordinary people were affected by the machinery of local administration. What tipped them off about Merceron they did not reveal, for when they started looking into him they could find 'no other tradition in the parish than that he [had been] an active and public-spirited local administrator'. But by going back to contemporary documents – parliamentary minutes, accounts of trials, handwritten reports of vestry meetings – they unravelled a story of brazen corruption at the heart of Bethnal Green.

A descendant of French Protestant, or Huguenot, immigrants, Joseph Merceron was born in the 1760s, probably on Brick Lane (where at least two Merceron families lived). Nothing else is known about him until in his twenties his name began to appear in the minutes of vestry meetings in St Matthew's parish church. His first mention was as a clerk to a lottery office-keeper in 1787. A few months later he was an assistant to a Poor Rate collector. A year or two further on he was appearing on 'all the committees, doing much laborious work for the parish, and undertaking the very onerous responsibilities of keeping its funds'. At first, the Webbs wrote, there was no reason to attribute to Merceron anything more than 'the usual English willingness of an ambitious and public-spirited man of ability to undertake unpaid work of local government'. But as the months and years passed, the vestry minutes revealed a politician with an increasing interest in power and money and a diminishing concern with public-spiritedness.

At the time, Bethnal Green still operated under the old vestry system of local government, whereby ratepayers elected their local representatives, and approved their policies, by a show of hands in the vestry of the parish church. It was a system open to abuse by anyone unscrupulous enough to pack meetings with ratepayers promised a few beers in return for their votes, which is what Merceron did. Within a few years he had been elected leader of the Vestry, director of the Poor, chairman of the Watch Board and Paving Trust, and commissioner of the Court of Requests, of Land, Income and Assessed Taxes, and of Sewers. He was also a justice of the peace and a licensing magistrate for public houses. Those posts he could not fill himself he gave to one or other of his 'little coterie of dependants and followers'. By the close of the eighteenth century, the Webbs recorded, he had become the 'almost irresistible dictator' of Bethnal Green.

For another decade Merceron's rule continued virtually unchallenged, until a new rector, Joshua King, was appointed to St Matthew's church in 1809. King was horrified by what he saw going on in the vestry of his own church and in the parish about him. He began to campaign against Merceron and in 1813 he managed to instigate proceedings against him for fraudulently altering parish tax and rate assessment – raising taxes for his enemies and lowering them for his friends, often simply by crossing out the approved rates in the tax books and putting in new ones in his own hand. The evidence was damning, but 'in a way in which the rector never understood' Merceron managed to get himself acquitted. King was shocked but not deterred. He continued to press government officials and when a parliamentary inquiry was held into law and order in the city in 1816, a good proportion of the hearings was devoted to witnesses, including King, giving evidence about Bethnal Green.

It was from the minutes of these hearings that the Webbs rediscovered the full extent of Merceron's abuses of power. Vast sums of public money went missing – including £12,165 to alleviate the distress of the poor in the parish – while Merceron grew unaccountably rich. As well as buying up cottages and houses which he rented out to potential voters, he purchased or assumed control of some two dozen public houses, which, with him as the licensing magistrate, were guaranteed their licences. Merceron's Bethnal Green, the Webbs' wrote, grew into a 'saturnalia of public disorder'. Pubs, many of them his own, 'kept open on Sundays, and far into the night, harbouring what were popularly known as "cock and hen clubs" resorted to by the young weavers of both sexes, and becoming "nurseries of depravity and vice" and centres of "annoying and disgraceful tumults".' Anyone who complained was liable to have his rates put up, or worse. A Mr Shevill was beaten up for suggesting that the parish accounts should be properly audited, while the silk warehouse of another opponent, a Mr Racine, was laid waste by a bullock driven in by 200 'violent fellows'. Such 'bullock driving' was one of Merceron's favourite sports. A bullock was bought from a drover and peas put in its ears or an iron rod inserted up its rectum to madden it. Then it was driven through the crowded streets and into buildings. One Sunday a bullock was driven into the churchyard while King was delivering his sermon.

As a consequence of the parliamentary inquiry, Merceron was put on trial again in 1818. There were two charges: corruptly renewing the licences of disorderly public houses in which he was personally interested; and fraudulently appropriating £925 from the parish to pay for the expenses of his trial of 1813. Merceron reportedly offered £10,000 to gain an acquittal, but he was found guilty on both accounts and sent to prison. King and 'all that was respectable in Bethnal Green' celebrated their triumph with a public dinner. An elementary school 'which Merceron had hitherto thwarted' was set up and other steps taken to improve the welfare of the parish. The victory was short-lived, however. By the time Merceron was released from prison in 1820, Joshua King had left his post at St Matthew's. By Easter of that year, Merceron had been re-elected a commissioner of the Court of Requests. The following year his son-in-law was made vestry clerk. Before long Merceron was 'once more in undisputed supremacy'. His imprisonment had not left him untouched, however.

He was now more careful about covering his tracks. Rather than opposing inevitable reforms of the vestry system, he co-operated in passing a new local act while making sure that the new system was one he could continue to control. His annual statements to the parish were masterpieces of public relations. He even bought up and destroyed 'the scarce reports of his trials' so that he might grow old in an 'odour of sanctity'. When he died a large plaque recording how he had lived to an 'honoured old age' was put up on the wall of St Matthew's church.

There is, in the Webbs' account of their 'careful analysis of the manuscript vestry minutes', a deserved air of self-congratulation. 'The Rule of the Boss' is a model piece of social history detective work, and a good story. I came across it early on in my own research for this book and read it jealously. It seemed a perfect fit for the narrative jigsaw I was starting to piece together. Merceron was born on Brick Lane and continued to live and work there most of his life. Of the twenty-two public houses he admitted to owning or controlling, no less than five were on Brick Lane: the Hare, the Turk & Slave, the Two Brewers, the Ship, and the Adam & Eve. This last, with its connotation in East End rhyming slang – 'would you Adam and Eve it?' – even suggested a nicely ironic title for the tale of a corrupt politician whose last act of debasement was to try to dupe history, and how he was caught in the act. The only problem was that the Webbs had already told it.

Nevertheless, I made a photocopy of 'The Rule of the Boss' and every few weeks I would pull it out and look at it again, trying to work out how some aspect of it might lend itself to my book. Eventually, more to allow myself to let go of the idea than in any real hope it might metamorphose into something I could use, I walked one afternoon up Whitechapel Road and the Mile End Road to the Tower Hamlets local history library on Bancroft Road, and ordered up the documents that had been the Webbs' own sources. Within minutes several large leather-bound volumes were set down in front of me. I opened the first one and a little frisson went through me, for it was one of the original vestry books of St Matthew's parish church: the actual stiff waxy pages, with their handwritten minutes of the vestry meetings of the 1810s, which Joseph Merceron must himself have handled almost 200 years ago, and which Beatrice and Sidney Webb had pored over a century later. I turned the pages slowly, finding reference after reference in florid ink letters to Mr Merceron or J. Merceron Esq. and the Revd J. King. As exciting as it was, after an hour or two I had found nothing that the Webbs had not recorded and I put the volume aside and picked up another one.

This was the *Minutes of Evidence taken before a Select Committee Appointed to the House of Commons to Inquire into the State of the Police of the Metropolis, 1816*. Reading it, I understood why the MPs were so concerned with the abuse of the public house licensing system. Pubs were where people met and drank and were, therefore, the potential breeding grounds not only of drunkenness, vice and crime, but of that even greater social evil: public disorder. If the system for licensing them, and therefore for keeping them under some sort of control, broke down, then the very fabric of society was under threat. But as I read on I also began to see, to my surprise, that 'The Rule of the Boss' had not told the whole story. On page after page, witnesses testified to Merceron's abuse of his position as a magistrate to deny or grant licences to landlords; but on the same pages the testimony also repeatedly referred to another local figure and institution: Mr Hanbury and Truman & Hanbury, the great Black Eagle Brewery on Brick Lane.

When one William Morgan applied for a licence for his pub he was visited by a clerk from the brewery and told that 'unless I should agree to a deal with Messrs Truman & Hanbury the house should never be licensed'. John Beaumont, another prospective landlord, was warned he would never get a licence for his pub unless 'I comply with the conditions of selling it or letting it for a term, much under value, to Messrs Hanbury'. A third landlord, when asked why he had agreed to serve Truman & Hanbury beer, replied, 'Messrs Hanbury would not, of course, be at the expense and trouble of using their influence with the justices, unless the trade was made over to them.'

The Hanbury in question was Sampson Hanbury, successor to the Truman family as the head of the brewery. He and Merceron, the members of the select committee concluded in their own comments, were 'close and intimate'. Joshua King put it more colourfully, testifying how he had often heard Merceron say that 'Hanbury is a devilish good fellow, that he was always sending him presents, that he supplied his house with beer gratis, and that a week before he had sent him half a barrel of porter'. It was, the testimony to the select committee made clear, a mutually beneficial relationship: Hanbury cornered the beer market of Bethnal Green while Merceron was in return showered with gifts and in some cases made manager of Truman pubs.

The hearings in the House of Commons exposed Merceron and led to his being jailed, if only for a relatively short time. But what of Hanbury? 'O tempora! O mores!' the members of the select committee commented at the end of one session. 'Does not the law prohibit brewers, distillers, and all persons interested in such trade, from acting at licensing meetings?' Yet Hanbury was never charged and when I turned next to reading one of the few accounts of Merceron's trial that the politician had not managed to destroy, I could discover no mention of Hanbury or the brewery.

I decided I needed to find out more about Sampson Hanbury, so I went to the British Library. Truman's ceased to be an independent business when it was taken over by Watney Mann in the early 1970s, but a few years before that the management had commissioned a history of the company to celebrate its 300th year. From *Truman: The Brewers*, I learned how Sir Benjamin Truman had built up the company during the eighteenth century only to die without any living sons. He left the eighteen shares in the company to two great-grandsons, and control of the business in the hands of his head clerk, James Grant. For the following eight years Grant continued to serve the brewery until he was finally able to acquire a single share from the family. What happened next reads like something out of a Sherlock Holmes story. In the summer of 1789 Grant went on holiday to Dorset and never returned. He died suddenly and the next thing anyone knew his share had been purchased by 'a young gentleman by the name of Hanbury' who came up to Brick Lane and took over the company.

Reproduced in *Truman: The Brewers* is a full-length portrait of Sampson Hanbury. With his long legs, large chest, raffishly handsome features and dandyish dress, he immediately reminded me of another nineteenth-century character: George MacDonald Fraser's fictional rogue, Harry Flashman. And it was soon clear the similarities were not merely in appearance. Like the Flashmans, the Hanburys had made their money trading with Virginia and Maryland. Though a Quaker, and therefore in theory a pacifist, Sampson Hanbury's grandfather, John, had armed his trading ships and put money into privateers, who were little more than pirates. He was renowned for cultivating political influence for his own financial gain.

How Sampson Hanbury came to purchase Grant's eighteenth share and assume such rapid and easy control of the company, *Truman: The Brewers* does not reveal, and I could discover nothing more on the subject myself. But by the turn of the century, Hanbury had increased his stake in the company to one third. That same year he bought a large estate with an imposing mansion and a beautiful deer park in Hertfordshire, and was soon made master of the Puckeridge fox hounds, a position he would hold for the next twenty-five years. By then he had also married Agatha

(Gatty) Gurney of the Quaker Gurney family of Norfolk. One of his sisters had previously married Gatty's father, a widower, and so Hanbury's wife was his own step-niece, as I learned from another book I found in the British Library, *The Northrepps Grandchildren*, by Valerie Anderson. This is a family hagiography and has scarcely a bad word to say about anybody – anybody, that is, except Sampson Hanbury. 'I wonder,' Gatty's cousin, Louisa Gurney, is quoted as writing in her diary, 'that such a charming person as Gatty should marry Sampson Hanbury.' Later Anderson writes of Hanbury's 'explosive rudeness' and how a cousin, Hannah, had 'always disliked' Hanbury 'so much'. She also recounts how another relative was exposed, while working under Hanbury at the Black Eagle brewery, to 'circumstances from the effect of which he never recovered', though she supplies no more detail.

It may have been that the legal case against Sampson Hanbury was not strong enough for the prosecutors, or that resources were considered more appropriately devoted to bringing to court the corrupt politician. But it seems fair speculation to wonder whether it was not easier for the authorities to go after the man of rough manners and immigrant background than the master of the Puckeridge fox hounds, 'famous in three counties', and head of what was by 1818 one of the largest breweries in Britain. Harry Flashman's great secret, it may be remembered, was that no one would believe that a man who looked and sounded like a gentleman would not behave like one.

Hanbury's position in society may explain why he was

never brought to book for his crimes. But what, to return to the Webbs, about written up in their book? The Webbs were making a study of local government and Hanbury, it is true, was a brewer not a politician. But surely the Webbs' story was even more revealing, their case against the old structures of society even stronger, if they could show how corrupt local government had been entwined with corrupt local big business. The Webbs were not merely historians. They were crusading reformers, using scientific historical research to expose failings in society and so challenge and change the way the country was governed. Sampson Hanbury ran the Black Eagle Brewery from 1789 until his death in 1834, virtually the same span of years that Merceron dominated local politics. For almost half a century the two of them had presided over that corner of London. Yet in 'The Rule of the Boss', as in Merceron's trial, neither Hanbury, nor his brewery, is mentioned.

My delving into what little I could find out about Sampson Hanbury gave no direct clue as to why this might be so. But in doing so I had come across another character in the story: Sir Thomas Fowell Buxton, MP, alias Buxton the Liberator. Buxton was one of the leading social reformers of the first half of the nineteenth century, campaigning within and without Parliament for prison reform, poor relief and, in particular, against slavery. When William Wilberforce left Parliament in 1825 he asked Buxton to lead the campaign for the abolition of slavery, which Buxton did until it achieved its end in 1833. Buxton was elected MP for Weymouth in 1818, but before that he had spent ten years working at the Black Eagle brewery. His mother, Rachel Hanbury, was Sampson Hanbury's sister and in 1807 Buxton married another Gurney, Hannah, the cousin who had so disliked Sampson Hanbury. Despite his wife's earlier animosities, Buxton went to work for his uncle and was soon made a partner and acquired substantial shares in the brewery, of which he remained a director even after he embarked upon his political career.

In the entry on Buxton in the *National Dictionary of Biography*, Buxton's work at the brewery is dismissed in a sentence. Instead the entry concentrates for that period on Buxton's 'charitable activities in Spitalfields, especially those connected with education, the Bible Society and the relief of the distressed weavers'. In 1816 one of the periodic crises in the weaving industry severely worsened that distress. Weavers were forced to beg in the streets and their daughters to paint their faces and walk into the West End to prostitute themselves to buy bread for the table and wood for the fire, as they had done in previous crises. With hunger 'widespread in Spitalfields,' the entry continues, 'Buxton delivered a forcible speech, based on his own investigations of conditions, at a meeting at the Mansion House which raised £43,369'. In this speech he spoke of entering the meanest houses and seeing the hungry and the naked of Spitalfields. 'I could detain you till midnight with the scenes we have witnessed. I could disclose to you a faint picture of such desperate calamity and unutterable ruin that the heart must be stony indeed that did not sicken at the sight.'

All these years later it is hard not to be moved by these

words. Yet after I had read them I looked again at the date: 1816. The very year that witness after witness had been testifying to Parliament to the devastating effect on a large swathe of the East End of the corrupt government and business practices of Joseph Merceron and the company whose full title had by then been lengthened to Truman, Hanbury & Buxton. With one hand Buxton was trying to raise up the poor of the district, but what was he doing with the other? Could he have not known how the machinations of the company of which he was now a partner, which now bore his name, were, in the words of a select committee of the House of Commons, 'oppressing' the poor? This is hard to believe. Buxton had not been brought into the company merely as a family favour. He was an intelligent and educated young man, winner of the university gold medal at Trinity College, Dublin. Moreover, as his son, Charles, would later write in a memoir of his father, Buxton had been charged with the task of 'remodelling the whole system of management' of the brewery.

The archives of Truman's are held in the Greater London Record Office and among them is Thomas Fowell Buxton's 'Observation Book'. This is an informal notebook, not a diary, but it contains personal thoughts about the business. In it there is no mention of educating the workers or of making sure that they did not labour on Sundays, as he made much of in his later writings. Nor is there any reference to the suffering of the poor of the district or to encouraging the company to engage in philanthropic activities. What it reveals is Buxton's 'wish that my name should be introduced into the firm' and his worries about profits. This was not surprising considering his shareholding. In 1811 he acquired two out of what were then thirty-six shares. In 1812 he purchased two more and in 1814 another three, the value of which depended on the profitability of the company. *Truman: The Brewers* tells us that 'under the authority of Sampson Hanbury, the Black Eagle Brewery prospered mightily'. Buxton's 'Observation Book' reveals a slightly different story. On 29 August 1812, he wrote how 'we have begun to have a more vigilant eye upon various departments of our business' and 'have made a profit of £30,858'. The next few years, however, were difficult. In 1815 he worried 'how are we to make a profit?' For 1816 he complained the prospects were 'but dreary'. The trouble was competition from other brewers, and he mentioned a proposal to reduce the quality of the beer in order to reduce costs, though he also wrote that he disagreed with this, noting that it would mean having to make 'presents to the publicans' to persuade them to take the lesser beer which their customers would not drink by choice. 'I am persuaded it is better to acquire trade now by good beer,' he wrote, 'than to have to seek it then by gifts and loans and purchases of leases.'

This reveals that Buxton was aware that sharper practices were being put forward within the company, if his own instinct was towards more ethical business methods. Yet how hard he campaigned for those ethical methods within the company is not clear. Buxton came from a good family but as a young man he had not been wealthy. A promised

Irish inheritance failed to materialize and in his later years he would write how he had 'longed for any employment that would produce me a hundred a year'. Sampson Hanbury hired him on £300 a year and allowed him to buy shares in the company that were, by the time he went into politics in 1818, worth £80,000: enough for him never to need to work again. That he used this freedom to devote himself to philanthropy is undeniable. But nor can it disguise the fact that he earned that freedom from a company whose success was derived in part from contributing to the very deprivations that created the need for the philanthropy of men like himself.

What, though, does this have to do with the Webbs' omissions in 'The Rule of the Boss'?

Sampson Hanbury died childless, though his shares passed to his nephews and Hanburys continued to be directors of the brewery into the twentieth century. But it was the Buxtons who made the greater success out of the riches of the Black Eagle Brewery. One of Sir Thomas Fowell Buxton's sons, Charles, was also an MP. One of his grandsons, Sydney Buxton, MP for Poplar, was a Cabinet minister and was eventually made Earl Buxton. He was given his first Cabinet post in 1905, about the time the Webbs were writing 'The Rule of the Boss'. Sidney Webb could be scathing about Sydney Buxton – 'the utter absence of original thinking in these men' he wrote of Buxton and a couple of others 'is deplorable' – but the older man had been a mentor and friend since 1891, when Webb had helped draft a sweatshop bill for Buxton, Beatrice Webb recording in her diary a number of dinners with Sydney Buxton in that year. On 29 July 1906 – the summer of the publication of the first volume of *English Local Government* – the Webbs attended a lunch party at Buxton's country house, among other social occasions with the 'Sydney Buxtons'. Nor was Sydney the only Buxton the Webbs knew. They were also friends with Charles Buxton and Noel Buxton, both great-grandsons of Sir Thomas Fowell Buxton, and both also MPs. So far as I was able to discover, the Webbs were not friends with any descendants of Joseph Merceron.

East London Female
Total Abstinence Society

160 Brick Lane

The monthly meetings of the Brick Lane Branch of the
United Grand Junction Ebenezer Temperance Association
were held in a large room, pleasantly and airily situated at
the top of a safe and commodious ladder.

CHARLES DICKENS, THE PICKWICK PAPERS, 1837

Something here. Linked to the brewery?

The most bizarre benefactor of the East End was its
home-born son Frederick Charrington. Heir to the prosperous brewery, based in Mile End, he voluntarily rejected
his filial role as inheritor to pursue the cause of Christ,
teetotalism and the extirpation of vice.

WILLIAM J. FISHMAN, THE STREETS OF EAST LONDON, 1987

A teetotal son of Truman's?

It is difficult to exaggerate the degree of interest in the

East End shown by settlers, philanthropists, religious missionaries, journalists, salvationists and sociologists.

P. J. KEATING, *WORKING-CLASS STORIES OF THE 1890s*, 1971

A missionary to the East End.

The story of Miss Angela Messenger, the heiress to the great East End brewery of Messenger & Co in the Mile End Road, and how she went to live among the struggling millions of the East, was inspired by the life story of Frederick N. Charrington.

GUY THORNE, *THE GREAT ACCEPTANCE*, 1912

Make her a woman?

You cannot escape from a big brewery if it belongs to you. You cannot hide it away. Messenger, Marsden and Company's Stout, their XXX, their Old and Mild, their Bitter, their Family Ales, their drays, their huge horses, their strong men, whose very appearance advertises the beer, and makes the weak-kneed and the narrow-chested rush to Whitechapel.

WALTER BESANT, *ALL SORTS AND CONDITIONS OF MEN*, 1882

Yes, a woman rebelling not only against the social ills of alcohol but oppressive Victorian patriarchal society in general.

Mr Charrington went to his father and announced his intention of absolutely giving up all share in the brewery. The opposition he met with may easily be imagined. Mr Charrington senior was amazed and angry. The thing seemed the height of quixotic folly. It verged on madness.

GUY THORNE, *THE GREAT ACCEPTANCE*, 1912

The story at heart a battle of wills with her father. He has the power but she has the conviction and imagination.

He was also very careful to prevent any work from being done in the brewery on the Sunday.

CHARLES BUXTON (ED.), *MEMOIRS OF SIR THOMAS FOWELL BUXTON*, 1848

It was the afternoon of a Sunday in early June.

You then find yourself before a great gateway, the portals of which are closed; beside it is a smaller door, at which, in a little lodge, sits one who guards the entrance.

WALTER BESANT, *ALL SORTS AND CONDITIONS OF MEN*, 1882

The great portals of the brewery were closed, as was the small doorway within the right-hand gate, but to the right of that was the window of the porter's lodge and that was propped open. The lane was never entirely quiet, even at three o'clock in the morning, but at that same hour on a Sunday afternoon the roadway outside the brewery gates was at its most somnolent, and with the warmth of the after-noon and the comfort of the lodge chair, it was not until a second knock was made on the window that the porter stirred from his reverie.

'Here,' he said, 'is the book for the visitors' names. We have them from all countries: great lords and ladies; foreign princes.'

WALTER BESANT, *ALL SORTS AND CONDITIONS OF MEN,*

1882

He continued to stare, mouth agape, until a light of recognition finally came on in his eyes and he blurted out gratefully, Why of course I know you. It's Miss—— isn't it? I signed you in myself. Only the other week it was. I've got your name right here, and he began to leaf through the pages of the leather-bound volume.

He led the way upstairs into another great Hall, where there was the grinding of machinery . . . and then they went to another part, where men were rolling barrels about as if they had been skittles.

WALTER BESANT, *ALL SORTS AND CONDITIONS OF MEN,*

1882

It was scarcely more than a month since she had taken her tour of the brewhouse, but then it had been a busy weekday and these halls had been brightly lit and filled with men and their voices and the sounds of their labouring and the

255

machines, and now she stood alone in the quiet and murky stillness.

This is an example of a traditional tower brewery, in which the initial ingredients are either hoisted or pumped to the top of the tower, from where they progress by the force of gravity between each successive stage of brewing.

GAVIN D. SMITH, *BRITISH BREWING*, 2004

She had begun by ascending to the top of the tower, where the water drawn up from deep in the earth began its return journey downwards, which her tour followed, through the floors and the various processes of mashing and stirring and boiling and fermenting that transmuted it into the darkened liquid on which this entire edifice was constructed.

By mid-century the Black Eagle Brewery had become the largest in London, brewing up to 400,000 barrels annually . . . the site now covered nearly six acres of ground.

TRUMAN: THE BREWERS, 1966

It was a journey as long as almost any that could be made within a single building in the city. It took her first into a hall filled with desks, where, on her previous visit, she had seen a score of backs bent over ledgers, pens dipping into inkpots, though now every chair was empty; and after that through a gallery stacked with sacks of malt and another with bulging wooden barrels.

The liquor was working and fermenting. Every now and then there would be a heaving of the surface, and a quantity of malt would then move suddenly over.

WALTER BESANT, *ALL SORTS AND CONDITIONS OF MEN,*

1882

A loud groan almost persuaded her to turn back the way she had come, but then she remembered hearing such a noise on her tour, when a bubble had broken the surface of the fermenting vats.

> Let Sarahs now arise,
> Let Miriams all come forward,
> With Hannahs truly wise,
> To prove their genuine worth.

'INVITATION TO FEMALES', NINETEENTH-CENTURY

TEMPERANCE HYMN

Still she had to draw several breaths before she could carry on and when she did so, to give herself courage, she sang one of her favourite songs from the meetings.

Porter had to be stored for a period and the use of large storage vessels was of great economic advantage ... as their greater dimensions allowed sediments to settle out and leave practically all the beer perfectly bright.

H. S. CORRAN, *A HISTORY OF BREWING,* 1975

She was still singing when she came under an arch and

stepped out on to the floor of iron bars, through which the tops of the great storage vats protruded like circles of wooden fences in the murk.

It became a matter of prestige to boast the largest vat in London . . . Whitbread named two of his cisterns 'King's Vault' and 'Queen's Vault' in honour of a royal visit. One hundred people dined inside one of Thrale's new vats . . . [Richard Meux's] final effort – in 1795 – held 20,000 barrels and cost £10,000.

PETER MATHIAS, *THE BREWING INDUSTRY IN ENGLAND*,

1959

The greatest of all, when she came to it, had the expanse of a circular ballroom. This was the Prince of Wales, so named because it had been launched the week the prince was born. She held on to the rim of the vat, its sides curving away from her, and gazed over its edge.

Surface a thick yellow crust, like a loaf. Yeast foam risen up and solidified on surface. Looks hard, though isn't.

NOTES FROM TELEPHONE CONVERSATION WITH FORMER

EMPLOYEE AT TRUMAN'S BREWERY

A foot or two below her was an uneven yellow crust: yeast foam, her guide had explained, risen to the surface and hardened, though when he had said hardened, he did not mean it could be stood on. Anyone foolish enough to try to do that would immediately sink into a lake of beer deep enough to swallow an elephant and no one be the wiser.

Gives off carbon dioxide, so can get dizzy.

NOTES FROM TELEPHONE CONVERSATION WITH FORMER
EMPLOYEE AT TRUMAN'S BREWERY

Gazing down she saw that her fingers had turned white where they held on to the side of the vat and she remembered what she had been told about the gases emitted by the beer, how they had been known to overcome even the most experienced of brewers, and she stepped back and took several deep breaths.

'Because, Angela,' said the one who wore spectacles and looked older than she was, by reason of much pondering, over books, and perhaps too little exercise, 'because, my dear, we have but this one life before us, and if we make mistakes with it, or throw it away, or waste it, or lose our chances, it is such a dreadful pity. Oh! to think of the girls who drift and let every chance go by.'

WALTER BESANT, ALL SORTS AND CONDITIONS OF MEN,
1882

How changed a woman she was, she thought, as she stood among those great vats, from the girl she had been barely a few months earlier; how far away that innocent creature now seemed; though now in her position of understanding she could see for how long she had felt a dissatisfaction with her life.

259

A soup kitchen was opened at No. 53 (now Nos. 114 and 116) Brick Lane, from which soup was sold at 1d. per quart and potatoes at 2d for 15lb to families whose need had been established. The members of the committee visited homes in the Spitalfields district to discover such cases, as well as personally supervising the making and distribution of the soup.

SURVEY OF LONDON, VOL. 27, 1957

She had been seeking, it seemed to her now, all her life, in her voracity for books, in her desire to be the most charming, the wittiest, to have the most handsome and clever men court her; though none of that had given her what she had found in serving a single ladle of soup to a poor man with hunger on his face and rags on his shoulders.

'As I approached this public house a poor woman, with two or three children dragging at her skirts, went up to the swing doors, and calling out to her husband inside, she said, "Oh, Tom, do give me some money, the children are crying for bread." At that the man came through the doorway. He made no reply in words. He looked at her for a moment, and then knocked her down into the gutter. Just then I looked up and saw my own name, CHARRINGTON, in huge gilt letters on the top of the public-house.'

GUY THORNE, *THE GREAT ACCEPTANCE*, 1912

She was waiting outside the soup kitchen so that her three companions might step up first into the carriage which was waiting to take them back home across town, when her eyes were drawn to a scene taking place outside the public house across the road. There, in the lamplight, a woman, with several children clinging to her skirts, was standing at the swing doors of the pub and calling to her husband, Oh Jack, do give me some money the children are crying for bread. At that the man came through the doorway. He made no reply in words. He looked at her for a moment and then knocked her down into the gutter. Just then she looked up and saw her own name in huge gilt letters.

'It suddenly flashed into my mind that that was only one case of dreadful misery and fiendish brutality in one of the several hundred public-houses that our firm possessed.'

GUY THORNE, *THE GREAT ACCEPTANCE*, 1912

In the soup kitchen they had spoken of drunkenness as blood brother of poverty, but it was not until that moment that she had made the connection with her own family's business. As a girl, indeed until that very moment, it had been a thing of innocent pride for her, how her name was emblazoned on so many streets and corners. But now, riding home in the carriage, after she and her companions had picked up the woman from the gutter, and taken her and her children inside the soup kitchen, and seen that they were fed and cared for, and she had pressed what little money she had in her purse into the mother's hands, she scarcely dared look out of the window for fear of what fur-

ther evils she might see being done as it seemed to her in her name.

Mr Charrington senior pointed out that he had been many years in business, and that during every day of them he had been studying the drink question ... [He suggested to his son that] he had suffered a kind of first nausea, just as young surgeons are supposed to do when they first handle the knife ... For his own part, Mr Charrington had made it his business to brew as good beer as could be brewed. His business was conducted with conspicuous regard to decency and order.

GUY THORNE, *THE GREAT ACCEPTANCE*, 1912

He was the wisest man she knew and she could not believe he had not considered these matters himself.

Of course I have, my dear, he said, after he had heard her story and offered her his handkerchief to wipe her eyes. I have been in this trade all my life and I have studied the drink question and can assure you that the brewery that bears your name is run with the most conspicuous regard to decency and order.

But Father, she said. If you had seen what I saw.

Do you think I have not? he said. Of course I have seen drunkards. What you are feeling is like the nausea a young surgeon experiences the first time he attends an operation, but that is no reason to suggest that the operating rooms should close.

It comforted the criminal about to be flogged, indispensably assisted dentists and surgeons before the days of anaesthetics, quietened crying babies.

BRIAN HARRISON, *DRINK AND THE VICTORIANS*, 1971

But Father, she said again, it is our beer—

And we ask no man to drink more of it than is good for him. Taken in reasonable quantities beer has been scientifically proven to be beneficial to health. Why else would we provide it to our own workforce?

Why, he continued with a laugh, when you yourself cried as a baby, it was our best porter that your mother gave you to drink, and I can assure you that it quieted you well enough.

Come then, sisters and countrywomen, unite with us in making a grand effort to ameliorate our condition and remove the plague spots from society.
    We remain,
    Sisters and Countrywomen,
    Yours in the Cause of Universal Redemption,
    The members of the East London Female Total Abstinence Chartist Association
    Association Rooms, 160 Brick Lane, Spitalfields, London
    January 25th, 1841

DOCUMENT FOUND ON INTERNET

She left his room comforted but that comfort lasted only the

few hours it took for her mind to rediscover its independ-
ence of thought. It was three weeks later that she
accompanied another of the members of the committee of
the Soup Kitchen to her first meeting of the East London
Female Total Abstinence Society, which as it turned out was
being held a few steps up Brick Lane.

'Ladies and gentlemen, I move our excellent brother, Mr
Anthony Humm, into the chair.'

The ladies waved a choice collection of pocket handkerchiefs at this proposition . . .

['I have,' said Mr Humm,] 'the unspeakable pleasure of
reporting the following additional cases of converts to
temperance. Betsy Martin, widow, one child, and one eye.
Goes out charring and washing, by the day; never had
more than one eye, but knows her mother drank bottled
stout, and shouldn't wonder if that caused it (immense
cheering). Thinks it not impossible that if she had always
abstained from spirits, she might have had two eyes by
this time (tremendous applause) . . .'

Anthony Humm now moved that the assembly do
regale itself with a song . . . It was a temperance song
(whirlwinds of cheers).

CHARLES DICKENS, *THE PICKWICK PAPERS*, 1837

Walking there meant passing beneath the tower of the brew-
ery, and she had shivered as she did so, but once they had
climbed the safe and commodious ladder into the large
room, pleasantly and airily situated, where the society met,
she felt the anguish in her head and her heart begin to lift.

Here was a whole gathering of people who felt as she did and were doing something about it. Speakers stood and bewailed the evil of drink, the devil in solution. Songs were sung, handkerchiefs waved, and plans were discussed for the next march.

Headed by Charrington brandishing his inevitable umbrella like a baton, a brass band thumped out popular hymns followed by a procession of the 'saved', carrying banners with boldy inscribed texts. It was the signal for the local drunks to attach themselves, swaying and dancing, to the rear, adding to the cacophony with bawdy music-hall choruses which went ill with the forward party's stern rendering of 'Lead, Kindly Light'.

WILLIAM J. FISHMAN, *THE STREETS OF EAST LONDON*, 1987

The march took place three Sundays later. A brass band led the procession, the marchers followed four abreast, blue ribbons on their hats, handkerchiefs in one hand, leaflets in the other, songs and hymns rising up into the air. She had been warned what might happen and that first time she drew only greater strength from the insults of the crowds, the shouts of 'coffee guts', the throwing of eggs and flour, the bawdy words given to their songs by the drunks who joined the end of the column.

Reaching the intemperate was the first and most critical task of the temperance societies. A common method of making this contact was for societies to hold free teas specially for drunkards. In return for free tea and food the imbibers were expected to listen to the experience of former drunkards who had reformed.

LILIAN LEWIS SHIMAN, *CRUSADE AGAINST DRINK IN VICTORIAN ENGLAND*, 1986

As the months passed, though, and all the society did was march and be mocked and hand out leaflets which were torn up or sneezed into in front of their eyes, and provide teas at which local drunkards ate their fill for free before taking their money down to the public houses, she began to grow frustrated at its impotence.

The Metropolitan Free Drinking Fountain Association erected and maintained drinking fountains, thus humanely furnishing the means of alleviating the feverish thirst which during the hot season impels so many to an excessive use of intoxicating drink.

HENRY MAYHEW, *LONDON LABOUR AND THE LONDON POOR*, 1851

Finally she went again to see her father. She had planned the meeting for weeks and carried with her pages of research and information on the provision of water in the district of the brewery, and its quality, and the cost of beer to a family.

'We use the Artesian Well, which is four hundred feet deep, for our Stout, but the Company's water for our Ales; and our water rate is two thousand pounds a year.'

WALTER BESANT, *ALL SORTS AND CONDITIONS OF MEN*, 1882

All I am asking, she said, is that we use some of the water that we are pumping up through our borehole anyway to provide a few well-placed drinking fountains so that people have the choice whether to drink water or beer.

Her father listened, nodding his head occasionally, until she had finished. Then he leaned forward and said, Do you know how much it costs to bore a well a thousand feet into the earth?

No, but—

I did not think so. Do you know, moreover, how careful we must be not to draw more water up from underground than is available there? The water table is not inexhaustible.

But, Father—

If we were simply to pipe that water out into the streets, the brewery would have to close in a month – the brewery to which you owe the position to which you were born, the freedom to waste your mind on these ignorant ideas.

I am not ignorant, she protested.

What you need, he said, wagging his finger at her, is to go and have a look around the brewhouse for yourself.

When they smelt the hops, it seemed as if their throats were tightened; when they smelt the fermentation, it seemed as if they were smelling fusel oil; when they smelt the plain crushed malt, it seemed as if they were getting swiftly, but sleepily, drunk. Everywhere and always the steam rolled backwards and forwards, and the grinding of the machinery went on, and the roaring of the furnaces; and the men went about to and fro at their works. They did not seem hard worked, nor were they pressed; their movements were leisurely, as if beer was not a thing to hurry; they were all rather pale of cheek, but fat and jolly, as if the beer was good and agreed with them.

WALTER BESANT, *ALL SORTS AND CONDITIONS OF MEN*,

1882

With every explosion of hot steam, with every grinding of wheels and new gaseous smell, with every new level to which the tour had taken her, the impression had grown stronger in her mind that she had been re-enacting Beatrice's journey down through the circles of Hell. Of course it had occurred to her at the time that the denizens of Dante's inferno were probably not as jolly and plump as the brewery workers, and nor, she had to admit now, could she imagine those denizens being given Sundays off. She stood in the stillness and silence, broken only by the occasional creak and groan, made aware all the more by their absence of the sheer plenitude of men who worked here. Not merely those involved in the making of the beer, but the bookkeepers and office boys and coopers and wheelwrights and carpenters and painters and draymen and farriers. They could not number less than a thousand, most of them no doubt married with children, and each one likely to lose his means of support should the brewery cease to produce its merchandise. It was an onerous thought and she had to delve deep into her resolve and strength to remind herself of the greater good that was her purpose this afternoon, the millions rather than the thousands for whom she was waging battle, the brave new world.

Oak vats or pine. Raised off floor on plinth. Plug in bottom, with chain hanging over side.

NOTES FROM TELEPHONE CONVERSATION WITH FORMER
EMPLOYEE AT TRUMAN'S BREWERY.

It was only for emergencies, her guide had told her. Below the vat was a valve with a tap connected to a pipe, through which the beer could flow out in an orderly fashion, but for emergencies there was the plug and chain connected to this crank.

On October 16th, 1814, in the Meux and Company brewery, in London, one of the twenty-nine metal hoops circling a beer vat twenty-feet high snapped. The explosion was heard as far as five miles away. A tidal wave of beer burst free, smashing through a twenty-five-foot high brick wall, washing away half the brewery, and flooding nearby streets and basements.

CAMDEN ARCHIVES

So what would happen, she had asked, if you were to turn this crank now?

It's like a bath, Miss, he had said. Pull out the plug and the beer'll pour out the hole, won't it?

Wave on wave with force surprising,
Temperance let thy waters flow.
Let thy mighty torrent rising,
Break the barriers of the foe.
Can aught stay this mighty river?

269

Can aught bind its passage free?
Flow its streams unceasing ever,
Till the world transformed be.

'TEMPERANCE RIVER', NINETEENTH-CENTURY
TEMPERANCE HYMN

And as she turned the handle, she sung out loud.

A letter

162 Brick Lane

They had been paraded and had their rifles and their kit inspected. They had filled their bottles with chlorinated water and been handed out rounds of ammunition, five to a clip. Later the order would come to move up to the line. Now all there was to do was wait. A group of them were playing a game of cards in the shade of the barn doors. Others were going through parcels that had arrived in the morning post-bag, the first to catch up with them since they had arrived in France, or reading letters, or repacking their kit, checking again their hard rations and field dressings, or like Private Solly Lewis were simply sprawled in the autumn sunshine.

Solly was sitting with his back against the barn wall, his legs stretched out in front of him to his bare feet. On his lap lay a letter of his own. He had not opened it but, every now and again he picked up the envelope and looked at his name in his father's spidery handwriting, and, once, he held it up to his nose before laying it down again on his lap.

He was still sitting there when Orpe appeared out of the

271

trees to say that there were some Hun prisoners down by the Calvary, on the road out from the village, and that he had shaken one of them by the hand. Orpe held up his own hand in the air as he said this, and stared at it with a puzzled expression, as if he was not quite certain that he had done what he claimed, and whether he approved of it or not. Some coarse remarks were made, about Huns, and about Orpe himself, which produced some sniggers, but nonetheless half a dozen of the men roused themselves to reach for their boots and their rifles, and with Orpe excitedly leading the way were soon making their way down the path.

Solly watched the last of them disappear into the trees, and then closed his eyes and turned his face to the sun again. Huns were exactly what he had been trying not to think about and he tried again to empty his mind, but in time the prospect of what lay ahead of them that night rose up again, and his hand strayed once more to his lap, to the unopened envelope that lay there.

It had been the first thing his father had said to him when he had come home with his news. His mother had begun to weep and his father to pray, and Solly had been on the point of walking out again when his father had grabbed hold of his sleeve. So explain to me, he had said, his voice thick with bewilderment, what these Germans have done to you or your family that you should want to go and kill them. Or God forbid, have them kill you? These Germans who welcomed us when we stole through the forest into their country. Who gave us tea and let us travel through their country without papers or paying them money.

And Solly had had no good answer. He might have repeated what was said everywhere, how the Huns raped women and bayoneted babies and defecated in the beds they had slept in when they moved on, but the truth was it had not been with any thought of Germans and their crimes, let alone any fighting or killing, that he had walked into that recruiting office and signed his name. He had done it because it had seemed the only way he could still the agitation inside him. And for all his parents' tears and words, it had stilled it. In the days afterwards he had felt that pleasurable exhaustion of relief that comes at the end of a long struggle, had walked the streets with a lightness he had not known a man might feel in himself. The first time he had put on his uniform it had been with something akin to wonder. Though in the weeks and months that followed had come the dully phantasmagoric realities of learning how to shoot and how to thrust his bayonet. The marches with the web of his haversack cutting into his shoulders and his feet inside his boots slippery with his own blood. The Channel crossing, his stomach heaving. The old French woman in Le Havre who had drawn her hand across her throat and croaked, Les Boches.

His first actual German he had seen a week after arriving in France. They were riding in a cattle truck and a cry had gone up and they had all rushed over to the side and pressing their faces to the slits in the wood had looked out at the hunched shoulders and dreary, unshaven faces. Since then they had several more times marched past prisoners on work details, and one night, they had even heard some Germans

273

singing and playing the harmonica, a haunting, beautiful sound that had quieted them until they had realized who was making the music and had drowned it out with their own songs about the Kaiser and sauerkraut. Though he had yet to stand face to face with a Hun, or shake one by the hand.

It's true, someone shouted, and Solly opened his eyes. It was Varley, now, running up from the trees, red-faced, and puffing out that there really were Huns down at the Calvary, for nothing that Orpe said was taken with a great deal of trust.

More men now began to stand up and button their tunics and soon even the card game stopped.

You staying here, then, Lewis?

Heads turned, eyes upon him.

Solly slipped the letter into his front pocket and reached for his socks, though by the time he had put them on and done up his puttees and laced his boots the others had gone.

The path was a short cut through a small wood. The line must have been closer at some point, or perhaps some of their own shells had landed here, for there were craters on either side and many of the trees were splintered, though others were untouched and still thick with red and brown and gold leaves. Birds sang in the branches and flitted from tree to tree, the splintered ones as well as the good ones; they did not seem to mind.

He felt almost happy to be walking here and he wondered what the rest of his family would be doing now: his father in his apron at the butcher's, his mother shopping, his brother in his tailoring shop sewing khaki tunics and trousers. It was only as he was almost through the trees that it occurred to him it was a Saturday, and they would not be working but were probably sitting around the Sabbath lunch table, eating the cholent made with the meat his father had brought home in his pocket: his parents, his brother David and his wife and their two little girls.

He saw the others as he emerged, crowded about the stone Calvary. There were eight or nine German prisoners. A couple of Highlanders were guarding them, one of whom saying – not for the first time, his tone suggested – that they were waiting here for orders, that they had been told to wait by the Calvary, and that was what they were going to do.

Solly edged round to get a better look, for the Germans were facing away from him. While he was doing so a voice spoke in English, an officer it sounded like, and Solly looked about nervously, for he did not think they were supposed to be down here consorting with German prisoners, though when the voice came again he realized it was one of the Germans who was speaking, a slender man with a small goatee beard and glasses. He was saying something about how he had worked in London for several years. At the Ritz Hotel. That's Pall Mall, one of the English soldiers said. No, it's on the Strand, said another.

This set off a conversation about London, in which the German with the English officer's voice was a free partic-ipant. Solly tried to move further forward so he could hear better, and see, but other men were doing the same, and his view was blocked. He was close to another of the

Germans now, though, and as he looked at him the feeling came to Solly that he had seen him before, and he wondered whether this German, too, had spent time in London, in the East End even. He squeezed closer, peering at him. It was nothing particular that made it come to him, no feature that stood out, but once it had entered Solly's mind he knew it was true. He could feel it as surely as these things are felt, by some mysterious ancestral knowledge.

He stared at the German, the dirt ingrained in his brow, the sunburned arms, the broad chest in the torn tunic.

Imagine, his father had said when he had come home on leave from training camp with his gun and his bayonet, that you stab this big sharp knife into a German's chest and from this German's mouth Hebrew prayers start to come out.

Stepping forward, so there was no one between him and the German, Solly said, softly, Gut Shabbes.

The German did not appear to hear him, so he said it louder, Gut Shabbes, Yiddish words, but Solly knew enough to know they were the same or almost the same in German.

Good Sabbath.

The German turned and any doubts left in Solly's mind were banished by the look of recognition on the German's face.

They stood like that, looking at each other, until the German made a noise in the back of his throat and expectorated what was in his mouth.

The spittle landed on Solly's chest, a green gob sticking to the pocket in which he had put the letter.

Solly stared at it, and while he was doing so, another of the English soldiers stepped forward and drove the butt of his rifle into the side of the German's head.

Shores

163 Brick Lane

The floor hinges up and a dark figure rises from the earth, the face shadowed by the brim of a hat pulled low, the body hung loosely with a long coat bespattered with something wet and cloying. A small lamp is set down, a long shaft, a glint of metal at its end, is propped against the wall. A hand reaches into a deep pocket of the coat and pulls out a moist package. The air is foul.

When she was young she thought that the shores were as much a world as the one above and though now she knows the limits of their extent, sometimes she thinks that still.

The hat is lifted off and though the hair is short the face is that of a woman. She hangs the hat and then her coat on nails on the wall and steps out of her boots and then reaches to her waist to undo the string that holds up her trousers. When she is naked she dips her hands in the bucket of water she left there this morning and washes herself, weighing her swollen breasts in her hand as she does so. Still dripping, she opens a door and steps out of the narrow chamber into a larger, more homely room, where she uses the candle from the lamp to light a fire, in front of which she dries herself. As soon as she is dressed she goes out to fetch him.

The first years her father went down the shores it was through the outlets into the river. An old man who had worked them that way all his life taught him the game: how to read the tides, how to find his way in the tunnels, the best places to hunt, how to keep alive down there. Then one day exploring the side shores beneath the streets where he lived he crawled down a narrow passage that ended in a wall and squatting there heard voices above. He measured out the distances so that he knew exactly where this shore was and when a basement in one of the houses that stood above it came up for rent he moved in. There were two rooms, one at the front, with a high window out on to the street, the other a small one at the back. Digging into the floor of the small room he was barely three feet down when his shovel struck air.

She plays with him for a while, sitting him on her lap and making him laugh until he starts to cry and she pulls up her shirt and feeds him, his hand clutching her little finger. He falls asleep on her and she sits there until her arm aches and her belly reminds her of her own hunger. She lays him on the bed and heats up the remains of the stew she cooked for herself the previous evening. When she has eaten she lingers over him and then goes into the small room and empties the

little sack into what is left of the water in the bucket and carries it through into the main room. She sets the bucket on
the floor and sitting at the table reaches into the water and
pulls out the first object.

She does not remember a time before she worked the shores,
though her father told her she spent her first years up above
with her mother, whom she does not remember either. After
she died her father tied her to his back and took her with
him. Soon he was setting her down and she was wriggling
into places he could not go, where no one had been before.
She can still recall the feel of her fingers closing round treasures twenty years ago: the half-sovereign standing upright in
a crack, the old cross down the ancient stone shore, the
master key that her father said was the most valuable thing
they had ever found. He put it on a metal chain and let her
keep it round her neck. In the evening she would sit drying
in front of the fire while he cooked their supper. Sometimes
two or three days would pass without either of them seeing
anything but that room and the shores.

When he wakes she holds him with one hand and with the
other opens the cage and lets the birds hop out on to her
arm and her shoulder. He laughs when one flaps on to her
head. They have always kept birds for the air in the shores.
She relies on her nose too, and the light of the lamp, but
when she is going into tunnels where she knows the air will
be bad she takes a bird with her in a tiny cage hung around
her neck. Her father would tell her not to cry when a bird

died, that it had done its duty and saved their lives, but he would be quiet that evening too, and pay particular attention to the other birds. His favourite was a crippled bird that would stand on its one good leg on the palm of his hand and sing to him. That one he never took down into the shores.

The work might not suit most people, her father would say, but he liked it fine enough. He wasn't the type to work between the same four walls every day of his life, a boss looking over your shoulder, your name written in pay books. Down here he could go where he liked, no day was the same as the last, you never knew what you would find. The muck was no bother to him, who had fought eight years in Boney's mud. Sometimes while they walked down the shores, or in the evening, he would tell her stories about the war and the places he had seen, the mountains, the city on the salt river with castles rising out of the hills, though the stories she liked best were about the farmlands where he had grown up, birds on every branch, berries in the hedgerows, corn growing out of the soil, the taste of pheasant and rabbit. At harvest time the men would cut the corn into smaller and smaller squares until the rabbits would make a break for it and the boys would hit them with their sticks and everyone would eat coney stew for supper that night.

She sleeps with him at her breast and when they wake she feeds him again, lying like that, on her side, looking at him frowning while he suckles. Afterwards she cleans him and takes him upstairs to Mrs Odling who watches him while she is gone. She eats some breakfast herself and then dresses in her shore clothes, the hat, the scarf to keep the spiders from her neck, the coat, the long trousers, the strong boots for the rats, though as long as you don't corner them they don't bother you. There is room enough for people and rats down there.

One day she and her father came round the bend of a main shore to see a horse pulling what she guessed from her father's stories was a plough and she thought they had found a farm, but the horse had come in a river outlet and was ploughing up the hardened muck so the waters could flush it out.

She climbs down the ladder and crawls along until she comes to where she can stand, wading first south through the wet slush then west in water down the main shore where she can reach out her hands on both sides without touching the walls. The lamp lights her way, hanging at her chest; she has not brought a bird today. Where she is not sure of her footing she feels ahead with the hoe, but most of the time she moves quickly, wanting to make it further west, where the pickings are richest. Often she and her father would make diversions down shores they had never been in before just to see what was there, happy to spend half a day exploring dead ends, but now she does not have time to waste. Her eyes follow the roll of the lamp, her fingers sensitive to the tap of the hoe, and only when she is far enough west does she stop to dip her hand into the muck or reach into a crack or an opening where the brickwork has fallen away.

She can go a whole week of days down here without seeing another soul and on another day it can be as crowded as Oxford Street with flushers and repair teams and other shoremen. The flushers keep the muck moving, raking it or digging it up where it has hardened. She has seen horses again several times since that first occasion, though only near the river. Some of the flushers she knows but others don't like the finders, accusing them of taking all the treasures or blaming them for weakening the walls that might fall and crush them. The other shoremen she is wary of too, though it was not so long ago that she was friendly with some of them. She stays clear of the repair teams she hears from far off and the rat hunters, hearing them by their dogs.

This is what she has found over the years: rope, bones, wood, iron, copper, nails, clay pots, jugs, coins, plates, knives, forks, silver spoons, mugs, a gold cup, rings, bracelets, hairpins, combs, brushes, boxes, pans, lamps, Bibles, letters, a bed, chairs, dead cats, dogs, birds, four dead people, two of them babies, one already a skeleton picked clean by the rats. Half the clothes she wears she has found down here. Shoes and gloves and other things that come in pairs she usually finds only one of, though once she found a gold earring and a full month later put her hand in the mud and came up with the other one. Most days what she brings home is worth more than a shilling but less than five. Once a month it might be more than a pound, once a year more than ten. Twice when she was a girl she and her father found tosheroons too heavy to carry. The first time they went home for a hammer and chisel and came back and the thing was gone. It took five years before they found another one that big, if it was not the same one: a ball of metal and coins and pieces of jewellery fused and rusted together by the water and the airs. This time she remained with it, the first time she stayed in the shores on her own, her father going back for the tools. They broke it up and carried it back piece by piece. One of the coins they took out of it had the date 1713 on it. There was gold and silver in that one tosheroon worth £18, even after the fence they took it to jewed them.

She watches for any weakening in the flame and feels ahead of her with the hoe. Every now and again she feels, too, for the key about her neck. She has never used it but often she has imagined what it would be like to unlock a cover and climb out covered in dirt into a street of fancy ladies. She has always meant to go west above but she never has, has never walked down Oxford Street, though she knows every shore and side shore beneath. Some of the shores are close to the surface and while she walks she can hear the tremble of the carts overhead and the sound of voices. When she passes under grates she covers her lamp so that the people above do not know she is down here. She knows them, though. Knows them in ways they do not know each other. What they throw away. What passes through them. She wonders how many

284

ladies' and gentlemen's doings she has felt between her fingers; whether she has ever touched the king's or queen's.

While her father was alive she never needed anyone else, but after his death she felt the lack of him in every moment and after some months she fell to talking to the shoremen and agreed to meet one in a pub after the day's end and after a few drinks went with him somewhere where he pressed himself into her. She tried this with several different shoremen. If she drank enough beer she did not mind their heaving, but it made no difference to the pain, so after a time she took to hiding if she heard them coming. Though one of them had left something inside her. He was born half a year ago, and since she did not know who was the father she gave him not only her father's Christian name but the Wilson part too. His first weeks she yearned to get back down here, for the peace and silence and for not being chewed on day and night, and as soon as she dared she left little Tommy with Mrs Odling and took up her lamp and hoe again. Then one day she went to fetch him and where he lay in Mrs Odling's arms the sun was on his face and he looked so beautiful that she wanted the sunlight always to be on his face, and now she hunts the shores so he will not have to spend his life down here in darkness.

She is nearly home, her pockets heavy, wading in ankle-deep water up the main shore, when she is met by a wave roaring down the shore towards the river on a rainless day. She swings the lamp from side to side but there are no passages or holes in the wall to duck down or press herself into, so she braces herself as her father taught her with her boots and hands and hoe. The wave lifts her as if she were a twig and carries her with it. The lamp and the hoe are ripped from her grasp. She is being taken towards a shaft and she feels at her neck and finds the key there, but she is swept past the opening. She holds her breath, tumbling inside the wave, trying to work out what the strange taste is in her mouth for it is neither water nor sewage and then it comes to her that it is beer.

A True and Faithful Narrative

178 Brick Lane

The town of Brainford was cruelly pillaged and plundered by the enemy, for they left neither beer, wine, nor victuals in the town, and carried away all the brass, pewter, linen and other things as they could, and cut to pieces other utensils of household which they were forced to leave behind.

LONDON INTELLIGENCER, 14–21 NOVEMBER 1642*

Letters reaching us from Cirencester do particularize how the Cavaliers did most barbarously and cruelly hew and pistol many women and children and carried away prisoner every man they found in the town that had escaped death (or being mortally wounded), tying two and two of them together and driving them along like cattle without shoes or stockings or hats to wear, and would not give

---

*Until 1641 the printing of domestic news in Britain was illegal, but with King Charles absenting himself from London to raise an army to wage civil war against the forces of Parliament and the impeachment of the Archbishop of Canterbury and the abolition of the Star Chamber, the machinery for controlling the presses evaporated. The first 'newsbook' appeared on the streets of the capital on 29 November 1641 and there was soon a multitude of rival weeklies and one-off tracts, most supporting Parliament, some sympathetic to the king, but all snapped up by a people hungry for news of the unquiet times and the bloody conflict drawing closer to the city with every passing day.

:m a bit of bread or let them drink upon a drop of water, and put no clothes upon them but a few such rags which would scarce cover their nakedness.

A PERFECT DIURNALL, 6–13 FEBRUARY 1643

About midnight last night there came an alarm to London, that the enemy was at large in the city, which occasioned a very great tumult and affright, every man betaking himself to his arms, and women and children running up and down the streets crying, until an infinite number of people were gathered together outside with lanterns, but nothing formidable appearing the uproar was silenced and the people did go home to their beds.

A PERFECT DIURNALL, 13–20 FEBRUARY 1643

The Lords and Commons, taking into consideration the great danger and distrusted times, have ordered that the Lord Mayor and citizens of London shall have power to entrench and stop all such highways and byways leading into the city, the suburbs, the city of Westminster and the borough of Southwark, and fortify the places aforesaid with forts and a circle of earthworks that will secure the city against the battering of ordnance.

WEEKLY SCOUT, 7–14 MARCH 1643

This day we heard of a discovery at the breastworks being put up by the good citizens of London in a field known as the Hyde by Whitechapel; an old stone waterworks was uncovered in the digging and in the earth beside it the skeleton of a newborn baby was found. From whence it came or how long it has lain in the earth we cannot say, but the bones were laid out and the residents were permitted to view them.

MERCURIUS LONDINIUM, 21–28 APRIL 1643

Just now to hand information of a disaster at the lines of communication being constructed near Brick Lane in Whitechapel, where after a rainfall a pile of earth collapsed into a trench and covered over two men, one of whom was rescued still breathing but the other when pulled out had given up the ghost.

A PERFECT DIURNALL, 26 APRIL–3 MAY 1643

Strange news from the eastern suburbs, *viz*, that men of the trained bands have perforce been sent to complete a stretch of the defences by Brick Lane near Whitechapel after citizens put down their spades and refused to dig. Two weeks past the body of a child was unearthed there and since that day two men were killed by a fall of soil into a ditch, another who was at the discovering of the child suffered such a tickling in his buttock that he scratched through his hose and made a great hole in his flesh; this being followed by the prodigious sight of an abundance of frogs and newts, which are creatures of corruption, and would have crawled into three cottages had they not been kept back by brooms.

MERCURIUS LONDINIUM, 5–12 MAY 1643

The weekly cheat from Oxford* puts out that certain

Mercurius Aulicus, a newsbook produced by the king's supporters in Oxford, where he had set up court, copies of which were smuggled into and sold in London. It was published on Sunday as a taunt to the Puritans.

events that we and other newsbooks have reported in our desire to carry to our readers the truths of these times are a natural consequence of the sins of Parliament and its supporters, the shamelessness and impudence of which claims can be judged by the date on the front page of that newsbook; rather than look to God for devilish matters we might rather look to the traitors and malignants who harbour themselves among the innocent citizens of this city and carry out their antiChristian plotting.

MERCURIUS LONDINIUM, 19–26 MAY 1643

You may remember how some weeks past the body of a child was discovered in the earthworks in Whitechapel, outside the liberties; well, on Tuesday last did come forward a woman who claimed the baby was her newborn that had been stolen or conjured from her; she had been ill since the day of her loss and only now had heard the news. Her neighbours did agree that she had been swollen with child but had none now; a bell forger's wife, she stood on the earthworks and pulled at her hair in her grief.

WEEKLY SCOUT, 5–12 JUNE 1643

It was two soldiers who, at the last, did stand up in the tavern and say that they would approach the matter and from there walked up the lane, for the cottage was only some small steps away; and when Judith Brown did open the door one set his carbine close under her breast and discharging the bullet it rebounded and narrowly he missed it in the face that was the shooter. At this, the other crying that they must need to pierce or draw blood forth from her veins to break the spell, they dragged her and knelt on her breast and scratched her face and when they had done this she knew that the devil had left her and she began aloud to cry, making a noise so piteous that they did finish the work they had come to do, such a stinking vapour issuing forth out of her mouth that the beholders were scantly able to endure it. That she was a witch all this proved beyond doubt and her neighbours said they had long suspected it; a foreigner to these parts, she was already in the shape of an old woman when first she appeared; crows and ravens were seen oft about her house; she would sit in her window brushing her long hair that was still her own; she frequented the playhouses until such were closed down in the name of God. When she was killed they searched her house and there was found in a chest within writings of a devilish fashion, which it was sworn were in her own hand, and quartos of banned plays the sort that no ordinary and good old woman or widow would keep; and which were taken and made into a goodly bonfire. If there be any doubters still who are against the prosecution of this witch they must be enemies of God, for was it not true that after a spring and summer when it seemed the country and this city must fall, not two weeks after the witch was dead the brave citizens of Gloucester did begin their defence of that city which lasted a whole month and ended in the lifting of the siege giving new hope to the Parliamentary cause and the citizens of London.

THE TRUE AND FAITHFUL NARRATIVE OF JUDITH BROWN, THE WITCH OF WHITECHAPEL, WHO DID BRUTALLY STEAL AND MURDER A CHILD AND BURY ITS BODY IN THE LONDON EARTHWORKS SO AS TO PUT A CURSE ON THE DEFENCES OF THE CITY,

L. H., 6 OCTOBER, 1643

Lolesworth

180 Brick Lane

It was still well over an hour before three o'clock when the bus turned down the long drive and deposited Brenda, alone, in front of the gates. She thought about getting back on and riding on a stop or two, but while she was making up her mind the doors closed with a sigh and the bus turned on itself and headed away up the drive. She watched the back of it growing smaller until it swung on to the road. She looked at her watch again. She had time to walk back to the last village, it couldn't be more than ten minutes or a quarter of an hour at most. There'd been a nice one there, she'd seen it out of the window, right on a little green. She could have a nip, two even, and still get back. She took a couple of steps forward, out of the shelter of the high wall and into the cold breeze blowing across the drive and the grass cut bleakly short on either side. She shivered and felt her legs wobble under her, achy from the journey. The last time she'd had a couple before going in he'd smelled them on her even with the packet of mints she'd chewed. He hadn't said anything, but he'd been cold to her the whole hour, and she

292

didn't want to risk that again, not with it being the first time here. So she promised herself one on the way home and turned back towards the window.

She could see them inside, laughing about something. Finally one of them came over. He made a show of looking at his watch before gesturing at her impatiently with his hand. She pushed the visiting order through the slot and waited for him to write down the details. Then he jerked his head at the door, and she went inside and sat down on one of the orange seats.

It wasn't bad, as waiting rooms went. Not too filthy, the walls recently whitewashed, though the ghosts of graffiti still showed through. A vending machine, too. She dipped into her purse and found a 50p piece and went over to get a cup of tea, which she brought back to her seat. She'd time it better next time, now she knew the journey. She was always early the first visit in a new place; better early than late. Twenty past eight she'd left the house to walk to the bus stop, the bus taking her to the station, then the train up to London, the tube almost to the end of the line, finally the bus that had brought her here. She'd done worse. When he was up at Wakefield she'd had to set out before seven and afterwards stay the night in a B&B. That was the only time she'd put in for money from HM, thought it was only right, what with her missing an extra day at the salon. The best had been when he was in Portsmouth, one bus taking her all the way, she could work the morning and still be back in time to cook Jan her tea and tuck her up. Not that the salon ever gave her any grief. It was only every other week, at most, and she'd been there seventeen years: an institution they called her. As for getting home late, it was a long time now since she'd had anyone other than herself to look after, apart from Larry, of course, the little she could do.

There were only two off the next bus: a girl, no more than sixteen herself she looked, pulling along a little boy. She didn't even look at Brenda, told the boy to sit down and behave himself if he didn't want a smack, though he hadn't done anything, and pulling out a compact started painting a set of lips on her mouth twice as thick as her own perfectly good ones. Brenda shuddered with professional disapproval. There were a dozen ways she could have told her to achieve a fuller look without doing that.

A larger group arrived and soon the room was filling up. Women most of them, as usual, though Brenda wasn't used to them being so young, and all these kids. She wondered what kind of place it was, how he was doing. She'd had her hair done and dressed herself up nice, as she always did, the way he liked, but she felt prim and proper sitting among these girls in their tight skirts and trousers and you-know-whats spilling out of their blouses.

A little boy peeked at her from between the seats. She smiled at him and he held up two fingers at her.

The first names were called and she sat up, ready. She was used to being one of the first, but that was in the old place. At least they'd told him he was being moved, so he could let her know. More than once she'd travelled half a day to find he wasn't there any longer, she'd had to turn round and go home, wait for his letter. She wasn't the last, but almost. She stood with her arms up while a female guard, a stocky little thing, patted her down. She held open her bag, though there was nothing in it but her keys and purse and some tissues and a little bit of make-up.

Mouth.

It wouldn't hurt to say please, Brenda said.

Do you want to go in or not?

Help yourself then, she thought, but she'd didn't say it. All she'd see were her teeth and fillings, she'd never brought anything in for him, not even a pack of cigarettes. He'd never asked and she'd never offered. Though when Miss Stocky said, All right and jerked her thumb, Brenda gave her a coldly superior smile. Like Larry always said, it's not what they do, it's how you respond.

He had his hands on the table and was looking round, impatiently, she could see, which wasn't the best start. She plumped up her hair and hurried over to him.

They kept you waiting, he said, up on his feet when he saw her, that look in his eyes.

It's a new place, Larry.

He pulled out the chair for her and then sat down himself, though she could see he still wasn't right.

I should have a word, he said. I haven't had a chance to speak to all of them here yet.

It doesn't matter, she said. I didn't—

But he was already turning to where the guards were standing and waving his hand.

Slowly one of them ambled over.

What's the trouble then?

This is my sister, Larry said. Mrs Wilson. She comes a long way to get here. She's never been late in twelve years, and I'm never late for a visit neither. I would appreciate it if in future we didn't have to wait until visits is half over to see each other.

A little smile began to form on the warder's face, as if his leg was being pulled, but then the smile turned to something else as he looked at Larry, puzzlement at first, and finally a realization. Brenda had seen it before.

Fair enough, he said slowly, nodding.

That's all, Larry said. The guard stood there a moment, trying to preserve what he could of his dignity, before turning away.

I see they've got a canteen, Brenda said, looking over to where visitors were queuing up to buy chocolates and crisps and Cokes. Can I get you something? You like a Mars bar.

I'm happy sitting here with you, he said. I eat too much as it is. He patted his stomach. If you want something, of course—?

Oh, no, no, I'm perfect, Larry.

You're looking nice, Bren, he said. As always.

Thank you, she said. He never failed to tell her this, or almost never, but it still sent a little quiver through her.

You too, she said, which was also always true: his hair combed, clean shaven, his shirt crisply ironed.

All well I trust? he said.

Yes, yes.

Janet and the little ones?

Yes, fine. Jan called last Sunday. They'd had a lovely day

on the beach. This seems like a nice enough place, she went on quickly. Talking about her daughter and grandchildren with him always made her nervous. It must be good to have a bit of country air. I saw some nice houses from the bus, gardens with little white fences, names not numbers. Your little bird must like it. The view, I mean.

She was prattling on, but he didn't seem to notice. He gave a faint smile and nodded his head.

It's a young crowd in here, isn't it? she said.

That's because it's a C cat, most are on short sentences.

Oh yes, she said. She had never quite mastered all the different categories. A, B, C, local, remand, trainers.

A bunch of pillocks. I've seen more trouble here in a week than you'd get in a year where I was before.

Oh dear, she said. Why have they put you here then?

He looked at her.

I'll be getting out soon, Bren, he said quietly.

She heard his words but it took her a long moment to take them in.

Out?

Well not right away, he said. I've only just moved here. But it's a beginning. If all goes well I should be in an open in a year or so, and after that, well—

The rest of the hour she was hardly aware of what he was saying or what she said for that matter. When it was time to go he gave her a kiss and she went out and stood in the cold, the dark coming in already. Kids ran around the bus stop and the girls about her laughed with each other, or wept.

She had a double at a pub next to the tube station and

another at Victoria and was glad to settle down in her seat once the train had started and she'd spent a penny. She'd always known that life didn't necessarily mean life, of course, but she'd never followed the thought through to him actually coming out. What would happen? Would he come to live with her? The idea made her hot and cold at the same time. She tried to imagine life with him, coming home to find him sitting on the couch watching the telly, bringing him his tea on a tray, maybe later the two of them walking down to the pub, arm in arm. Then she thought of the flat she'd left behind this morning, her bed unmade, her women's things all over the bathroom, the bottle she kept out on the counter so she could have a nip of a cold day before she went to work, and another when she came home. And what about her Sunday visits? She'd never told Larry about them, nor told Arthur and Stephen about Larry neither. Thought it best. But if he was living with her he'd want to know where she was disappearing to every Sunday morning.

She closed her eyes, thinking she might sleep, but she was too stirred up for that now. Thinking about everything. Larry and Arthur. They'd always been the poles of her life. Light and dark, sweet and bitter, chalk and cheese. But that was the war, wasn't it? Bringing people together who'd never normally have given each other the time of day. She'd often thought if it hadn't been for the war Arthur might have done something proper with his life. Though, of course, then she'd never have met him.

It was that sweetshop, if memory served her right; Larry

and Roy had been scheming how to get in ever since rationing had begun, and they roped Arthur in on account of his size. There was a tiny window round the back and they squeezed Arthur through it and he opened the door and they scarpered each of them with a couple of jars tucked under their arms. They got caught when they started handing out the sweets at school, or Larry and Roy did. Arthur was at a different school, he'd been more careful. With the family reputation Larry and Roy were straight up in front of a judge and he gave them eighteen months at approved school.

The next time she saw Arthur, he wasn't small any more. Still thin as a whippet, he was always that, but he must have grown six inches in a couple of months, and grown handsome too. She was thirteen, she didn't know she'd turned into a woman until she saw Arthur walking towards her with a smile on his face.

She was practically living on her own then: the boys off in approved school, her mum either at work or blotto, her dad on the trot since the day he'd got his papers to report to the Tower. He'd slip in over the fence for an hour every now and again, and the boys before they were sent down would take messages to where he was kipping, or money, or if they were lucky bring some back, or something. You always knew what he was into by what there was suddenly a lot of in the house. Brussels sprouts one month, boots the next. Come to think of it she was surprised he hadn't tried to make a few bob out of those flowers.

They were something else, they were. It made her smile

just to think of it. The summer of flowers, they'd called it. She'd never seen anything like it before, and if truth be told not since. From one day to the next every house the bombs had blasted to rubble bursting out in a carpet of red and gold and purple. Butterflies everywhere, those little furry caterpillars crossing the road in their hundreds. There was one site she and Arthur had made their own. The other kids didn't like it there, the way the houses on either side leaned over it, held up by those huge pieces of wood, but she and Arthur didn't care. He'd found a mattress in a boarded-up house and had dragged it behind the stump of a wall out of sight of the street. Stuck a piece of wood in the rubble and scratched Hyde Park on it in chalk. The real Hyde Park couldn't have been more beautiful, lying there on that mattress, seeds floating about them like snow, him putting flowers in her hair, in his shirt button too.

That autumn Larry and Roy skipped over the wall and came home. The coppers were round looking for them a few times, but the boys'd learned how to keep their heads low from their father and soon the police gave up. There was a war on after all. They never went back to school, started lifting lead from bombed houses, and when that ran out they turned to what their dad did, only better, Arthur going in with them. By the time the war ended the three of them were making more money than their mum and dad ever had. Stephen happened by accident but she was sixteen by then and old enough to be married. They were happy years, those, with Stephen, then Jan born, their own little house three doors down from Larry, Roy always somewhere around, money never a problem, respected wherever she went.

What happened that night down the pub she never really knew. She'd never liked that place, all those whores, put her off her drink. She was in her bed when Arthur shook her awake, telling her they had to wake the kids, get out of there.

The war's over, she said, still half asleep.

I thought it was mine, he said.

What?

All that blood.

By now she'd turned on the light and she saw it on him, like he'd spilled paint on himself.

It was his knife, Bren, you've got to believe me. One minute we were having a drink and the next it was in his hand.

Who are you talking about? she said.

Roy, he said, like she was an idiot. Who do you think? It was about nothing, Bren. Nothing.

She took off his clothes and cleaned him up and woke the kids and grabbed what she could. It never occurred to her to let him go without her. She'd made her choice all those years ago on that mattress in Hyde Park. They were on the street when he ran back in and came out again with something tucked inside his trousers, though she didn't know what it was then.

It wasn't till they'd jumped on the first night bus going down Whitechapel High Street that they realized they had no idea where they were going. If that bus had been heading for King's Cross maybe they'd have gone north somewhere but as it was they sat on it all the way to Victoria terminus. They took the first train pulling out, Arthur still looking over his shoulder, which was how they'd ended up in Havant. I'm not staying here, she told him, but he kept saying, It's perfect, Bren, who'd look for us here? Even the name's right, this place practically doesn't exist.

They spent the rest of that night in the waiting room, the next in a room above a pub. The landlady took to Brenda, guessed something was wrong though she never asked what. She let them stay a week without paying, then let Brenda make it up serving behind the bar in the evenings while Arthur looked for work, which he finally got labouring. It was hard on them both, they were used to better, and Arthur wouldn't let them go to the council. Nothing official, he said, no names. He was petrified it would get back some-how. The kids kept asking when they were going home, when they'd see Uncle Larry and Uncle Roy again. But you can get used to anything, she was testament to that, and they soon found themselves new uncles among the regulars to buy them lemonades and packets of salt and vinegar. Those first months she and Arthur lived from day to day, afraid every time the pub door swung open, but when a year passed they thought maybe they were safe in Havant.

Between them they were earning enough to think about getting their own place, moving out of the pub, but Arthur wouldn't think of it while she was still working behind the bar – him sitting at home with the kids while the customers chatted her up. As grateful as she was to the landlady she'd had enough of it herself, with her sensitive skin and all that washing up of glasses, her hands were as red and hard as chickens' feet. She'd seen a notice about a beautician's course, she'd always been good with make-up, but it was £250 and the most they ever had left over at the end of the week was a couple of quid. Then one Sunday Arthur said he was going down to Portsmouth to see Pompey play and he came back with a fistful of notes. He said he'd won it on the game, but she knew straight away what he'd done. While he was having a drink to celebrate she went up to the room and looked behind the cupboard where she'd found it months earlier, wrapped in a piece of cloth. A squat black thing, heavier in her hand than it looked, with a pair of silver snakes on the handle, though it was gone now.

She passed the course and got her first job, it wasn't much money but her hands weren't always in soapy water and she was home in the evenings. They moved into a little flat, only two rooms but it felt like a palace after the pub. She bought some cheap material and made curtains. At night she'd cook instead of them eating pub food and they'd sit with their tea on their laps in front of the television. When summer came Arthur'd take Stephen across the road to this little park to play football, her watching from the window while she made the dinner. Laughing at Arthur like one of them storks or flamingos, birds that were all legs and bones, little Stephen hurtling about after the ball. She was looking out when she saw them stop their playing and stare across the grass at the four men, the one standing a little in front of the others. It must have been a hundred feet from where she was, but she could see what he had in his hand as clear as if he was standing beside her, those snakes glinting in the sunlight. She shouted, but it was too far. He lifted up his hand and Arthur crumpled to the ground. Then his hand still up he moved his arm round and pointed it at Stephen. She couldn't believe he was going to do it, she'd never have let Stephen grass up his own uncle, whatever he'd done.

It was like a car hit him, lifted him up in the air and threw him back. He'd always looked so much like Larry, too. You'd have thought he was Larry's boy, not Arthur's.

It was on account of Stephen the police went after him so bad, and why the judge gave him such a stiff tariff. She never said anything, of course. Said she'd been watching the television, had thought it was a car backfiring. It was all over the local papers, national ones too. Everywhere she went in Havant people stared at her. But she'd buried her men there, once the police had released the bodies, and after that she couldn't leave.

She hadn't been the one to make contact, she'd never expected to see him again. Then four years after, she got the letter. He was in Portsmouth, just down the road, if she ever wanted to visit. He didn't mention Arthur and Stephen. For a month she did nothing, but then she got herself a visiting order and went down. Jan never forgave her for going, for keeping going. It was why she moved to Australia, Brenda knew. But Jan had Phil, and little Arthur, and Gary, while Larry had no one except her.

The train was halfway to Havant when the trolley came round. She bought one of those little bottles and a few minutes later when the trolley man came through again she bought another one, slipping it into her bag for later. For comfort.

Poor Larry, she thought as she poured the rest of the first bottle into the plastic cup, when was the last time he had a nip? There was that hooch they made themselves, with marmite and orange juice, but he'd told her once how horrible it was, and now, anyway, he couldn't risk that. The slightest thing could spoil his chance of parole for years, she knew that much.

Of course she could send him some. A couple of these little bottles would be perfect, wrapped up in brown paper. She wouldn't put her name on it. Wouldn't send it from Havant either. She could drop it in a postbox next time she was passing through London.

Oak tree

199 Brick Lane

THIS ENGLISH OAK TREE WAS PLANTED
BY THE YOUNG PEOPLE OF
BOUNDARY COMMUNITY SCHOOL (BCS)
21ST FEBRUARY 1996
THIS PROJECT WAS INITIATED BY SHAKUL ISLAM,
CO-ORDINATOR OF BCS, TO RAISE AWARENESS OF THE
YOUNG COMMUNITY MEMBERS, OF THE ENVIRONMENT
AND ITS EFFECT ON OUR WORLD.
BCS AIM TO FOCUS ON THE TREE'S DEVELOPMENT IN
PORTRAYING EDUCATIONAL ACTIVITIES, BY ENCOURAGING YOUNG
PEOPLE TO TAKE RESPONSIBILITY FOR THEIR OWN ENVIRONMENT.
FUNDED BY: SPITALFIELD MARKET COMMUNITY TRUST
BOUNDARY COMMUNITY SCHOOL (BCS)
BOUNDARY ONE STOP SHOP

The canary trainer

outside 216 Brick Lane

I first came across 'Willy' Wilson in the early 1990s, long before I started writing this book. I had recently come back to London from working in the East and was still hankering after all things oriental and tumultuous, and on Sunday mornings I would get up while most of the city was still asleep and lose myself for a few hours in the noise and grimy disorder of Brick Lane market.

Of course calling it that would have annoyed Willy. The pet market on Club Row was closed down by the council in 1984 and the market no longer even extends into that road, but to Willy – as to most locals – the whole thing was still known as Club Row. At least that's what I've read him as saying. I never actually spoke to him myself. When I first started frequenting the market I had no reason to do so, and by the time I returned there, working on this book, I had formed some ideas of my own about him which I wasn't ready to put up against his version of his life.

Of the real Willy all I knew was what I'd seen on a couple

of Sunday mornings spread over a decade or so: a scrawny, bird-like figure himself, with yellow skin and dark eyes, selling birdseed for a pound a bag. I noticed him because he was always there: sitting on his fold-up chair next to his fold-up table on that stretch of pavement where you seldom found the same stall or grubby sheet spread with useless and broken items two weeks in a row; though it was seeing him looking out from the page of a newspaper that really fixed him in my mind. It was a picture story in one of the weekend magazines, black and white photographs with little bits of text under each, and one of them was of Willy with his bags of seeds. 'Willy' Wilson, it said, the birdseed man of Brick Lane market, with a couple of quotes he'd given about how the market's real name was Club Row and how in the old days it had been the actual birds he'd dealt in, not just the seed.

After that, in the way of these things, I felt I had some personal connection with him, and I would watch out for him when I went to the market and be glad when I found him there. I even saw him on television once, in Japan of all places (the East again I now realize). I was flicking through the channels late at night in some cramped hotel room in Osaka and there he was, being interviewed by a Japanese film crew, though I couldn't hear what he was saying, or even hear his voice, because of the Japanese voice-over. After that, he was virtually an old friend, and when the first inklings of this book came to me I thought of Willy: what I could make of him, how I could work him into my fiction.

Briefly, I entertained the idea of making him of Huguenot descent (the name an anglicization of Viljoen or Villion, perhaps). It was the Huguenots who brought over the habit of keeping songbirds: the weavers operating their silk machines to the songs of linnets or woodlarks or greenfinches in wooden cages by their latticed windows. But like other Huguenot habits – oxtail soup, a love of gardens – keeping birds long ago infiltrated the national culture, and anyway I was soon piecing together different origins for the Wilsons, as well as for Willy's other side.

Imagining how the birds came into his life followed easily from that. The way I saw it as soon as he was old enough to let himself out of the flat on Sunday mornings, while his mother slept off her Saturday night gin and tonics, a boy of seven or eight, he would have found his way to the animal market. This was the early 1950s, when you could still buy almost anything there, not only kittens, puppies, rabbits and guinea pigs, but goats, tortoises, snakes, even a donkey if you wanted one. Perhaps it was the birds themselves that first caught Willy's fancy: their warbling songs or their bright feathers in a world still dulled and shattered from the war (though as it happens the best singers are the dullest to look at, like the nightingale) or the feel of their hearts beating in their fragile chests when he held them in his hands; though to my mind it was the bird sellers who initially attracted him. Gnarled men on their stools beside their cages, old soldiers most of them, some even from the previous war, glad themselves to have a young'un interested in their birds. Mornin' Willy, they'd say, when he came shyly along, his hands in his pockets. Want to hold a goldfinch then? Soon he was helping to clean out the cages and keeping an eye on a man's birds when he went round the corner for a piss, or a cup of tea, or something stronger. In time he learned the birds' names, and where they migrated from, and what to feed them, and how to look after them and coax them to sing.

He didn't have many friends at school – any real friends, the way I saw it – and the bird men became his friends, gave him a place, once a week, where he felt he belonged. You couldn't earn a proper living out of birds, though, not unless you had a shop or were sharp or underhand. For most of the bird men it was a hobby, the couple of quid they might make on a Sunday going on birdseed and a pint or two at lunchtime. So when he left school I imagined him working in the other market, Spitalfields, which hadn't moved out further east yet, casual labour, shifting boxes, helping out with selling the fruit and veg. He would still have been living with his mother, who had her disability pension from her leg and whatever else she earned, and he didn't need to bring much home, other than seed for the birds he kept in one room, Annie letting him as long as they didn't come in the other. And every week there was Sunday to look forward to.

In the 1960s, however, the law began to catch up with the Club Row bird sellers. The trade there had never been in bred birds, but wild caught ones, which was illegal, and with inspectors now raiding the market the game began to be about keeping one step ahead of them, and money rather than the birds. A new kind of bird seller took over the market, flogging garishly coloured birds which, when the paint wore off them, turned out to be plain brown finches brought over by the thousand from India. Most of Willy's old friends stopped coming and the heart of the bird trade moved from Club Row to the Knave of Clubs pub on Bethnal Green Road. There the thing was song competitions, birds in tiny cages put up to sing against each other for money, with bets on the side. The best singers – those who 'jerked' the most in a minute – changed hands for tens of pounds. Willy went there a few times until one afternoon a cage was thrust into his hand as the police burst through the door. He was arrested and fined £10.

After that, instead of going to Club Row or the Knave of Clubs on Sundays, he took to catching the train out of London: riding it until he saw grass and trees, and getting off at the next station to walk out into the fields and woods. The first times he had an idea he might come home with a few birds in his pockets, but while he had heard talk about catching them often enough, the relative advantages of nets, or traps, or lime, the only birds he'd ever caught himself were those he'd thrown his shirt over when they wouldn't go back in their cage, and the wild ones were too quick and canny for that. He spotted them, though, and listened to them singing, and once he spent the night out in the woods with them, having missed the last train. He slept on the ground, shivering through the night even with his coat wrapped about him, though in the morning when he stood up and started moving he felt more awake than he ever had after a night in his own bed. For breakfast he ate fat ripe blackberries that no one else seemed bothered to pick, sharing them with the birds.

It was around that time that he fell in with Cooky and Kev and the others. He was older than them, twenty-four or twenty-five by then, while most of them were scarcely more than kids, some even still at school – in theory at least. In practice they spent their days loitering about the streets, or in Doyle's, the shoe shop where they bought the cherry red boots that were part of their uniform (cherry reds, Levi jeans turned up at the ankle, Ben Sherman shirts, braces, hair shaved to a bristle), or the second-hand record shop off Bethnal Green, or, after Willy started hanging out with them, at his place. Willy's flat was one of his attractions to them; his job, and the money it earned him, being the other. His work at the market started at four in the morning and was over by lunchtime, and afternoons they would buy a few cans, Willy paying, and go back to his room to let out his birds and drink.

Willy was still mourning his mother then. Annie was hardly more than fifty when she died, but she'd had a 500 lb bomb almost crush the life out of her, and then there was the gin, which she'd always liked, but to which she'd become even more partial after Willy's father took off. In her last years, without her teeth and her lip curling even more, it had been difficult for people to understand what she said. It wasn't only loneliness, though, and filling a hole in his life, that drew Willy to Cooky and Kev. How much he would have known about his own origins, or how much he admitted to himself, was a question I turned over in my mind. It was the real Willy's sallow colouring that had given me the idea in the first place: he could have been of Italian origin or Jewish, but when I first saw him I'd been living in India for a couple of years and travelling round the sub-continent and I remembered thinking there was something of that part of the world in him. Annie wouldn't have talked about it, of course. Once she had worked out that Charlie wasn't coming back, she would have cut him out of her thoughts, pretended he'd never existed, lived the rest of her life as if Willy was the product of an immaculate conception. Probably Willy never even knew where his father was from (Charlie never wrote so he would have had no idea where he'd gone back to), but he was old enough when his father walked out to remember his brown face, old enough to miss him too, to hope that he'd come back – and when he didn't, to hate him for not doing so, as well as for the words the kids at school called him.

He must have been aware that Cooky and Kev weren't proper friends, not like the bird men, that they were using him, and probably mocking him behind his back, if not to his face. But he was used to being at the edge of things, and the uniform made other people look at him as they looked at the rest of them. And then there was what they talked about, how it excited him the way touching himself did. Like after he did that, when they had gone from his flat, when he was picking up the cans and putting the birds back in the cages, he would feel a certain dirtiness, a shamefulness, but by the next afternoon he would be ready again to hear what they said, and say it himself.

Of course, they were mostly just talk, bravado. They would stand at street corners calling out their words and occasionally jostling a brown-skinned man or scaring a woman or a kid or two. That day would probably have passed like any other if Cooky hadn't seen something in the face of one of them scuttling by that had made him say, 'Ere, Kev, who does that Paki remind you of, then? It's Willy isn't it, he could be your effing cousin, Willy. And Kev had laughed. And Willy had snapped. Had run after the Paki and when he caught him jumped on his back and knocked him to the ground and kicked him where he lay there making his noises.

That was the moment, in my mind, that the young Willy of my imagination turned into the old Willy I used to see in the market. Shrunk in size, and shrunk into himself. Devoted more and more to his birds which had been given the freedom of his flat. After Spitalfields market moved out to Leyton, he survived on benefits and the few quid he made from his birdseed. Maybe he went along to a National Front meeting or two – they used to gather on the corner of Brick Lane and Cheshire Street on Sunday mornings, not far from Willy's pitch, to sell their newspaper while the Socialist Workers stood across the street shouting their own slogans – but for Willy it had been personal not political anyway. If he had any creed of his own it was an inarticulate longing for a simpler existence that was connected to his passion for his birds and the joy he had experienced the night he slept out in the country, waking up to breakfast on blackberries picked off the bush, and which manifested itself in a fascination with apocalyptic visions for the future of the city.

The last image of him I have is a few months before his death, coming across a torn book laid out on one of the grubby sheets near his own pitch, beside a comb missing half its teeth. It is titled *Living off the Land, or Food for Free*, and surprising himself, Willy buys it for 30 or 40p. It is probably the first book he's ever bought, and I doubt he actually reads it, or at least more than the lines on the back about the nutritiousness of wild fruits and nuts. It fits in with his own visions, though, of a time after the city's destruction, the buildings gone, and most of the people, nature regenerating itself and the birds and the animals in ascendancy. He's had these visions since as long as he can remember. In truth the landscape of his childhood was a bit like that, half the East End a bomb site, playing his solitary games among the rubble and weeds. He'd grown up in the knowledge of the bombs that had fallen on his mother. Then when they got their first telly there'd been the pictures of The Bomb, that great mushroom, and after that programmes he'd watched about asteroids, plagues, this global warming, and most recently, this terrorism. The pictures of the planes flying into the buildings in New York excited him in a way nothing had done for years, he watched them again and again, and it may have been them that persuaded him he shouldn't wait any longer, that he should let the birds go. For when they found him, a week dead at least by then, the smell unspeakable, there were no birds in the flat, only the crusted layers of their droppings and feathers, along with the tins of beans and soup and boxes of crackers he'd been hoarding, and a half empty sack of birdseed, neatly stored in a corner, by a fold-up table and fold-up chair.

Bull

246 Brick Lane

The birds flapping up into the hot midday air alert the members of the troop, who bark out their own alarm, standing on their hind legs, mothers making urgent throaty calls to their young. A few of the monkeys, their nerves breaking, make a dash for the tree, where they cling to the branches, peering through the foliage, but most of them have seen what it is now and they grunt reassurances to each other and as the intruder draws closer chatter at it indignantly, though if the old bull hears them he gives no sign of it, neither altering his course nor looking up, but continuing on his slow, swishing way through the grass.

It is two days since the bull, grazing on the far side of the plains, lifted his head and sniffed at the air. Whether there was some scent there or his memory was stirred by some other sensation, a taste in the leaves he was chewing or a prickle in his skin, after a time he lowered his head and turning away from the bushes set out into the grasslands. He walked all the rest of that day, as he walked all day yesterday, and has been walking since dawn this morning, stopping only to feed and drink and sleep, following dusty paths where they have taken him in the direction he wants to go, otherwise cutting across the grasslands through herds of ungulates, parting to let him by and closing in behind him, as the monkeys also settle back to their business when he has gone. An hour after he passes them he comes over a rise and stops. His eyes are poor and he cannot see the great winding river at the bottom of the gentle incline below him, but he can smell it. He has not drunk since yesterday afternoon, but it is only in part the prospect of the cool water that draws a rumble from his throat and a shake of his head, and hurries him on.

Soon the smells of the river grasses and the oozing marshes thicken and the ground softens under his feet. He stops and scents the air, drawing on old memories, before turning and pushing through the reeds towards a channel where in past years he has drunk clear water without having to wade too deeply into the treacherous muds. How long it is that he has been coming to these marshes at this time of year is not something that troubles his great head, though within him still is the memory of the first time he smelled and tasted the soft brown plants. It was chance that brought him here then, in his solitary wanderings, during the brief season when the plants grow among the grasses that are his more normal food, though for many years now when the air or the leaves or the earth tells him it is time he has turned away from whatever he has been doing and made his way here.

When he has drunk his fill he flings mud on to his head

and back, for even his thick hide can suffer in the sun. Then he lifts his feet from the sucking mud and squelches back towards the edge of the reeds and with a shudder of anticipation begins to snuffle about in the shorter grasses until he finds a first clutch of the flat-headed plants. He reaches down and touches them with the sensitive flesh about his nostrils, breathing in their rich scent, before taking one into his mouth and chewing it slowly, enjoying again its familiarly strange crumbly texture and nutty flavour. When he has savoured it he reaches down for more, eating two or three at a time now until the whole circle is gone and he moves on in search of more. In this way he passes the afternoon, shuffling slowly along the edge of the marshes, ingesting several dozen of the plants, though they are small and he is great in size, and it is not until the light is fading that he begins to feel the changes.

First comes the warmth in his skull and then the melting to the extremities of his limbs so that he forgets about eating any more for a time and stands there, swaying gently, letting the waves pass through him, sometimes lifting a leg and shaking it. When these sensations fade he lowers his head and continues his search in the darkness, his eyes closed, relying entirely on smell even when a three-quarter moon begins to rise; though as the hours pass it is other odours that come to him: first those of his mother, and then the other members of the herd, the females and the young males, in which he spent the early years of his life. They rumble to him, and he rumbles back to them, rubbing against them as they move around him, flank against flank, head to head.

Later still he smells and hears other things, his rumbles growing louder, and once he throws back his head and trumpets at the moon.

Morning finds him standing in a patch of reeds, hypnotized by a pile of his own steaming dung, his legs covered in black mud, his body trembling slightly. He remains there, breaking up his dung with his feet, sniffing it and taking pieces of it into his mouth, while the sun climbs above the trees. Only when the heat begins to beat down on his back does he become conscious of the thirst in his throat, and he leaves the dung and weaves unsteadily through the reeds to the channel where he drinks. He feels strange, his hide tingling and his legs weak, and he is lightheaded, for he has not eaten much other than the soft brown plants for several days, though he has no desire to eat now, lowering himself instead into the marsh and rolling gently in the mud. When he tires of that he lies there rumbling to himself until his eyes close and he sleeps.

He is sleeping still when the men appear over the rise.

They stop as the bull did yesterday and then move forward again in a long line, the monkeys they killed earlier in the morning over their shoulders. For the past hour or two they have seen signs of the bull's passing along the way and they are alert for his presence, but though they scan the riverside ahead of them the bull is hidden where he lies sleeping by the tall marsh reeds and all they see is the green vegetation stirring gently in the faint breeze and the glinting brown river beyond. Approaching the marshes they make for a tree on the dry ground before them. The men throw down the monkeys in the shade and before even they drink they fan out across the dry earth and the softer ground close to the marshes. Soon one of them shouts and they come to where he is kneeling over the large round slough in the ground. They look out again into the reeds, thinking they must have missed the curve of grey back they had expected to see, but still there is nothing, nor any movement, and though even their dull noses might have scented the bull, the mud he has wallowed in has covered up his odour. Eventually they agree he must have passed out of sight along the river or perhaps swum across it to the other side, for they know that his kind swim well, and satisfied, they drink, and then make their way back to the tree. When the women have cooked the monkeys the men eat, and afterwards they sleep, for they have a long night ahead of them.

The day is beginning to cool when they rouse themselves, those still sleeping being woken by the others, for the light will not last for ever and they have the dream plants yet to collect. Gathering fruit and nuts is normally women's work but these plants are men's business and they search along the edge of the marshes, for they know the plant only grows where the ground is moist, but not too wet, and not too well shaded by the longer grasses. When they find the remains of some plants with the marks of the bull all around, they wonder whether perhaps some other men were here before them and were chased away by the bull, but they see no sign of any men. Then an untouched circle of plants is found, and soon another, in grasses where the bull did not search, and soon they are absorbed in their gathering. When dusk begins to fall they call to each other and carry back the bounty they have gathered in curved pieces of bark to the tree.

Only one, the oldest and wisest among them, has not taken part in the gathering and they place the dream plants on the earth in front of him, where he sits, and receive back from him the portion he measures out for each of them, some more, some less, for only the strong can wrestle with strong dreams and not be defeated. When each has his share they sit in a circle and eat the plants, slowly, savouring them, while the old man first, and then some of the others, tell of past dreams and their meanings, the light of the fire flickering in their eyes and dancing on their skin. For a while nothing more happens, but then one of them stands up and begins a loose-limbed stooping dance around the fire. Soon he is joined by another, and then another, until they are all on their feet, even the old man, moving in the same loping way, and when one begins to chant they all take up the song, their voices like the howls of animals. In time they pick up stones and sharpened pieces of wood and scratch deep furrows in their skin, smearing themselves with the blood.

The moon rises as it did the night before and they dance in its light and its shadows, now and again one of them breaking the circle to empty his stomach or to defecate, for the dreaming brings on cramps. One among them, a young man for whom this is only his third dreaming, walks further from the fire, the world bathed in the pale light of the moon. His thirst reaches him even in his dream state and he wanders out into the reeds, enjoying the feeling of the mud between his toes, though when he comes to the water he forgets his thirst and stares at the reflection of the moon on the black surface. He is still staring at it when he hears a growl. He turns in the direction of the sound, the dreaming dampening his fears. It comes again though this time it sounds more like a snore than a growl. He moves forward, hearing it again, pushing aside the reeds until he sees the great moonlit flank of the bull.

It is a while before he arrives back at the fire and can make the others understand what he has seen, or makes a few of them, for most appear not to hear him, or if they do, they merely incorporate his telling into their dreaming. Eventually with five or six following him he makes his way back into the reeds.

Is it dead? one says, when they come to the bull.

No, says the one who found him. It sleeps.

As if in agreement the bull snores, the sound startling all of them except the one who found him, who steps forward and pokes at the bull's flank, first gently, then harder, the bull responding by giving out another long rattling snore.

They stare at him some more and then one says, What a feast we can make of this beast.

It is dream time, says another. We cannot kill until the sun has risen and set and risen again.

This disappoints them for it is many months since they have eaten the flesh of the bull's kind, and even more delicious, the fat.

Maybe it will sleep till then, says another.

For two days?

It has eaten the dream plants, another says, remembering the prints around the remains of the circles, and they agree this must be the case, for they have never seen any animal, let alone one of this fierce kind, sleep like this while men poke at it.

If it ate the dream plants then it will not feel this, the one who found him says, taking the chipped hand stone with which an hour ago he was cutting his own chest and arms, and scouring a deep line in the hide of the bull, jumping back after he has done so, though when the bull does not react, he laughs.

I will do it also, says another, taking the stone and making another cut, and after him another does the same.

Then the one who found him says, We can cut out some fat without killing him.

This seems an ingenious idea, so he reaches forward and cuts out a chunk of skin and fat as big as his fist and takes a mouthful of it before passing the rest to the next man.

In the moonlight they see the blood well out of the wound.

Another of the men takes the stone and cuts another chunk and they eat this, still hot from the bull's belly.

A third man steps forward to cut his chunk, but this time the message of pain from the bull's nerves manages to reach his brain and he stirs and lifts his head, and the men cry out and leap back, the one who was making the cut leaving the stone embedded in the beast. The bull lifts his head at this noise, and smelling the men gives out a call of terror and alarm, though there are no others of his kind to hear it.

It frightens the men, though, the courage the dreaming gave them now turning to a nightmarish horror, and they fall over in the mud and grab at each other in their efforts to escape.

As they do so, the bull pushes himself to his feet.

He is huge against the pale moonlit sky behind him and he lifts his head and trumpets and in their fear the men shout back at him, and he, risen from his sleep, feeling now the burning pain from his mangled belly, takes fright and rears away in panic. He picks his feet from the mud and charges as quickly as he can away from the men and out into the marshes.

Seeing this the men stop and watch him until he disappears beneath the tops of the reeds.

He sleeps again, says one.

No, says another. It is the mud.

They wait there, half afraid he will suddenly reappear out of the grasses, but eventually they pick their way carefully through the marshes and reeds, until they come to an open patch and see the bull sunk up to his belly in black mud

By the time they make it back to the fire, the sky in the east is beginning to lighten and day is coming. An argument breaks out between those who went to see the bull and the ones who were left behind, who are angry that the others broke away from the circle and did not continue with the dreaming; and there are calls to wake the old man who has gone to sleep. But as they listen to the story of the bull the others forget their anger for they have never heard of such a thing and it seems a dream in itself.

Now they all go back into the marshes to see the bull, who has sunk even further. He twists his head and trumpets weakly, struggling in the mud, which pulls him further in.

They watch him for a while longer, all the time the mud sucking him deeper in, but eventually they leave him to go back to the shade of the tree, for the day is growing hot and they are weary themselves and even if they were permitted to kill him on this day they would not risk the sinking mud. One by one they lie down and fall into their own deep sleeps.

It is later in the day that a couple of the boys slip away from the sleeping men and the watching women and follow the men's tracks through the reeds. Two or three times they almost slip into the mud themselves but they are determined to see the bull they heard the men speaking about, and eventually they come to the place where the men had stood watching.

At first they can see nothing, but then one of them points to something protruding from the mud. It is the end of the bull's long nose and as they watch, it shudders slightly and a snort of moist air puffs out of it.

Sylhet House

Swanfield Street at Brick Lane

I don't know, she says, turning away from the spectacle of him sprawled in all his pale nakedness on the bed. I mean their only son is in— she couldn't bring herself to say the word— and now you're expecting their only daughter to bring her white Christian boyfriend home to meet them?

A brave vessel

174 Swanfield Street

Some forty years ago the northern end of Brick Lane was torn up by the council. This had always been the least constant part of the lane. It was the last section to be built up: maps from the mid-1700s show a rough track winding through orchards and meadows, among them Swan Fields. When it was developed it was as Turk Street and Tyssen Street before the name reverted to Brick Lane around 1880. In the 1960s, however, this upper reach of Brick Lane was effectively dammed by the building of a large council estate and the course of the road diverted westwards for a shortened last fifty yards to a meeting with Swanfield Street. Modern council housing was put up along this new stretch of the lane, as it was down the entire eastern side of Swanfield Street, with the exception of one plot, on the corner with Brick Lane, where a single private house was spared redevelopment, and stands there still.

There is no shop sign on this house (nor does one hang from the black metal hook that protrudes out towards the street), but during the day a battered sandwich board is set up on the pavement outside, offering for sale the foam cushions and pillows that can be seen in haphazard piles on the floor or leaning against the dilapidated walls, through the open front door, which itself could do with a lick of paint. Nor is the exterior of the building in any better state of repair, which in these preservation-conscious days is something of a surprise, for beneath the flaking paintwork and crumbling stucco are the bowed wooden shopfront and fine wide windows of what a recent council publication called 'the last remaining weaver's house in the area'.

Further south, on Princelet Street and Fournier Street, entire rows of eighteenth-century houses have survived intact and have recently been lovingly and expensively refurbished. But on Brick Lane itself rather less remains from its prosperous silk weaving days, when the lane was filled with French voices and taverns with names like La Tête du Boeuf and L'Etoile. The prominent exception is the Huguenot church at number 59. Though its interior fittings have gone – the organ donated by George III was transferred elsewhere when the Machzike Hadath synagogue took over the building in 1897 and the remaining pews and galleries were stripped out after it became the Jamme Masjid mosque in 1975 – the exterior of the building is much as it was when the date of its completion, 1743, was set in the wall, along with a sundial and the Latin inscription, *umbra sumus*: we are shadows. But the church – now mosque – apart, piecing together Brick Lane's history from its buildings is a task for the architectural detective.

Across Fournier Street from the mosque, for instance, at

57 Brick Lane, is a grade two listed house, originally built in 1728. Its essential fabric and much of the brickwork remain from this time, but it has been subject to a good deal of reshaping and rebuilding. The ground floor was refronted as a shop in the early nineteenth century. Several windows have been bricked in on the Brick Lane front and two more lengthened. The window arches have been rebuilt with new bricks and the glass and woodwork replaced. The slate roof is of a later date, the chimney nineteenth-century.

Further up Brick Lane, at the corner with Sclater Street, is a house built even earlier and occupied by 1728 by Pierre Fromaget, a weaver. This house is also grade two listed, though mainly because of the unusually grand sculpted street sign on the wall, which says 'Sclater Street 1778'. The house was rebuilt at this time and it was probably rebuilt again or at least heavily reworked in the early nineteenth century. Earlier doorways have been blocked in and new ones knocked through. An attic beneath a pitched roof has gone. A shopfront was put in at the ground floor when the usage changed from weaving to pawnshop in the 1840s and was remade in the twentieth century. Of the actual 1720s house, all that remains is a patch of pockmarked and eroded brickwork at ground level on the Sclater Street front, some six bricks high and ten bricks wide, the bricks probably baked in a kiln further up the lane.

In comparison, 74 Swanfield Street, with its intact shopfront and protruding row of six thick wood-framed leaded lights on the first storey – which have something of the look of an eighteenth-century sailing ship's stern galley windows – and upper storey weaver's windows, seems to have escaped the reworkings of time. Every time I walked past I would stop and admire it wonderingly. Sometimes, when the door was open, I would see the old shopkeeper – a Bangladeshi, I presumed – sitting on his chair amid the pillows and bags of polystyrene balls. Finally, one afternoon, I walked in and introduced myself. Mr Kirby, as he was called, turned out to be of Indian descent from the isle of Mauritius. He had come to England in 1953, at the age of twenty-one, after completing his national service in the army, Mauritius then still being a British territory. He had worked in the shop when it was a timber merchant's and furniture maker's and had taken it over when the owner, a Jew named Goodman, had retired.

Looking around at the bare brick wall on one side, and the painted tongue-and-groove wooden panelling on the other, I asked about the origins of the house.

Oh yes, it was a weaver's house, he said. Built in the eighteenth century. By a sea captain, as you can see from the windows. He gestured upwards with his hand.

It had all been old buildings when he'd first come here, he continued. Where Brick Lane was now had been St Philip's church – the lane ran right through where the nave had stood. On the other side were Victorian tenements. The council pulled them all down, church and tenements, to build new housing. They tried to pull this place down too, but he was having none of it.

I suppose it's a listed building now, I said.

He made a noise and shrugged, and at that moment his

wife came down from upstairs to tell him his lunch was ready.

When I'd first started researching this book, I'd contacted English Heritage and they had sent me a thick pile of sheets detailing every archaeological find or architecturally inter-esting building in the Brick Lane area. It was from these Sites and Monuments Records that I had read about the Roman burial amphora unearthed a few yards from Brick Lane in 1887, and the Saxon finds of 1906 and 1992, as well as the locations of the spring known as Snecockswell which supplied St Mary Spital through an underground culvert and the defences built across the lane during the Civil War (though it was from early fifteenth-century deeds referred to in the *Survey of London* that I learned about the lease of four acres of 'Sputelhope otherwise Lolesworth', known as 'le bryk place', to 'Hugh Brampston, fishmonger'). When I got home I pulled out these sheets and went through them, but while there were entries for 57 and 125 Brick Lane and a handful of other listed buildings on the lane, there was nothing for 74 Swanfield Street.

A few days later, I was down at the local history library on Bancroft Road. Chatting to one of the librarians, I asked if he knew anything about the house. He disappeared and a minute later came back with a little pile of photographs. One, from 1975, showed the house standing on its own, looking in even worse repair than it does nowadays. I turned it over. On the back, it said, '18th-century weaver's house'. An earlier one was taken just as the demolition had begun. The Victorian tenements were still there on one side. On the other was the church, half-gutted, but still with its imposing front. Huddled between was 74 Swanfield Street.

Curious to find out more about the house, I wanted to look up its earlier usage in the commercial street gazettes, which were first produced in the 1830s. But I knew that Swanfield Street was a recent name and the street had originally been called Mount Street, so in order to find what number Mount Street the house was, I asked the librarian to bring out some maps. The first was from 1894–6. It showed the land cleared by the London County Council for the building of the Boundary Estate, an early social housing project. The plot where 74 Swanfield Street stands was easy to find, as it was right next to the church. However, the map showed it as land cleared for the new estate. Thinking this must be an error, that perhaps the house had been condemned and then reprieved, we turned to the next Ordnance Survey map, from 1907. This showed the whole of the Boundary Estate now built, including the Victorian tenements on the eastern side of Mount Street, which were called the Streatley Buildings. Between them and the church, however, was still an empty plot. We turned to a later map. This did show a house there and gave it a number, 57 Mount Street. I went to the shelves where the street gazettes are kept. There was no entry for this address until 1911, when it was a chandler's, or general grocery shop, its proprietor an Israel Polsky.

By this time the librarian had put on the table a report by English Heritage from 2000 on eighteenth-century houses in Bethnal Green. I leafed through it until I came to: 'No. 74

Swanfield Street is an interesting curiosity – a house of c1900 that reflects the area's earlier local tradition so well that it has been mistaken for a remodelled 18th-century weaver's house.'

Further poking about in the library, and returning to speak to a surprised Mr Kirby, put together more of the story. In the 1890s, after the slum that had occupied the land had been pulled down, there were various plans for the new estate. One involved a grid of streets, though in the end it was decided to build in a circular shape, radiating outwards from a little park with a bandstand in the centre. The eastern side of Mount Street proved to be just outside this circle and the Streatley Buildings were put up as a separate experiment, more expensive, with lavatories and kitchens inside each flat rather than shared, and yards and workshops at the back. The cleared land was deep enough for this along Mount Street until the plot where 74 Swanfield Street now stands, which was foreshortened by a hall behind it in the precinct of the church. This plot was therefore left empty. When I told Mr Kirby what I had found he dug around in his papers and pulled out the results of a Land Register search he had made. This recorded the 1903 lease, at £3 a year, for eighty years, of the plot on which his house stood, by the London County Council to a William Henry Adams.

The subsequent history of the house is easily told. From 1911 to 1961 it was a chandler's or grocer's, first under Israel Polsky, then Philip Nirenstein, later Philip Newman (perhaps Nirenstein anglicized), and lastly Stanley Webb. After that it was taken over by the Service Lumber

Company, which was owned by the Goodman for whom Mr Kirby worked. The origins of the building, though, are more of a puzzle. In 1910, the *Book of Duties on Land Values* for the area, held in the local history library, has Israel Botsky (presumably a misspelling of Polsky) as the proprietor of the shop. The electoral roll for the same year lists Israel Krasnopolsky – again one assumes the same man – who must therefore have been living in the house. The owner, however, was an Adam T. Biggs.

Who was this Biggs? Did he build the house? Or was it the Henry William Adams who took out the original lease? The records held by the local history library yielded no more information and a search of the National Monuments and Records archives produced little more (and a little less) than I already knew: that it was 'A house of the 1890s [it was actually a decade later], built of brick with two storeys and garrets. The building was originally one-room in plan, with upper-storey "long light" windows, as if in imitation of the area's earlier weavers' tenement houses.'

What were the reasons for building this house in this way? In one of the poorest parts of London? There are no other houses remotely like it in the area. Its mock eighteenth-century features – the bowed wooden shopfront and the row of ship-like windows on the first floor in particular – would have significantly added to the cost. Why would Webb or Adams or whoever it was have gone to this expense only to rent it out to an immigrant grocer?

Whatever the reason, something about the house – perhaps

its appearance of age and fading grandeur – has enabled it to survive when all around it has been pulled down and replaced with characterless modern red brick council housing. Standing alone on its quiet corner, cracked and peeled by the wind and rain, with its stern-galley-like windows on the first floor, there is something about it of the direful spectacle of a shipwreck.

Acknowledgements

Some of what is described in 'Feldman's Post Office' actually happened to Samuel Chotzinoff's family as related in his memoir, *A Lost Childhood* (1956). Much of the factual information in 'P. Norwich & Co.' is drawn from Philip Sugden's *The Complete History of Jack the Ripper* (1994). I am also particularly indebted to Katy Gardner's account of a year in a Bangladeshi village, *Songs at the River's Edge* (1991); Anthony Birley's *Band of Brothers – Garrison Life at Vindolanda* (2002); William J. Fishman's *East End Jewish Radicals, 1875–1914* (1975); and the papers of J. Edward Lousley and Prof. E. J. Salisbury on the flowering of bombed London. Much of the material in this book I discovered in the treasure-house that is the Tower Hamlets local history library on Bancroft Road, with the unerringly knowledge-able help of its librarians.

Jack Henry told me the true events that form the basis of 'A letter'. That story is for him. Kate Gavron and Rushanara

Ali read parts of the typescript and gave very useful advice. My thanks, again, to Clare Alexander and to Ben Ball; to Temple Clark; to Cristina Ferreira for the gift of time; and, as always, for so much, to Judy Henry.

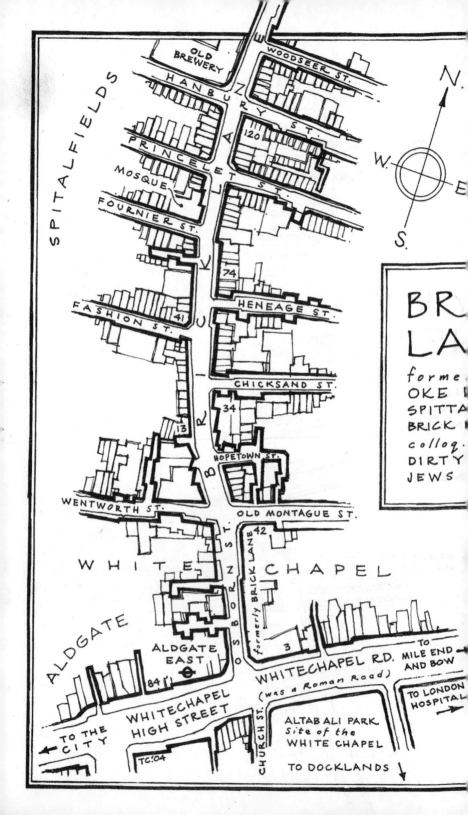